The Broken Dream
Book Two of Northern Fire

By Ian H. McKinley
Published by Lugar Común Editorial
Ojo de Vidrio Collection

THE NORTHERN FIRE PENTALOGY

Harbinger
The Broken Dream
The Winter Wars
The Rune Slate
Tears of the Ghosts

The Broken Dream
Book Two of Northern Fire

Ian H. McKinley

The Broken Dream: Book Two of Northern Fire
© Ian H. McKinley, 2016
© This edition Lugar Común Editorial, 2020
Gerardo Barajas-Garrido, Collection Editor for Ojo de Vidrio

Library and Archives Canada Cataloguing in Publication

ISBN 978-1-987819-87-8

First Published in 2016 within *Harbinger* by the same author
2nd Edition Lugar Común Editorial, Collection Ojo de Vidrio

Ottawa, Canada, 2020

www.lugarcomuneditorial.com
info@lugarcomuneditorial.com

Canada

for Prince Pinot,
Duke of Bordeleau, Count of Pine Hill,
Baron of Bogotá, Earl of Suesca, irreplaceable,
the spark of life in our lives that was always
"just passing by,"
forever remembered by those who
you had the grace to touch with paw or shoulder.

Table of contents

Dramatis Personae

The principal characters:
- Lars Sorenith, son of Renith and Rena;
- Cairn Soleigh, son of Leigh and Fallig;
- Lora Dauilig, daughter of Uilig and Loska;
- Thay Sorig, son of Rig and Thülla; and,
- Elkor the Grim, a Straelish man of multiple talents.

Noble personages:
- Lady Oda, a Straelish noblewoman; and,
- Korgash Hasselmann, a *herg* (lord) of North Straeland.

Some other Straelish personages:
- *Frouw* (Madame) Singrid, a shopkeeper;
- *Herr* (Mister) Wolfgar, Singrid's husband; and,
- *Herr* Monsfried, a woodcutter.

Notes on Fjordlander theology

For those readers who may wish to refer to them, at the end of this book appear some notes on the pantheon of Fjordlander gods.

Map of the Northlands

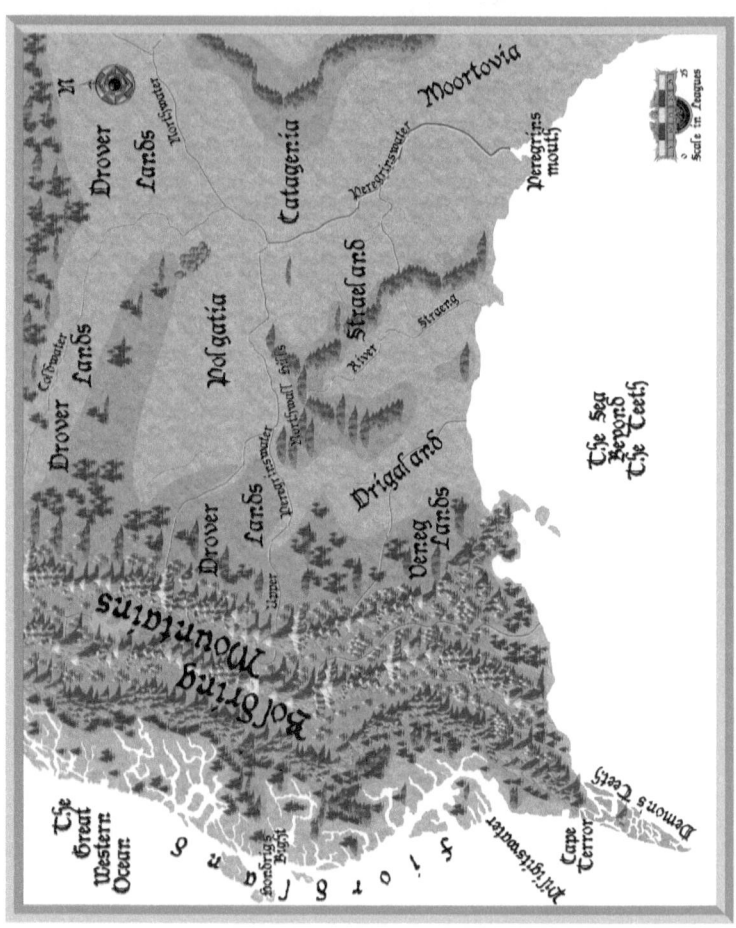

Map of the Kingdom of Straeland

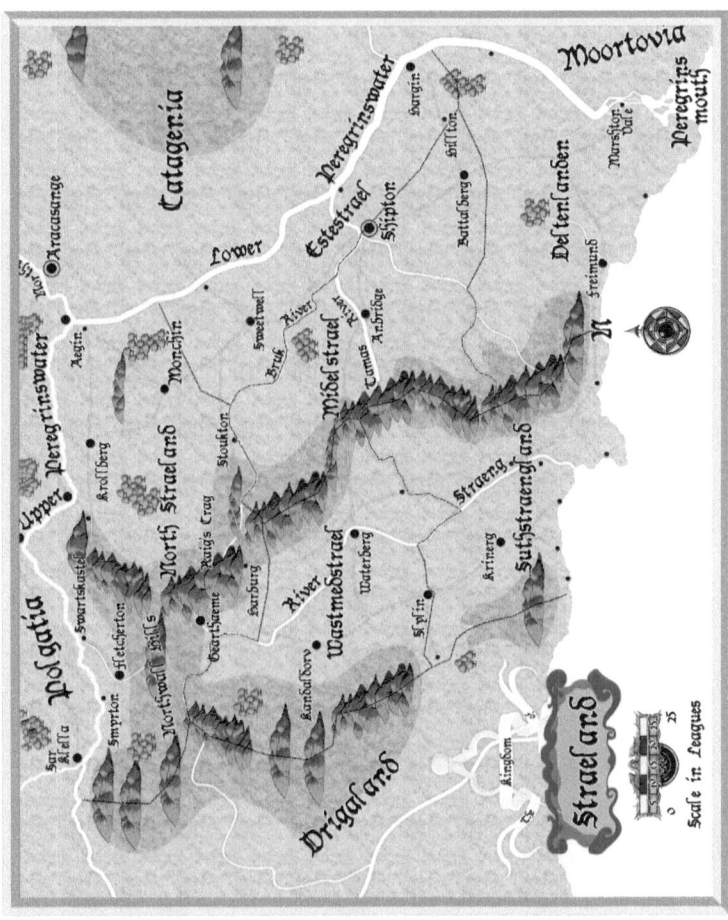

Prologue

The gravedigger didn't like the man but he liked the coin well enough. Ugly as a curse cast under a sickle moon, the man's face was thankfully hard to see for the raised cowl on the black cloak and for the moonless night they had chosen for their task. The man scurried more than walked, and his odd gait was all the stranger for the way his back bent forward. Underneath the cloak bulged a hunch. Arriving at an agreement to creep into the graveyard in the middle of a night at the beginning of winter hadn't been a pleasant experience neither; the man's ugly mouth, chock-full of rotten teeth, could evidently only spew ugly words. The gravedigger was used to insults - they came with the work - but the man seemed to delight in hurling the vilest slanders. Just as well the man was willing to hurl a bit of coin along with the insults.

"Hurry up! Put your back into it."

The gravedigger leaned on his spade. "If you's in such a hurry, why don't you put *your* back into it."

"Because I'm not in the habit of paying my hard-earned coppers in exchange for indolence, that's why," the man snapped. "Now, if you haven't already mistakenly buried your wits, use them to recall that there's supposedly a band of accursed Thorn People in the woods. I've been a slave to Fjordlanders; you do not want to fall into their hands. More likely again is someone coming along. Remember, if we're caught here, we're like to hang. Hurry!"

The gravedigger huffed, "Them's just rumours, that business about Thorn People! I'd be more afeared of the fairy folk. Woods are their haunt. Strange things happen in woods."

He stretched out his back, and bent to his work again. "Besides, seems to me you should be recalling some things too. I'm swift enough to get away if someone comes a calling." He shovelled in silence for a while; like it or not, the man was right, the longer they took, the greater the likelihood of getting caught and it wasn't a good night for a dash in the dark along icy pathways and over snow-bound land.

"What you want this grave opened for anyway? It's a poor grave in a poorer graveyard. Even a Drover wouldn't bother digging this one up."

"I don't pay you to ask stupid questions. I'd normally say the less you know the better, but I'm afraid that ..."

The hood rose and swivelled.

In a sudden flourish of movement, the cloak galloped off among the frost-encrusted earthen mounds towards the graveyard's far wall. The gravedigger paused to watch just long enough to hear the gate creak and a voice barking an order. He dropped the spade, turned, and dashed off.

Clambering over the stone wall that separated the graveyard from the village, the gravedigger spotted movement against the snowy ground. He cursed under his breath and dropped down into a snow-encrusted garden, hoping the pair of spearmen hadn't seen him. *Warriors! Galivith-accursed warriors!* He dashed between two cottages and down a track that led to the *tonplatz*, the village square. Once there he found a path of hardened tracks in the encrusted snow that would not betray his passage, and, although icy, he scrambled along them to the street that wound out of town. Rounding a bend, he heard voices ahead of him. He skidded to a halt, losing his footing and falling to the ground.

"You hear that?" a man's voice asked.

Another man's voice replied, "Aye, I heard something."

The first voice made a clicking sound and the gravedigger heard a horse's clip-clopping. Casting his eyes left and right, he saw a ragged woodshed against a cottage and he slipped inside, forcing himself into the tight space among the cord of wood stacked all around.

The clip-clopping drew closer and it was made by not just a single horse, but two.

There were gaps in the woodshed's planking, so the gravedigger pressed himself against the logs and knelt down, making himself smaller and hopefully harder to see. Torchlight glinted through those gaps as the horses and the torch-bearing rider rounded the bend in the street.

"I don't see anything."

"I thought I ..."

The man's words were cut off by a shout from back towards the *tonplatz*. "Wulfhere, did anyone come this way?" The voice was a woman's.

One of the horsemen called back. "We didn't see anyone but we maybe heard something."

More flickering light drew closer, coming from as many as two or three torches. The gravedigger felt a growing weight in his gut that was overwhelming his pounding heart. He suppressed a sudden sob. When he wiped a sleeve across his runny nose, he felt tremors shake his arm. Through the gaps in the planking, he saw a woman trussed up like a hunter and she was followed by three warriors. *It's an accursed* weroth! *What in Galivith's good world is a war band doing poking around here in the middle of the night?*

The woman, now right outside the woodshed, said, "We saw at least one flee in this direction and we found tracks by the wall. I swear to Galivith that I heard something hereabouts."

A different voice, a man's, said, "Fan out."

Just then wood clattered about the gravedigger. He swallowed a shriek as something moved in the dark and the woodshed door creaked open half a foot-length. All talking stopped outside as something waddled out into the night.

"There's your culprit," the woman said, chuckling. "A racoon!" Chortling arose from the searchers. Then the woman added, "Whoever they were, I don't doubt they're long gone."

"Aye, but I wonder if they're gone for long, if you take my meaning," said the man who had sworn he had heard the gravedigger's fall. "Mark my words; we'll get another report of a missing sheep and soon enough we'll be riding out on another cold winter night looking not only for outlaws, but damned Thorns as well."

"Well, you've missed your chance to get a good racoon-skin hat. Your culprit's waddled off into the night," the woman said, drawing chuckles all around. The hilarity halted abruptly as more horses drew up.

"My *herg*," said the huntress. "If someone came this way, they're long gone."

A herg? A noble out here on a winter night? The gravedigger prayed to Galivith for salvation.

A voice, deep and resonant, proclaimed, "What a pity. We lost sight of the other grave-robber at the riverbank. But Yarrow, here, tells me the person might have been a hunchback and that he moved strangely. We might have something much more serious than those sheep-rustling Thorn People to deal with."

They're hunting Thorn People? Those wasn't just rumours?

The *herg* continued, "As I recall, my shire reeve informed me that a hunchback arrived in Stoukton this past autumn. Despite his own deformities, this man set out his shingle as a *læknir* and that sometimes he was seen arriving home as the sun would rise. I now suspect he isn't a healer at all, nor even a grave robber, but something far, far worse. We might have a necromancer at work in our lands."

A dead-dancer? I was in the hire of a dead-dancer?

The resonant voice - clearly the *herg* - continued, "Luckily, I am the Sword of Galivith and the impure cannot stand before me. Do not lose heart. We will rid North Straeland of this dead-dancer's stain soon enough. Then we can turn our attention back to those vile Thorns."

The *herg* and his war band moved off into the frigid night.

Before dawn, cold, shaken and shaking, the gravedigger slipped from the woodshed and made for home. Thereafter, despite his wife's complaints, he laid out a bowl of milk every night for the racoons who lived near his cottage.

Part I

The Misshapen Man

Chapter One

Lora shivered despite the bearskins heaped upon her. "…
needs proper food," she heard Cairn say, though she didn't
understand why. She saw him above her but he sounded
so far away, as though he were across a meadow. She could
see Lars too, though his eyes seemed strange, near dead, but
again, she didn't understand why. Of all the eyes around her,
only Thay's burned with an inner dragon-fire as he looked
down at her. The stink of damp fur filled her nostrils. *Fur?*

"We all need food," Thay muttered, and as he did so, Lora
noticed that she could see the vapour of her friends' breath as
they spoke. Above her, the boughs of the trees hardly hid a
grey sky, try as they would to intertwine skeletal fingers above
her. She realized that she lay upon her back and felt a root
digging into her spine. They all had thick cloaks draped over
their shoulders and Lars' looked like a bearskin.

"Is it winter?" she asked, but she did not hear her voice.
"Where did you get furs?"

"What's that?" Cairn asked, looking at Thay.

"Sorry?" asked Thay.

"I asked you what you said."

Thay looked up and replied, "I said that she wasn't meant
for such an end." He seemed to float higher and higher above
her, nearly catching himself in the web of skeletal wooden
fingers. "I'm going to get her some food." She hauled her eyes
over towards Lars, but they didn't get there. All that she could
see contracted, darkness claiming the periphery; she chanted:

> Summer's harp   pushes the hull,
>   joyful strake-song,   baleen-driver;
> but Winter's horn   sounds doleful dirge,
>   Norrgi-song allots our chores.

"What?" Cairn asked.

"I didn't say anything," replied Thay. "What's come over you?"

Then she heard Lars' voice cut in as the darkness closed about her, "Lora did. A cold wind's coming." Lars heard. Cairn oft times too frantic, Thay - sweet Thay - turned inward, listening to himself. But Lars always heard. He knelt down looming over her. His white-blonde braid couldn't keep the dark at bay.

§

"Of course it'll work," Cairn declared. "The man's a fool for not having a boy and a dog look after them sheep. *My Da* never took such a risk."

"Well, they're there, and they don't look like they're guarded," Thay observed. Then he shivered and whispered, "By Florri's beard, it's cold! Colder than back home."

Cairn said, "But it's drier here. I doubt the Tears of the Ghosts fall much here. Like winter up in the plateau."

They studied the farmstead for a while before Cairn said, "Say a prayer." Cairn closed his eyes and murmured a few words to Florri before declaring, "Right. Let's go." Thay nodded and scooped up a pile of kindling surmounted by a couple of faggots he had prepared. They pulled themselves to their feet and lurched across the snow at a jog on the snowshoes they had made the week earlier when the snow had first fallen. They burst from the thicket and strode rapidly to the outhouse. Thay yanked the door open and dumped a pile of kindling inside and set about striking a flame from his flint while Cairn lumbered off in the direction of the barn. The flame caught quickly and then Thay bolted after his friend.

By the time the farmer reacted to the deep-of-the-night chaos - his sheep bleating, his dog barking from under the bed like a valiant saviour - he immediately sent his daughters and wife to hide in the larder, took his axe from beside the hearth and poked his head out the door of his farmhouse. The outhouse was on fire, the barn door was open and the animals in the barn were raising Galivith, having scented smoke. The sheer absurdity of the vandalism, more than anything else, prevented the sheep farmer from pursuing the perpetrators, though the lack of reinforcements also played a role, including the craven dog still raising hell from under the bed.

Feeding Lora helped her regain strength but her fever did not break. She was not well enough to walk so the boys loaded her into a stretcher made from blankets they had stolen from a farmyard during the autumn and together they carried her through the woods. To keep her warm, they draped over her one of their bearskins - also stolen, this time from a cottage at the edge of a town in late autumn. The snowshoes helped them make their way overland, but after another day of living off mutton, they came to a wide river that had not yet frozen over in the first onslaught of winter. They weighed the wisdom of building a raft before Thay pointed north and led them upriver. Nigh on a day later they came to a stone bridge wide enough for carts but seemingly isolated from any town. They watched the cart track leading to the bridge for a while to gauge the danger in attempting a crossing, but they saw no one, so they crept from their thicket near dusk and lumbered in a lurching gait to the bridge, their snowshoes kicking up powder as they passed. During the crossing they came upon a man lying crumpled upon the bridge's stones.

Dressed in torn, dirty black robes and a thick black Straelish cloak riddled with holes, and largely balding except for the patches of long, thin, grimy soot-coloured hair clinging to the base of his skull, he had a large hump protruding from the middle of his back. Droplets of blood had mixed with the dirty snow beneath his open mouth and his claw-like hands clutched his sides as if to protect himself from a kicking. The man had ruddy blotches on either side of his forehead, left perhaps by blows, but Thay could not but think of two budding, demonic horns pushing at the man's flesh from the inside. The face matched his scalp; blotchy and asymmetric to the point of parody. The boys slowed as they came upon him and looked questions and answers at each other.

Lars shook his head.

Cairn shrugged a reply.

Thay narrowed his eyes, twisted his head and bit his lower lip.

Lars shook his head again.

Thay furrowed his brow and nodded with determination.

Lars rolled his eyes and looked at Cairn with big eyes.

Cairn shrugged again but added rolled eyes.

Thay set down his end of the stretcher, careful not to shake Lora from her fevered sleep, and knelt beside the man. He saw an exhalation of vapour in the cold dusk air as he reached out to check the strength of the man's pulse, but when he touched the scrawny neck, a claw like hand shot up and dirty nails dug into Thay's wrist. The man wheezed words in Straelish with more venom than force, ending with "off." Thay slapped the hand aside and pulled the man into a sitting position. Eyes opened, spilling first hate, then recognition as he took in Lars' mien - tall, white-blonde hair with a braid dangling at the temple, ice blue eyes, faint fuzz of a young man's beard, furs hung over his shoulder. Then his eyes spilled out even more hate. One eye was brown, the other bloodshot green, but they didn't look in quite the same direction. "I said, 'bugger off.'"

Thay shot up and stepped back. Lars gasped, "He speaks Fjordlander!"

"Florri's frigging teeth," spat the man. "You're a real bloody genius, aren't you?"

Cairn chuckled and observed, "You're right, Lars, he does speak our tongue, and he speaks it like us!"

"Who *are* you?" Lars demanded.

The man raised his head to glare at what Thay thought was both sides of Lars' head. "I'm a *bad* man. I'm a devil. I'm … what do you call it in your savage tongue?" He raised his scabby hands to both sides of his head and shook them in the gesture of mock scariness, "I'm a medicine man. Now bugger off and leave me alone."

The boys looked at each other again. Lars nodded.

Cairn nodded back.

Thay looked first at the stretcher and then arched an eyebrow at each of the others. Lars pursed his lips, hesitated, then nodded.

Cairn nodded as well. Lars and Thay each grabbed an arm and shifted the strange man onto the stretcher beside Lora. "Get your hands off me!" gasped their new burden, but he lacked the strength to resist. Lars snatched up a sack that lay beside the man and slung it over his shoulder, generating a metallic clang. Thay hauled the stretcher up with surprise; the man did not add much weight to the load. They set off again to the sound of the snow crunching underfoot, the periodic ravings of Lora, and the constant cursing of their new acquaintance.

§

"You Fjordlanders're a bunch of in-bred, superstitious bastard barbarians, the lot of you."

Cairn furrowed his brow while he chewed and then he replied around a mouthful of elderly, well-exercised, terrified-when-slaughtered mutton, "I wouldn't say we're so barbaric."

"You said you were a medicine man," Lars interrupted, leaning over the small campfire and pointing a dagger at the man. Cairn thought the desired effect was lessened by the bit of mutton skewered on the tip of the blade. "So, make medicine and make her better."

"She needs a … a …" he switched back into the Straeling tongue and said a word that sounded like "dock tor." He quickly added, "… *fisik* … a *læknir* … a *leech*, that's how you idiots say it! Not a lean-to. And a good bed, a heap of warm blankets and lots of fluids. She'll die out here. What did you goatfuckers think? That you could really expect her to get better as you dragged her about in the freezing cold? You're fucking idiots."

"If you're not good at medicine, then what are you?" Thay asked. "Why were you lying on that bridge?"

"That's none of your bloody business," the man snapped.

Lars popped the mutton into his mouth and rummaged around in the sack before pulling out a kettle. He examined it before shaking his head, "What kind of man puts holes in the bottom of his kettle?" The man peered daggers into Lars - one into the chest and, from as near as Cairn could tell from the man's skewed gaze, one into the left knee. Lars pulled out a pot. "Now *this* is interesting. A pot that doesn't just not have a handle, but the metal's cut open where a handle would hinge. Now, if you had a handle on it, as it was made, you could hang it over a fire, but you can't even do that because there's no place to attach a makeshift handle.

"Not only can the pot not be hung," Lars continued, "but you can't even set it on a rock *next* to a fire because someone's dented the bottom so badly out of shape that it'll only tip on its side." Again, the man peered violently at Lars with only pursing lips to betray an erosion of emotional control. Lars gazed at the man for a long while, nodded to himself, and then upended the sack, spilling its contents onto the slush beside the fire. There was a thick, filthy grey blanket that had been cut into strips and from the folds of which fell the tiny corpses of at least two fleas that Cairn could see. There was a set of grimy, black rags - perhaps some shamed soul would call them a robe, underclothes and vest, but only someone used to impractically tailored clothes because of the slashed-open design that would leave important bits dangling in the open. There was a length of rope hewn into perhaps a dozen lengths about eighteen thumbs long. There was a collection of glass shards. There was a fork, or they suspected it had been a fork for the prongs had been hacked off. Finally there was a frozen turd that looked like it came from a human.

Lars recoiled at the turd and kicked the pile towards the stranger. The man, huddled against one of the largest trees in the thicket for some measure of support, stared at the pile, despair clearly written across his distorted features. "Oh," Lars exclaimed, holding the sack aloft with his left hand and mock surprise giving a lilt to his voice. Cairn could see that something large had not fallen through the sack's mouth. Lars pulled out a perfectly crafted, round metal water jug with a cork stopper on it. "We have one thing left. It's not like everything else you own. Where'd you steal it?"

The man moved with such speed that he took Lars completely by surprise. Thay was quicker, perhaps having suspected something, knocking the man back down on the ground with the butt of his axe, but not before the man had seized the water jug and sent Lars sprawling. Lars sprang to his feet and hauled out *Harbinger*, aiming its point at the man. "I didn't steal it, you ignorant barbarian!" the man yelled, sitting back down against the tree. "Not everyone in this world acts like you bloody thieving brigand bastards."

When the man made no further attack, Lars set aside his sword, but both he and Thay stood their ground. "It's *mine* and I'm bloody thirsty, so I'm going to take a drink of *my* water." He pulled off the cork and took a swig. His bloodshot, skewed eyes shot wide open and he sprayed the fluid over the fire. The Fjordlanders laughed as they caught the scent of singed piss. The man crumpled to the ground in a heap of weeping.

At length Thay pulled the man into a sitting position, despite much cursing and flailing, and thrust a waterskin into the man's arthritic, knobby hands. The man uncorked the stopper and sniffed the contents. He took a pull of the water, rinsed his mouth out and spat around the side of the tree. He then drank greedily, downing as much of the waterskin as he could before the ice inside blocked the remaining water from escaping. "Who are you?" Thay asked.

"Elkor," the man whispered in reply. "Elkor the Grim."

"Aye, that y'are," Thay agreed, "but can you help her? We know enough about you now, man, to know that you need help. You help her, we help you."

"Will you help me kill that bloody man?"

"Aye. We can do that. What bloody man?"

"Korgash! *He* bloody well did this to me. It's not enough to drive me from my bloody town, he had to track me down thirty bloody leagues from home to bloody beat me! And steal my books! My *books*! And destroy the rest of my belongings just to remind me of who I bloody am, and that I'm bloody powerless to stop him, and that I'm not fit to breathe his bloody air. Most fuckers like him would have simply bloody well killed me, or had the stupid bloody peasants of my town do it, for being a warlock. Well, he *knows* that *he* doesn't have to bloody well kill me, or have me killed, does he? No. He bloody well knows that suffering can be prolonged, doesn't he?"

"You're a *what?*" Lars demanded.

Thay gave Lars a warning look and turned back to Elkor. "So, we help you kill bloody Korgash after you help Lora, right?"

The man gazed up at Thay, incredulity and hatred equally spilling from his eyes. "He pissed in my bloody water jug! What kind of deranged goatfucker does *that?*"

"A deranged goatfucker we'll help you kill if you help our friend."

Cairn thought Elkor's bloodshot eye looked at Thay while the other stared at the darkened woods. "Get out of my way," Elkor ordered as he pushed past Thay and went over to Lora. He looked her up and down, placed a gnarled hand against her forehead and two scrawny fingers on her neck. He prized open her eyelids to look at her eyes. Finally, he said, "She's as good as dead unless you get her into a bed, get fluids into her, and get her some herbs that *I* no longer have. You've got to get to the nearest town and bloody well hope there's an inn that'll let you stay. I'll warn you, though, they don't bloody well think much of brigands and thieves in these parts."

Lars stormed forward, closing on Elkor and raising his fist to strike the man. Thay grabbed Lars' arm. "We're no thieves!" Lars yelled.

Elkor rolled his eyes and retorted, "Of course not. Corpses can't bloody well have possessions, can they? So if you take things from a corpse, how can it be called thievery? It becomes something noble, doesn't it! It becomes fucking plunder! Bow down and pray to it! And why not throw a few fucking slaves onto a bonfire to consecrate it!"

Lars surged again, enough that Cairn finally hauled himself to his feet to help Thay hold their friend back. "*You'll* be a corpse right quick if you keep slandering my people!" Lars yelled. Elkor finally turned his gaze from Lora to Lars, or at least part of Lars.

"*Slander?* Well, if that word means what I thought it meant in your barbaric tongue, then you'd better open your eyes boy! Let's see, is there a synonym? Ah, yes! 'Besmirch.' Is that what you meant? Well, you beardless fool, it's no besmirching, no slandering." He poked a dirty finger into Lars' chest, "What is this raiding you do? You storm ashore on some un-suspecting village to force the inhabitants to bloody well sit in circles with you, sing songs, and add to your collections of dried flowers plucked lovingly from people's gardens?"

By now Elkor had the stunned attention of all three boys and he continued, "When I was your age I got captured by one of your raiding parties and served as a slave on a longboat for five years." Then he yelled, "Five bloody years! Pulling on frozen oars, not allowed the luxury of a simple pair of gloves.

Look what it did to my hands!" Again he prodded Lars with his twisted, swollen fingers. Then he continued in his usual, oily tone, "And the Sea Wolves only allowed me to live, me, a shit useless oar-puller, because I could navigate on open water better than any northern sealfucker.

"Oh *yes*, you people deflower those you raid, but it's not in a song circle, is it? No, it's done over blood and wailing and burning and slaughtering and it bloody well is done over *thieving*. And those wenches that suffer from it and have the misfortune of living have to deal with your little presents, don't they? And then those little presents get to learn that they're hated. And they get picked on by other children, and they get beaten by their angry, bitter mothers, and they get blamed for misfortune and they're forced to go fishing even though longboats are seen off the coast. And if they ever get home again, they get called *warlocks* or *sorcerers* or *necromancers*." Elkor stared into Lars' eyes, but then Cairn thought that the man's gaze shifted to Thay and he said, "Open your fucking eyes, boy."

Thay swayed on his feet and Cairn, still clutching the now pacified Lars, had to catch his friend's arm to prevent him from falling. Thay held a hand to his head and winced. "Are you well?" Cairn asked.

Thay shook his head and returned Cairn's worried look. "That's rare."

"What?"

"A crimson dream. While awake."

§

The boys sat huddled together around the fire. They had banished Elkor to the edge of the thicket to keep watch, despite him seeming neither all that willing nor even all that well ... he certainly whinged about it until Thay pointed out that it was a good way of making sure his enemy, Korgash, didn't come upon them unseen. Lora shivered in unconsciousness next to the fire on a pallet made from their wooden target shields and blankets. "He's right," declared Thay. "That's why I had the dream. It was to tell me to listen to him. We've got to get Lora to a bed."

"What was the damned dream you had anyway?" Cairn asked.

"It was just a glimpse of a vision. The future. Or a possible future if certain paths are followed. I know it was. I saw this Elkor the Grim with Lora, but Lora was old and he was decrepit. And they were blessing *Harbinger* and it glowed a fierce emerald fire, a northern fire like in the winter skies at night back home."

"Blessing my sword?" Lars asked, wonder mixed with incredulity written across his face.

"Aye. And there's more. I saw … well, something impossible. If you can believe it, I saw him with Asgear working on the sail of a longship. They were putting the Scales on a black sail."

"The Scales?" Lars asked, wonder written on his features. "You mean the stars? Like this?" He drew *Harbinger* so the three of them could see the nine gems set into its pommel to mimic the constellation so beloved by Hondrig.

"I don't understand." Thay said, rocking back and forth on his heels and gazing into the fire. "Look, I know we don't ken much about this man. But he's learned. He's had books! Lars, I know you don't believe me, but I did listen to Kyre every now and then. He oft spoke to me of *books*! Like, boxes of knowledge that you open up and the magic flows into you! He's as much as admitted to being some sort of medicine man or sorcerer. He appears to ken what he's about when it comes to Lora. I say we give him a chance." The others nodded, following Thay's gaze into the fire.

Lars said, "If you've seen him with my sword and setting the Scales into a sail, then it forms part of a bigger whole, right alongside Helgya's vision. The wielder of my sword will be our *Kunungr* and I'm the wilder of the sword."

Cairn nodded. Then he said, "But he's an ugly, slimy bugger and he hates our kind, us Fjordlanders." The others nodded.

"He seems to have just cause," Thay replied. Lars turned his head and stared at Thay but Thay just kept staring at the flames. At length he added, "He seems ready to deal with us. He speaks our tongue. Right enough, he's as ugly as a *tosk-hyr*, his eyes put shivers up my spine, and he wants us to help kill a man who likely was on to something when he thought he'd found a necromancer, but I'm sure he can save Lora and I am sure he's yet to do something in the future with her that will be important."

Cairn declared, "Any man who pisses in another man's water jug deserves to die." The others nodded.

"The turd was funny, though," Lars replied. The others nodded.

"And the fork," Thay added with a grin. "Who'd think to do that?"

"One twisted Sk'van worshiper, that's who," Cairn declared. The others laughed.

"And did you see the look on his face when he saw the kettle?" Lars gasped between bursts of laughter. The others laughed harder. Soon the three of them were writhing around in the slush laughing hysterically.

The racket brought Elkor shuffling back to the camp to stand and watch with distain. He whispered to himself, "Laugh while you can, sheepfuckers. Laugh while you can."

Thay was the first to get to his feet and go to Elkor. The strange man shot Thay a contemptuous look but the young lad was undeterred. He grabbed the sleeve of Elkor' cloak and guided him to the edge of the thicket, where they could keep watch while they spoke. "We've talked it over," he said.

"I didn't know wallowing in mud was how you folk talked things over but I'm not surprised."

"Lora needs help; you need help too. It smacks of Rulla's

work, or perhaps Tanat the Rogue. Either way, we're agreed. We'll see about killing this Korgash fellow whenever you meet him next, but in the meantime you obviously need protection, so we're your muscle. Can you get us into an inn without people chopping off our heads and mounting them on harpoons?"

"Do I look like a fucking miracle worker?"

"Kind of," Thay said. They stood together, staring off into the night for a while before the young Fjordlander stated, "It's Darknight ... what some call midwinter night. Lora'd have known if she had her wits about her. The others have forgotten. It's our birthing day. We turn seventeen as night gives way to dawn."

Elkor turned his head at this and at least one eye stared at Thay. "You're quadruplets? Elkshit! You don't fucking look it."

"No. Each one of us was born to a different mother."

"On the same night?"

Thay nodded. "Aye, on the very same night. Very nearly at the same moment."

"You're a stinking liar," Elkor said, but there was no venom in his words.

Thay turned and, after deciding which of Elkor's eyes to look into, said, "We'll be seventeen on the dawn. We're hundreds of leagues and three large mountain ranges away from our home. All the people between here and there want to kill us. We're born on Midwinter Night, but we know enough to know that it's the easy bit of winter that's behind us. It gets harder from here on in. Without your help Lora might not even make it to her seventeenth birthing day. But I think you'll help us tonight. I have seen it."

"You've seen it?" Elkor chuckled. "You're raving as much as she is."

"No. I think the promise of helping you kill this Korgash will sway you. And the fact we were all born on the same night."

Elkor huffed and stared off into the night. Finally he asked,

"Do you have a robe with a deep hood?"

Thay nodded. "It's a bit ratty, but it'll do."

Elkor huffed. "Right then, have that idiot Lars stand behind me and smile, and yes, I can probably get you into an inn. Do you have coin?" Thay nodded. "Do you believe in that goddess bitch of yours - what was her name? - that mistress of fates ... Rulla, the one with the owls?"

Again, Thay nodded, though this time he warned Elkor, "Calling Rulla anything but wise around us is dangerous."

Elkor snorted, "Odd how it's never gods, themselves, who strike people down, but their rabid followers. Listen, I can give your prayers a fighting chance. But you'd best keep praying. We should leave. Now." Thay nodded and turned on his heels. "Wait!" Elkor hissed, grasping Thay's cloak. "You said something when that blonde idiot was going to thump me. You said you'd had a ... a ... What's a crimson bloody dream?"

"Sorcery," Thay replied before cracking a smile.

§

They crept from the thicket in which they had hidden and crossed snow-covered fields, Lora again lying in her stretcher, though Elkor could limp along without help. Thay could see that there were scattered steadings set back from the woods, clusters of darkened buildings - a house or two, barn, granary, shed, outhouse - surrounded by well-maintained hedgerows rather than lines of carefully piled stones like they would be back home. They made their way to what Elkor called a "road," and though he swore it was far more elaborate than anything of which the Fjordlanders could boast, it appeared to Thay to be no more than a broad cart track. When the youngster said as much, Elkor huffed and retorted, "It might not be a Polgati road, but it's a hell of a lot more than one of your goat tracks ... when there's not snow on it."

They came to the nearest town around midnight, a place Elkor said was called Harburg. It was not what Thay expected. There were a great many more buildings; easily double what he had seen in Sangspit back on Caljürd's Arm. It began with a ring of smooth-walled cottages and some larger, rectangular wooden structures that looked like big smoke houses. Those then gave way to bigger buildings built one abutting the other, much like the buildings that he had seen at the end of the summer in Marshton Vale close to the Peregrinsmouth, ones that rose beyond the height of a single man. Then those, too, gave way to tall, long buildings that appeared divided into family dwellings that lined the way, giving him the impression on the dark night of being in a narrow fjord, with cliff walls rising up on either side of him.

They rounded a corner, then another, and finally found themselves in an open space, on the north side of which a broad, round building brooded in darkness, and from which rose a narrow spire illuminated by the half-full moon. Elkor took them to a building on the edge of the open space that had a sign hanging over the door that he said announced it as an inn named "The Drover's Maid." The inn was locked up against the cold winter night, but a few bangs on the door brought a middle-aged, balding man to the threshold. The man was shocked at Elkor's cloaked and hooded figure with obvious outlanders behind him, but he soon accepted coin and let them in. Elkor got the boys a room to share and took another with a bed and a pallet so that he could keep an eye on Lora, but he soon found out that the northmen intended to take turns watching over the girl. After talking with the man, Elkor went out again into the night. He returned a while later, frost clinging to his greasy strands of hair, and, with Thay looking on, he brewed up a tonic in the inn's kitchen from the chopped-up leaves of herbs and measures of fine powder.

"You just stir all that into boiling water?" Thay asked.

Elkor glanced up, a look of stupefied contempt on his distorted features, and spat back, "No-oh. It's not *just stirring it into boiling water*! It's a great deal more than that; the measure of liquid requires precision, only slightly less than the measure of the herbs. There are other ingredients I need but that are surely here, so I don't need to risk my life obtaining them. But if you think this requires the ritual sacrifice of a virgin, or a deaf, two-headed otter, then I'm sorry to disappoint you; some people know better."

After administering the concoction - thankfully, by spoon through the mouth rather than any sort of necromancer ritual involving a dagger opening veins - Elkor said the only thing to do was keep a watchful eye on Lora and press a cold compress against her hot skin. Seeing as Lars was doing that, Elkor rolled into bed and fell into a deep sleep.

Though he could not darken his hair, Thay used his dirk to shave the next morning and he dressed in Straelish clothes they had stolen from a score of clotheslines during the autumn, all to appear less foreign to the innkeeper's eyes. Thay's Straelish was sufficient to get food brought up to them. In so doing, he learnt that The Drover's Maid was otherwise empty of clients. For the coin that Thay offered, they were able to have the man and his family take care of their every need as they watched over Lora.

During that day, Elkor administered his tonic, piled greater numbers of blankets on Lora's bed, and spoon-fed her beef broth at regular intervals. Lora passed two bad days, but the only person who seemed concerned was Elkor. Thay's vision had convinced the northmen that she would survive. Their most alarming moment came not from worries about Lora's health, but late in the morning of the first day in the inn when a group of the men of Harburg, under the leadership of a priest of some sort, demanded to see them. The meeting occurred in the inn's small dining room, but not before Thay and Cairn had threatened Lars that if he did not shave and cut his hair, they would claim he was a Fjordlander slave. Of course, Lars refused.

"Then you're not coming," Thay declared.

"Because I look like who I am? Stand aside."

"No. I'm not joking. You could get us killed."

They stared at each other for a long time.

"I'll stay here with Lora. Go!"

When they met with the townsfolk, Lars remained in their room. Elkor went with them and did most of the talking. Despite its raggedness, Elkor wore the ratty black robe that Thay had given him the previous evening and kept its hood raised, claiming disfigurement from a cooking fire in childhood. He assured the villagers that they had nothing to fear, that he and his party would respect the Queen's law and the Word of Galivith. He further informed the men that the northmen were travellers, "Veneg savages" from the lands just east of the Boldring Mountains. The claim was outlandish, but it explained the Fjordlanders' height and unease with Straelish. Even so, the fact that Thay spoke Straelish reasonably well and the others enough to get by, set the villagers' fears at ease. The locals were all dark-haired and Thay made a mental note to make sure Lars always wore a woollen hat to hide his brilliant white-blonde hair complete with braid dangling past his left temple.

Thay did wonder in passing why the townsfolk could tolerate "Veneg savages" but not Fjordlanders.

He escorted the priest - he went by the title *revered* - and the townsfolk to the threshold of the inn and while the villagers dispersed, the priest lingered on the doorstep. He wore normal clothes beneath a red cloak trimmed with black, upon which was embroidered a sheaf of wheat in yellow thread. When no one was in earshot he turned to Thay and said in a hushed voice, "You are strange folk and I would have you know that Galivith teaches us to trust only in those we know and to be on our guard with those we know not."

Thay reached back to his time learning Straelish with Aganas, and later with Yens, and remembered that Galivith was the Straeling God. The priest continued, "He says, 'A trusting man dieth more frequently upon the sword.' But Galivith also teaches us that to survive we must offer hospice to those who need it and that in the offering to the one, we offer to the collective. For my part, you will have no trouble and I shall preach Galivith's words regarding hospice on his next Name Day.

"But there are others not only more cautious than I, but more inclined to enjoy the persecution of strangers, all in Galivith's Holy Name. There is one, a *herg* and a warrior of some renown and a wealthy man, though I know not whence comes his coin. This man is trying to turn this part of Straeland into his domain. He says the *oberherg* we have is too old, too weak and has no heirs to protect the north of the realm. He says that *Oberherg* Holgarth should be set aside, with honour, so that 'someone' with more energy can protect those who live here from outsiders. He delights in showing his prowess, leaving no doubt who that someone might be. Some, in towns such as this, make sure he knows if there are strangers that they fear. He makes a great show of protecting the folk. If I were a stranger passing through these parts, I would give no one cause for anyone to be afraid and then send word to this man. Also, there are others as ready to pick up the sword, or the pitchfork for that matter, and offer its point rather than offer hospice. Tread softly, young man. If you and your friends are still here come the next Name Day, you would be welcome to join our adoration ceremony at the temple."

Thay nodded. The priest turned to go on his way but then turned back and added, "That hooded man you're with. He speaks Straelish like us, but he could easily be perceived as every bit as much a stranger as you. He has an ill feel to him. Were I you, I would rid myself of him. At the very least, advise him to remain in his room."

After that, their stay in the inn went undisturbed, but the very next day, Thay and Cairn went to the town's trading houses to look for clothes of Straelish make, including some winter fur-lined coats. Thay was worried about how to conceal Lars' hair and had settled upon the idea of woollen hats, but he was particularly worried about how he'd persuade his stubborn friend to wear whatever they might find. He hoped Straeland's winter, harsher than that in Fjordland, might strengthen his argument.

It took them half a day, first visiting a shop whose keeper referred them to a cottage on the end of town, whose resident crone told them that her friend on the other side of town might have what they needed, who indeed confirmed that she would have what they needed after the passage of two moons, but if they wished they could try with a farmer who had good reputation for producing quality wool, who finally admitted that he just sold the wool sheared from his beasts but who referred them back to a carter who sometimes moved rare goods, after all of which they finally got their hands on woollen hats.

As the sun set, they entered a narrow building behind the round, spire-mounted hall in search of fur cloaks. They found themselves in a half warehouse, half shop stuffed with blankets, animal pelts and lengths of leather. The shopkeeper was a balding man with a crooked back and a pronounced limp. He was suspicious of the youngsters and yet welcoming in equal measure. He didn't need to introduce himself, as his wife's hollering from the parlour at the back of the house did the job for him. Thay's Straelish wasn't good enough to catch all of what the shopkeeper's wife yelled, seeing as she yelled it so quickly and ran the words together, but it sounded like, "Wolfgar! You're a dolt if ever there was one! Did you see the state of these clasps you bought? Well? Did you? Wolfgar! I'm speaking to you! Don't you go ignoring me or I'll *Wolfgar* you all the way to Herrybock! Do you hear me?"

Wolfgar shrugged at the hollering and asked, "So what is it that you lads need?" Then he duly fetched the goods that Thay and Cairn asked to examine. The man seemed to warm up to the Fjordlanders, or was keen to put his wife's continued hollering out of his mind by attending to the young men's needs. Wolfgar showed them his fur cloaks and heavy blankets, to which Cairn nodded his approval. Thay picked out a decent thick woollen vest that fit him, Cairn got himself measured for one of his own, and they selected thick blankets to take with them, and the shopkeeper's mood improved to the point that Thay could not perceive even a trace of suspicion in the man.

At length the hollering abated and the lads thought nothing of it until a small woman burst into the shop with the force of a gale. Waif-like, with her long raven-coloured hair braided into two strands that dangled over her shoulders and past her slight bust, she had a fair face covered with freckles. She stomped over to the table upon which the men had been inspecting a selection of blankets, a two pace-wide roll of coarse cloth that looked like a tree trunk slung over her shoulder. She stood there for a moment before bobbing her head at the blankets and declaring, "Do you mind giving a hand, or are you beneath something as menial as *work*?"

"Ah … yes! Of course," stammered Wolfgar before gathering up the blankets. He glanced up at the Fjordlanders and added, "My beloved wife, *Frouw* Singrid."

"Don't you 'beloved wife' *me*! What are you trying to sneak past me? Haven't you learnt by now that I'm wise to you?" She laid out the cloth on the table before declaring, "You'll be wanting this."

Both Thay and Cairn glanced down at the cloth and then at each other. Thay reached back to his schooling with Aganas growing up and managed as polite a phrasing as he could, "Might I ask why the esteemed lady says we shall want this?"

"*Lady*, is it?" Singrid huffed. "I'm no *lady*, though a better woman than most *hergs*' wives, especially that Lady Oda who's been sniffing around with her ruffians." Thay and Cairn glanced at each other again in puzzlement. "It's burlap."

"Why do we want *burlap*?" asked Cairn.

"It's durable," she replied, "More than tough enough for an overland trip, and yet breathable, which means you won't have problems with dampness."

"Overland trip?" asked Cairn, just as Thay asked, "Dampness?"

Singrid rolled her eyes to the ceiling and heaved a sigh. "Galivith above, help me!" Then she swept her hand towards her husband and the goods they had been inspecting. "Well, you're sizing up cloaks and blankets, asking about provisions and you talk funny, especially *him*," she declared, thrusting her chin at Cairn. "It's less costly and lighter than *canevaz*, though more porous if you're caught in rain. It'll do you good as a liner to a makeshift shelter, as an outer covering over your blankets if you hole up in a cave, and you can carry things in it."

Thay and Cairn glanced once more at each other, pulled a measured, considering frown, and then, shrugged and nodded.

"Good, that's settled. Wolfgar, you're limping again! You're back to your old tricks of pushing yourself too hard! Put the kettle on the boil and sit down before you drop dead on me, will you?"

"Yes, my little kraken of the deep," Wolfgar replied before tottering off.

Singrid swiped at her husband, but for all he might have a limp, he could dodge a blow as well as Lora. Then she glanced at the Fjordlanders, rolled her eyes, and declared, "A cord of wood fell on his leg, but you'd think it'd fallen on his head!"

Wolfgar's voice carried back to them through the curtain that closed off the shop, "Ah, had it only fallen on my head! Maybe then my hearing'd be gone!"

Singrid huffed. Then she said, "Wolfgar'll get us some broth. In the meantime, what else do you need?"

The perusal of goods became more efficient with Singrid directing the process. A short while later, as they passed a shelf by the shop's far corner, Thay came across a bolt of smooth, shiny cloth and asked Singrid what it was. "That? That's the most expensive item in the house. Comes from the Chayan Empire. There's some what like wearing it for special ceremonies but there's not much demand for it at the best of times, never mind in the middle of a quiet winter. No lad, you don't want that, not that young ones like yourselves could afford it."

"If there's few who can buy it, why sell it?" Thay asked.

"For sale?" Singrid exclaimed. "No, that's not for sale lad."

"Not for sale?" Thay asked, bringing Singrid's attention back to the bolt of cloth.

"No lad, that's special, that is. That's waiting for *Oberherg* Holgarth's fine *lady* wife to pass through the village. Or even the Queen! She's a good Estestraelish girl like me. She'd remember me if I made her a present of that bolt of cloth. In the meantime it tells everyone for a league about that I can procure. People look at that, just like you're doing lad, and they know I can get them anything, or at least that Wolfgar can. Even though we might do it better than any man, women can't be seen running a shop now, can we?"

"I don't know," Thay replied, his brow furrowed. "Why can't you run a shop?"

Singrid rolled her eyes to the ceiling again and called out, "Wolfgar, where's that broth?"

In the end, Thay handed over a hefty weight of silver - a portion of Lora's *bondgyld* that Kindron had secreted away in his chest - in return for the blankets and the woollen vest. That precious sum also secured them five fur-lined coats, for which they got measured immediately - Singrid said she would drop in at The Drover's Maid to take the measurements of the other three people needing the coats. They promised they would return at some point for the burlap, and they left with Singrid's and Wolfgar's blessing of Galivith upon them.

Chapter Two

Four days after their arrival in Harburg, Lora's fever broke, though she remained weak and slept a great deal. That evening, to Thay's surprise, Elkor told him to stow his coin, "get off his arse," and find them a billet in which they could stay as well as some work. When he asked why, Elkor responded, "Think about it, fool," and went about preparing more broth for Lora.

Although Thay was puzzled by Elkor's behaviour, he nevertheless persuaded an aged widower to let them two rooms in his cottage and he convinced a woodcutter to take them on for a few days. The woodcutter, *Herr* Monsfried, was tall, had grey hair, a grizzly beard and a perpetually clenched jaw. Thus, for the week that Lora recuperated, the lads worked dawn until dusk hiking into the forest, felling trees, sawing branches, fixing tackle and harness, and leading teams of horses back to the yard in town. It was back-breaking work, but they had experience doing it from the previous winter spent on the plateau under Fallig and Leigh's tutelage. They applied themselves to their tasks and they could see how much their months at the oars had hardened them. Monsfried said little to them that was not a barked order, but Thay thought the man liked them well enough and he appeared impressed by the northmen's snowshoes.

One day, when a storm blew through, they spent the day working in Monsfried's yard, sawing logs and chopping branches into faggots. Over a lunch of beef and potato stew beside the stove in the work shed, their patron asked to have a close look at their snowshoes. "That's mightily impressive," he declared, holding one at arm's length and peering at it down the length of his nose. "I've never seen snowshoes this broad and light before. They must be good on deep powder. The bitter cold makes the snow here hard and crusty right quick. No one 'round here has such a thing." Then he passed it back to Cairn, took up his bowl, and added around a mouthful of stew, "Though I've heard the Thorn People have snowshoes of wood and gut to race across fresh snow." Thay watched Monsfried closely to detect any accusation in the man's eyes, but the veteran woodcutter carried on chewing a chunk of beef while digging around in his bowl with his spoon in search of a thick slice of carrot.

"What's a Thorn People?" asked Lars.

Thay thumped his friend's left biceps and snapped, "Don't be daft! You know right well who the Thorn People are." The warning glance he shot Lars only met with a confused stare.

Cairn chimed in with, "Oh, *Thorn* People, I thought he said, 'Torn' People."

Thay glanced back at Monsfried in time to see the man smirk and spoon the carrot into his mouth. "Well," he said, "I'd like a pair of those there things, but I'd be careful to wear them 'round hereabouts where folk know me. I wouldn't want to be taken for one of them raiders. Might be I'd get stuck on a spear."

Lars made an "O" with his lips before nodding and saying, "Mmm, I see your meaning." They ate in silence for a while before he asked, "Do people here not do a wee bit of raiding?"

Monsfried nodded. "Oh aye, there's a bit of lifting of cattle from time to time; bandits on the roads if the Queen's men take too much time between patrols; every town has its thief, but there's one thing none of them will take, by and large."

"What's that?" asked Lars.

"Lives. Our *hergs* don't allow murderers free rein or else the Queen calls 'em to court." Monsfried gathered up the bowls and said, "Right, back to work lads. I'm not paying you to sit about."

§

"So, what have you three lugs been doing with yourselves?" Lora asked in greeting after Cairn, Lars, and Thay came back from their sixth day in the woods. She was up and about and had obviously had the opportunity to bathe and comb out her auburn hair. The northmen had left the widower's house first thing in the morning, long before dawn, so they had not seen Lora since the previous evening. The improvement in her health over the day was remarkable. Her eyes sparkled in the lamplight and her voice held energy in its playful cadence. She had jumped up from a stool in front of the hearth in the cottage's main room when she heard the main door open and her friends stomp snow off their boots. Elkor was nowhere to be seen.

Cairn shrugged off his heavy cloak, hung it on a peg by the door and replied, "Nought but a bit of hacking, chopping, splitting, more chopping, trudging, hauling, pulling, tripping, bleeding, and cursing. Apart from that, not much."

"You're looking well," Lars observed, running a hand through his white-blonde hair to sweep off a powdering of near-indistinguishable snow. "Where's Walster?" he asked, referring to the widower, as he tramped over to the fireplace.

"He's stepped out to get the evening bread. You'll have to fetch your own beer," she said with a smile. "It's not as good as mine, of course, but it'll serve. A bit sour."

"You've been *drinking*?" Thay asked, astonished.

"Just a cup to wet my lips," she said with a sly smile.

"Does this mean we can leave Harburg?" Cairn asked. He flopped into a chair by the hearth. "I'm sick of hacking, chopping, splitting, hauling, pulling, tripping, and bleeding."

"You've never liked hard work, Cairn," Lora stated with a smile, patting her burly friend on the shoulder.

"I don't mind the cursing," he replied.

Thay joined them, rubbing warmth into his hands and then holding them to the fire. "Elkor seems to have cured you once and for all."

At that, Lora sat down on her stool, glanced around the room, and leaned forward like the lead conspirator in some unwholesome plot, although Walster and Elkor had both stepped out. "Who *is* this Elkor anyway? He only goes about in that black robe of his with the hood up as though he wants to hide from the world. He *speaks* our tongue! - though he doesn't have a civil word in him. And his hands are all twisted! This town has the strangest healer ever."

Lars arched his eyebrows at Cairn and Thay.

Cairn's eyes bulged and he blew a deep breath out between pursed lips in reply.

Thay furrowed his brow and shrugged, turning the palms of his hands to the roof.

Cairn lolled his head from side to side, biting his lower lip. Thay nodded.

In resignation, Lars swiped the air with his hand and then gestured to Cairn and Thay to carry on.

"Well," Cairn declared, "he's not exactly the village healer. Tanat busied Himself with us and put this Elkor the Grim in our path." They then told Lora about how they had found the strange man on the bridge, how they had helped him, and how they had asked him to help her. "He's ugly as sin and people don't like him if they see him, so he's happier in the robe. But he helped you, right enough."

Lora rocked her stool back and forth, peering into the fire for a time. The young men let her be. At length she told them, "This Elkor character is to come home with us."

"What?"

"You can't be serious."

"That's the daftest thing I've heard since Cairn roped himself to his bench on *Rignil*. Ow!" Thay rubbed his biceps; he hadn't dodged Cairn's retaliatory punch.

"I *know* it's daft; about as daft as four seventeen year-olds stuck beyond the Teeth in winter hoping to get home overland when their only foreign tongue is accented Straelish, they can only navigate on cloudy days by moving away from the dawn and even *that* gets unreliable at midday if it's snowing, and they have *no idea* what lies between here and home. There are tales of the savage Veneg and *tosk-hyr* in the only thing we *know* lies in our path, the Boldring Mountains, three ranges so high and deadly our people don't bother guarding against attack from that direction in the winter. So, I agree with you. It's daft. It's all daft.

"But this Elkor the Grim, now *he* might know a thing or two," she continued, "like how to speak Polgati or whether we should pass through that land to get home. He might teach us things, and, Rulla knows, perhaps keep *another* one of us from dying, like he has done with me.

"From what you've said, he's hated 'round here. Mayhap the offer of a *lifgyld* coupled with the first kind word he's heard on a regular basis might convince him to come with us." She looked into each of the lad's eyes in turn before adding, "There's one last thing if that isn't enough to convince you ... I just *know* we need him." At that moment, her gaze transformed. Her eyes glazed over. She chanted:

> *Burning hate, hidden face,*
> *   formless cloak, forlorn hope.*
> *Aspect grim, sly and slight,*
> *   from the cowl come cold cruel truths.*
> *He spurns the world, turns the kerns*
> *   with words that gird when truly heard.*
> *They prod and prick, they pry and prompt,*
> *   deplore old lore from foreign shores.*
> *Heed his harsh hints; home's the harvest,*
> *   fjords and fields, falls and freshet all.*

Lora's words hit them. They all reflected on them for a while, with the only sounds in the cottage being the faint howl of the winter wind outside and the hearth popping and crackling inside.

Finally Cairn declared, "He calls himself Elkor the Grim and you've gone and chanted 'Aspect grim.' Odd. I suppose he might indeed teach us a thing or two, as you say, but he *hates* us, Lora! The Sea Wolves made a slave of him. He might just decide to teach us how easily we can have our throats slit in the middle of some dark night."

"Or in the middle of some dark *rite*?" offered Lars.

"Sure, slitting throats would come at the *end* of a dark rite," Cairn countered, shaking his head. Then, turning to Lora, he asked, "And what do you mean by 'home's the harvest?'"

Lora rolled her eyes. "You know how it happens, Cairn. The words and images come, not necessarily the understanding. Farmers who sow barley work all year for their harvest, do they not? Maybe it means that home'll be *our* harvest if we heed him." Then she turned to Lars, "What say you?" It seemed to Thay that her eyes did not sparkle as they had earlier; now they were afire, as though the fever had returned. "*You* know how important this is."

"How should *he* know?" Cairn demanded.

"He *hears* me. He understands."

Lars nodded. "She sees true. It's just like the old tales ... of what folk said about Helgya."

"And you, Thay, you have something of my gift in your crimson dreams," Lora said. "You have dreamt it, have you not?"

"And *you've* seen *that*?" Cairn asked, incredulity tainting his tone.

"Aye, I have," Lora retorted.

"Just like you saw something ... how did you put it? ... 'long and enduring' with Asgear?" Cairn pressed.

That brought Lora up; she sighed and conceded the point, "Aye, you're right enough. Perhaps my *Sight* can fail me ... though the strange thing is I still see that with Asgear."

"Then it'll come true," Lars declared.

Cairn pulled a face, "Oh come on! He's dead, just like the rest of our oar mates."

"Just because we didn't find any of them doesn't mean one didn't escape," Lars declared.

Thay put an end to the argument simply by getting up, walking over to the small draughty window, and looking out into the snow and wind. When he turned around, Lora's eyes looked normal again, but they bored holes into him as he said, "Elkor'll come back with us, right enough. It's necessary. But I reckon more for the practical side of the thing. As Lora says, for the knowing *how* to get us home."

§

"You stupid bastards think that I'd want to spend one fucking heartbeat more than I have to in your charming company? I've been bloody well flattering you when I named you idiots. It doesn't bloody well do you justice. You've all got dung for brains." It was late and Elkor was shuffling back and forth in front of the fireplace at Walster the Widower's home. Thay and Cairn had resolved to speak to Elkor of their request, accosting the man upon his return trip from the outhouse before going to bed. The two Fjordlanders sat at the rickety table between the hearth and the kitchen.

"Look," Cairn pleaded, trying to sound reasonable, "you'd get *lifgyld* for helping get us home. You'd also get *lifgyld* for saving Lora from the fever. You could buy a thousand turds to carry around in your sack." Elkor halted his pacing and peered daggers into the big lad. Thay leaned over and thumped Cairn on the back of the head. "Ow! No, listen, I'm serious. Well, all right, not so serious about the turds, but you could buy passage back here, hire a thousand men, and sack your whole home town if you cared to, never mind kill this Korgash fellow. You'd be rich."

"You goatfuckers don't know what rich is."

"Sure we do," Cairn replied. "We've been counting the worth of foreign plunder for generations."

49

"Your kind would feed a Hengezan lore cloak to your bloody herds of rats or knock a fence post into your fucking frozen tundra with an Imperial burial urn."

"We don't actually keep herds of rats," Cairn stated.

"Intentionally," added Thay.

"Intentionally," Cairn agreed, nodding.

"Oh, yes, sorry, I for-fucking-got. Rats are too bloody clean for you filthy bastards."

"No," Cairn said. "They're too hard to herd."

"The Vallhunds go crazy when they see rats," Thay agreed.

"Listen to yourselves!" Elkor shot back before resuming his pacing in front of the fire. "You're trying to bloody well entice me to your self-confessed rat hole just so that the incessant bloody yapping of dogs that look like ticks with pointy ears can vex my every moment."

Thay let silence fall on the room before he mumbled, "We'd let you do whatever you do."

"Do *what?*" Cairn and Elkor asked in perfect unison., their heads turning to the tawny-haired youth.

"Whatever it was that got you cast out of your town. As long as it doesn't actually require us to sacrifice our children or endure the summoning of demons. I'm certain that I could get you a house built with that *lifgyld* Cairn keeps speaking of, and I'm pretty sure that I could make it so that no one would get in your way or turf you out. You could collect these book things you seem to think are important and keep them safe. It mightn't be a bad life. Or you could just take the *lifgyld* and sail back home."

"You've both bloody well suffered serial frigging blows to the head," Elkor declared.

"Very likely," Cairn acknowledged, shaking his black-haired head. "Very likely indeed."

§

The boys worked for another week woodcutting for Mons-fried before they felt Lora had gained enough strength to move on. Elkor said he had travelled once as far as the Drover lands and hoped never to return, and that if he did, he wanted it to be in better company, and during a better time of the year, but if they were determined to go, well, then, he would certainly not stay behind as his fortune of *lifgyld* trudged off through the snow without him. He also threw in a great many curses; at least four "goatfuckers," a "roe for brains," which was new, and an "earwig-sucking seal-wanker." The Fjordlanders took this for agreement to guide them home. Lars pointed out that the Drover lands still sounded like they were a long way from home, but they nevertheless felt confident that Elkor could do it. Elkor told them that he could get them seventy leagues without them having to stay more than one night at a time camping, greatly reducing the chances they might freeze to death. He also said, "I also know a capable woman who can get us over the Peregrinswater, as long as we can *find* her."

"What do you mean?" Cairn dared ask.

"You've a brain, *use* it! It means she's someone who doesn't like to be *found*, and she's good at it. I hope you're better at searching for smugglers than thinking."

"Smugglers?"

"Yes, she and her gang are some of the best along the Per-egrinswater." With that, Elkor seemed to think that he had fully explained everything.

"One more thing," he added. "From now on you all speak only Straelish, even among yourselves. Your people are rightly hated in these parts. I'll not put my skin at risk helping you, only to have an errant word make the entire land rise against us. Maintain the fiction that you're Veneg or make your way home without me."

Monsfried gave them their wages and those were enough to cover all the cost of the rooms they had rented from Walster the Widower. Monsfried also gave Lora a goodly sum for a pair of snowshoes that she had made during her recovery. With that coin, and bulk of the wealth remaining from Kindron's small chest, she did the rounds of the shops and was able to exchange some silver for things she reckoned they would need on their journey - two flasks of oil, some herbs for her healing bag, a lengthy coil of horsehair rope, and - with her mind thinking back to Knab, her Darnok chieftain - a small pouch of nails that Cairn could turn into caltrops.

She dragged Elkor to the half warehouse, half shop that Thay had described to pick up the fur-lined coats that they had ordered. *Frouw* Singrid also displayed her full selection of winter hard goods. Lora bought them each fur-lined, cow-hide mittens and, once exposed to Singrid's views on the many uses of burlap, a length of that coarse cloth. She also bought some hardy winter clothes for Elkor, though he refused to take the greens and reds she suggested, saying he would only settle for black. Elkor got fitted for breeches and tunics, and Lora handed over a tidy sum for clothes as close as Wolfgar - who could work dyes - could come to so tricky a hue as black. Singrid was well-pleased with the unexpected midwinter earnings, Lora enjoyed being out and about, and even Elkor seemed to swear less.

They also resolved to hold a feast that night in The Drover's Maid to celebrate their departure and they invited Walster the Widower, who seemed only too eager to celebrate their leave-taking. They also bade Monsfried join them as well as Singrid and Wolfgar. The innkeeper and his wife worked hard the entire day preparing the meal and the fare was certainly ample. They had a merry time, with Singrid and Wolfgar the life of the celebration. The banter between the two never ceased, Singrid haranguing her husband and her husband quipping about his suffering under the whip of the slave driver, under the evil spells of the woods witch, under the decrees of the Empress of Chaya

Herself. Cairn certainly didn't let his limited Straelish get in his way and waxed ineloquent and imperfect about how he would never again do as much hacking, chopping, splitting, hauling, pulling, and tripping as he had under Monsfried's own whip, though he acknowledged that, as an aspiring warrior, he might yet do as much bleeding. Monsfried retorted that he hadn't seen very much hacking, chopping, splitting, hauling, pulling, and tripping, before clarifying that the bleeding was no more than Cairn deserved. Lora, under the influence of the beer, kept chuckling at the quips flying back and forth and declared winners of the individual bouts of competing wits. Lars broke into a Fjordlander drinking song, but Elkor, clad in his new black cloak with its hood up to cover his ugliness, promptly kicked the youth under the table before the chorus; Thay smiled to himself … the chorus lauded *"ale flowing from the kegs like blood from outlander necks."* Their invitees might not understand the "Veneg" verse, but Thay thought Elkor's precaution wise.

When they had eaten as much as they could, they pushed themselves back from the table and sat sipping their beer. Old Walster claimed tiredness and bade them all a good night, but not before reminding them to fold up all the bedding before leaving the next morning. Wolfgar and Singrid also begged their leave, quarrelling together even as they thanked the youths. "For my part," Singrid declared, "I'd just as soon stay on for another cup, but if I let Wolfgar have another, there'll be no getting him up tomorrow. I'll never get a good day's work out of him."

"A good day's work? You always say you've never gotten a good day's work out of me!"

"Well, I'd certainly not get one tomorrow if you had another cup! At least now I still have hope."

They departed like a fading thunderstorm. Monsfried smiled as the couple left and observed, "They're perfect for each other and twelve years of marriage hasn't changed them a bit." He drained his wooden mug and set it on the table before turning to Elkor and asking, "Why is it that a man hides himself so?"

Silence reigned at the table until finally a sucking breath sounded from Elkor and he thrust back his hood, revealing his misshapen face, crooked eyes, and the patches of red high on his forehead as though there were horns trying to burst through the skin. "There!" he snapped. "Are you well-contented now? Are you pleased to see for free the face of the deformed hunchback that you'd pay a penny to gape at during Summer-fest? Sate yourself! You'll never see *my* like again!" He glared at Monsfried, his expression daring the woodcutter to comment.

Monsfried pursed his lips, reached across the table for the jug of ale, and poured a mouthful first into Elkor's goblet and then into his own. The Fjordlanders looked to one and other: Cairn cut a last slab of meat from the roast, stuck it with his knife, popped it in his mouth, and set about chewing as though his life had no other purpose; Lars hummed a rowing song he used to sing with his dad; Thay studied Elkor's countenance; Lora stared into the fire, all her giggling gone. At length Monsfried took a swig from his goblet, set it down, looked at Elkor, and said, "By all accounts from my new friends here, you nursed yon girl back to health when she was on death's doorstep, and did so when you hardly knew her. My young friends are grate-ful, and the girl's crafted me a nice pair of snowshoes, so I am grateful, regardless of how a man looks. If life be easier for you with your face hidden, friend, so be it."

"I have no friends," Elkor retorted.

Monsfried ran his fingers through his beard and replied, "Perhaps not, but it don't mean *I* can't consider *you* one." He pushed his chair back from the table and got up. "I must get myself home. 'Tis a cold night and I don't want to let it get no colder for my walk. Go well." Turning to the youngsters he said, "Don't let anyone take you for Thorn People." He em-braced them one by one before pulling on his winter coat. Then he nodded to Elkor and smiled at the youngsters, "May

Galivith's blessing be on you." Then he left, closing the door softly behind him.

"Why do you hate everyone and everything?" Lora declared more than asked after they heard the crunching of Monsfried's steps on the crisp snow fade into the night.

"I only give what I get," Elkor hissed.

"He treated you kindly," Lora retorted. "I didn't see much kindness in return."

"*Kindness?* Pah! He was pointing out to you that you've selected *unsavoury* company for your trip!"

"He was doing no such thing!"

The argument covered the sounds of more feet crunching across the cold snow. Elkor was hissing out a retort when the door flew open with a crash as it slammed against the inside wall. A half-dozen large, fur-clad shapes burst into The Drover's Maid with swords drawn. Two each lunged at Thay and Lars, and the young Fjordlanders found the points of swords against their chests before they could react. Two others bounded around the table like wolves, cutting off any escape. Cairn lumbered to his feet, sending his chair clattering to the floor, and he grabbed the only weapon at hand - a carving knife. He pulled Lora behind him. "No fighting! No fighting!" cried the innkeeper. That cry brought his wife bursting from the kitchen, the door opening with a bang that added to the cacophony.

Thay and Lars held their hands up, surprise and fear written on their features. Lora stepped forward beside Cairn, *Íss* levelled at one of the men in front of them, her big friend keeping the other at bay with the carving knife. The two assailants' swords greatly outmatched the knives, but the cramped quarters littered with knocked-over chairs and bounded by a solid table gave the newcomers pause for reflection. Elkor simply pulled up his hood and bent his head towards the table as though in prayer.

Silence fell, and into the inn strode a pair of figures; first a woman of medium height, and then a tall man with his dark hair matted by clumps of ice. The woman pulled off a fur hat and shook free long, chestnut-coloured hair that hung in elegant curls. She had a narrow face with brown eyes, a long, thin nose surrounded by a smattering of freckles, and that face was pale, though Lora did not think it was a result of the frigid air outside. She wore a sable cloak over a coat of purest ermine, from under which flowed a blue woollen skirt embroidered at the hem with green vines. She also wore black leather gloves, oddly dainty given the winter weather. The image of a winter queen flashed through Lora's mind; cold, graceful, and perilously beautiful.

The man was not just tall, but big, though his appearance may have been accentuated by the heavy cloak draped over his shoulders, made from the pelt of a great black bear. That cloak glistened with ice crystals and was fastened by a black, circular brooch adorned with gold flames. The glimpse of the brooch made Lora shift her eyes back to the woman. Sure enough, she wore a silver brooch with a springing stag upon it.

As the woman rubbed warmth into her thighs, the man stamped snow from his boots and then, almost courteously, wiped them on the mat at the inn's doorstep before turning and closing the door on the freezing outdoor air. Then he walked slowly, deliberately across the room, as though strolling on a spring day. Lora glimpsed chain mail and black boiled leather armour underneath the cloak. Given the cloak, mail, and boiled leather, Lora realized the man wasn't as broad as she first believed. He stopped in front of the hearth, carefully removed a pair of fur-lined gloves, and held his hands to the warmth of the fire. Finally he turned around. His stubbly, long face broke into a smirk and he slapped his gloves into the palm of his left hand. Lora would have thought him handsome, even with his broad nose askew, were it not for his brown eyes; they glimmered with contempt and all Lora could feel was fear. On his back was hung an ornate double-bladed battle axe gleaming as though forged from steel.

The man walked back to the table. He yanked the woollen hat off Lars' head, revealing all that blonde hair, complete with the braid that dropped down from above the Fjordlander's temple. Lars made to lunge at the man but Thay pulled him back down to his chair. The potential for violence made the man smile. Once satisfied he didn't need to fight, he walked around the table and stopped in front of Elkor's trembling figure. Then he tapped his foot - tap, tap, tap, tap, tap, tap, tap - and said in calm, reasonable tone, "A good man, a loyal man, warned us about outlander barbarians in this town, but he didn't mention *you*. Well, you're possibly braver than I thought, though undoubtedly much less wise. Either you enjoy pain or cannot learn. Which, pray tell, is it?"

"You've no cause to threaten me, Korgash!" Elkor hissed.

The smirk on the man's face deepened. "Do I not?" he asked. "As I recall, I heard about a grave robbing necromancer active around my lands. I investigated the surrounds and learnt about a foul plague troll posing as an apothecary in Stoukton. When I arrived there, I heard it had already fled my righteous judge-ment. But I caught up to it some weeks ago on a bridge not far from here, taught it a lesson, and gave it some advice. I elected to let the beast live, to serve as a warning to all such plague trolls, though I warned it not to trouble these parts again. But then, you would recall, would you not? You were there. Did you not think my arguments carried enough weight?"

Elkor mustered a hiss in response.

The man set his gloves on the table. "I'm *glad* you ignored my advice. Holy Galivith Himself has delivered you into my hands, for I find you with Thornish friends! Now I name you a plague troll *spy* in collusion with foreign enemies. You know what the punishment for treason is, no? I am sure Galivith will provide me with the rope I need to hang you and your friends."

At this the woman walked over. She breezed past Korgash to stop in front of Elkor. She reached out a dainty hand to the cowl of the misshapen man's robe and brushed it back from Elkor's face. Elkor recoiled but the woman had already be-held his visage. "Hideous," she declared, making a great show of shuddering, though to Lora's ear distaste hardly touched the woman's lilting cadence. Her voice was fire to Korgash's steel. "Of course, you're right, my *herg*, we should have him hanged immediately! But it *is* such a pity that *Herg* Panzler is so vocal and strong in support of *Oberherg* Holgarth."

There was a pause, only the crackling fire in the hearth sending noise into the room. Lora's eyes darted back and forth between these two potent figures, saw puzzlement flash across the man's face, and then recognition of that puzzlement in the eyes of the woman, who added a question, "How do you think *Herg* Panzler would take to you adjudging cases here? We're neither in my demesne nor yours."

Korgash turned his eyes from Elkor to the woman. "Your sense of propriety does you honour, my lady, though in this case it is misplaced. I could convince the Queen of the need to have acted swiftly and decisively. This man, if man you call him, is evil. He is a self-styled necromancer who seeks to bring his dead father back to life."

"That is a filthy lie," Elkor shot back. "I am nothing of the sort. And I swear by any false god you believe in that if I could find a way to breathe life into my father again it would only be to kill him myself."

Korgash chuckled and retorted, "It's hard to kill plague trolls. You'd be hard put to do it, to kill your dear old father, if you succeeded in breathing life back into him." Then he added with another smirk, "But it's not so hard to kill a plague troll that I couldn't kill *you*. And did you hear, Oda? The blasphemer rejects Holy Galivith!"

No sooner had Lora's eyes caught movement at the windows than the door opened again, letting another blast of cold air into the room. Singrid stamped in, leading Monsfried and two young stablehands, all three men brandishing pitchforks. Finally, Wolfgar shuffled in as well.

"Oh dear!" the woman declared in flat tone. "I fear we have disturbed the villagers, my dear." Then she turned to the newcomers and commanded, "Set aside those ... *tools*. You'll either hurt yourselves or force us to hurt you for your effrontery."

Monsfried stepped forward, still brandishing his pitchfork, and retorted, "You're not my liege *herg*, Lady Oda." The way he let her title and name fall off his tongue left no doubt for the distain that he felt for her.

Now it was Korgash's turn to step forward, his hand moving to the haft of his axe. "Do not insult the lady, peasant!"

Singrid placed her fists on her slight hips and retorted, "*Peasant*, is it? I'll have you know that we're burghers, loyal to *Herg* Panzler and *under his protection*."

"Petty gentry! How lovely!" Lady Oda again exclaimed in her mocking manner. "Please do shut the door," she called to Wolfgar. After he complied, she said, "Thank you, dear *herr*. Now, why are you interfering in these affairs? Are you acquainted with these … *people?*"

Monsfried shot back with a, "Why are *you* bothering honest folk in our *herg's* demesne, lady? You've no business drawing your arms here!"

Korgash took another furious step forward, causing Monsfried to bring up the glinting tips of his pitchfork. Lady Oda put a delicate hand on Korgash' forearm, forestalling any further escalation in violence. She turned her gaze on Singrid and said, "Have you *truly* come to defend this horrid necromancer and these young foreigners?"

Singrid replied, "There's been no necro-anything going on around here and these young folk are good people! They wouldn't mix with a dead-dancer. They are all under the protection of the Queen. If blood is spilt here, it will be your friend there who'll need to account for it."

"If he lives to account for it," snapped Lars.

Oda exclaimed, "It speaks! How quaint."

Korgash had also turned his hawk's gaze on Lars. Now he laughed at Oda's quip and said, "You're at the pointy end of a broadsword, pretty boy! Though I'll allow that your fighting instincts are good. Do you want to come at me? Now's your chance. I promise not to damage that braid of yours, though I might wring your neck. Come on! I'll have my men step aside."

Monsfried shot out his hand, forestalling Lars' lunge, but he never took his eyes off Korgash. "He's trying to goad you, lad. Don't take his bait. What you don't see is he's scared of the Queen's writ, right enough. Don't let him claim to *Herg* Panzler's sheriff that you attacked him." Then to Korgash he said, "The Queen's laws cover even people from Outside. Whatever grudge you hold against this man Elkor, you'd best think on how it is you're going about pursuing it."

At this Korgash let loose a deep, merry laugh. "I never thought Elkor here could ever produce someone to vouch for him! No, indeed not. Who would want to stand beside a necromancing plague troll spawn?"

Lady Oda sighed. "This bores me, my dear. Send them on their way so I may go up to my room." With that she turned to the innkeeper and his wife by the kitchen door, "Your little inn *does* have rooms, does it not?"

The innkeeper managed a nod. His wife, spotting the opportunity to bring the dangerous stand-off to a conclusion, stepped forward and said, "If you'll follow me, my lady."

Lady Oda did indeed follow, sending an order over her shoulder, "Send Jenna to my rooms when she comes in from caring for my horse." The sound of her boots echoing up the stairs behind the innkeeper's wife faded from the room.

Korgash smiled a smile that sent shivers up the spines of those present and spoke to the stable hands who had accompanied Monsfried. "If these Thorn People or if that disease beast there give you any trouble in the future, send word to us. From tomorrow, we'll be up at Raig's Crag." Korgash smiled again, then spun on his heels, and strode over to the stairwell, pushing aside Monsfried's pitchfork as he climbed the stairs, "Put the plague troll and his pets outside and bring a supper to my room."

Chapter Three

They left Harburg that night, forsaking even a short sleep. Monsfried told them to use his woodshed, where he stored some tools and provisions in the stand of trees he was felling. They packed quickly and soon were on their way, northwest, trudging along, afraid, angry, and weary. They reached the hut well before midnight and found it was just large enough for them to lie close-packed, huddled in their cloaks and blankets. Sleep came quickly to all but Elkor.

When they stirred again, the day had dawned cold, but sunny, with a crisp, ice-blue sky. Cairn used the fire pit beside the hut to make a hot porridge. Elkor brooded in silence, worrying over the previous evening's events. For their part, the youngsters felt better; though the bite of the dawn wind was ferocious, they breathed it in deeply, glad of its sharpness for it chased the darkness from their minds. The vapour of their breath hung in the air and at length they laughed as Cairn hurled snowballs at Lars. Then they lashed on their snowshoes before showing Elkor how to do the same with a pair Lora had made for him during her convalescence. Finally they prayed, begging Florri for good luck and Norrgi for good weather; Elkor shook his head and sighed.

From Monsfried's hut they struck off due north. Although he had a hard time adjusting to the snowshoes, at one point Elkor declared, "I've used Straelish snowshoes before ... and they're easier for walking, but these big ones you barbarians use work better on this new snow."

The youngsters cast questioning glances at each other and Lars finally replied, "Did you just laud something Fjordlander?"

"Has that woollen hat not warmed up your wits? I most certainly did *not*! I named you barbarians and said you used better snowshoes … your flea-ridden ancestors no doubt pilfered the technique."

Lars snatched off the hat and threw it at Elkor, hitting the Straeling in the face and triggering a curse. Elkor tried to kick it back but the snowshoe caught in the snow and he pitched onto his face. The youngsters all laughed but Thay made sure to pick up the hat and press it into Lars' hands.

While Lora had lost some of her fitness, only Elkor found the going truly hard as he bent under the weight of his pack. And yet, despite his difficulties, the youths thought he was well-contented to have left Harburg from the lack of invective spilling from his hood. At length, he directed them to veer east so as to come to the road, though it was but a rutted track barely wide enough for a hay cart to pass through the trees. The passage of many feet had packed the snow down enough that the five of them could walk on hard snow instead of wading through snowdrifts. This was a relief because they weighed more now that they carried more equipment and trudging through the knee-deep snow off the track was difficult, even with snowshoes. Thus they were happy to get packed snow under their feet and strap their snowshoes onto their backs.

Elkor had agreed to guide them at least to Polgatia, across the Peregrinswater from Straeland. They had discussed his rationale for choosing to strike out north before heading west; bearing directly west would take them to Drigaland, where they would continue to rouse hostility for being Thorn People. Elkor said the Polgati fell victim less often to Fjordlander raids and thus might not be so immediately suspicious of the youngsters. Moreover, the Polgati would not peg the Fjordlander's accent in Straelish as being necessarily foreign, so they might even pass as Straelings. Between the Polgati lands and the mountains, he said, lay Drover territory, and come spring they might get themselves Drover horses to speed their way home.

Cairn wondered why Elkor would want to guide them given their obvious intent to get home rather than first hunt down Korgash. He guessed that Elkor was biding his time: Korgash could wait, in the meantime Elkor had food, new equipment and protectors who could prevent beatings by locals - apparently a common occurrence in his life. Finally, Cairn suspected that the prospect of *lifgyld* for getting the youths home perhaps took precedence over revenge. But as they trudged through the afternoon, Cairn found his mind returning again and again to Elkor's motives and the depth of Elkor's hatred of Korgash. Finally, he gave voice to his thoughts, asking over his shoulder, "Will he come after us again?"

"I fucking well *hope* so," Elkor declared with a force that surprised the youths despite the time that they had spent with the strange man. "Indeed, I'm relying upon it."

Cairn frowned. Then he said, " 'Relying upon it?' Well, you've just lost me."

"*There's* a surprise! Well think about it, unless you're content to be a fucking oarsman or a goat-herder for the rest of your life. For good or ill, you've a brain. Use it."

Cairn snarled, spun about, grabbed Elkor by the cloak and thrust the strange man ahead of him, giving himself an easier walk and making Elkor's more difficult. Up front, Thay rose to the bait, calling over his shoulder, "Right, let's see. You're an exiled priest of darkness." Elkor did his best imitation of Cairn's snarl but otherwise did not interrupt. "So, you know lots of things, but not how to live off the land in winter or track your enemy over long distances."

"Wrong. I *know* how to do such things, but I do not do them well."

Thay shrugged. "It's all of a kind. So, you find yourself with four Fjordlanders you reckon are no more than striplings. You figure it'd be much simpler to have your quarry come to you thinking he's the hunter and doing the hardest part of your work for you."

Elkor nodded. "Very well, as far is it goes. What comes next, my pubescent genius?"

Thay narrowed his eyes and said, "So, it either works or it doesn't. If it doesn't, well, you delay having to decide what to do by taking us as far as Polgatia. But if it *does* work, you won't know the when or the where, so we give you more eyes and ears."

"Just so. Certainly not more wits."

"Who needs wits to herd goats or pull oars?" Lora piped in from behind Cairn.

"Again, correct. The pretty thing may just have a brain after all."

"The *pretty* thing has a twelve-thumb-long seax and the *ugly* thing has a death wish," Lora riposted in sweet tones.

Thay ignored the side skirmish and continued his thinking, "But your man, Korgash, he's got his followers and when they come at us, they'll overpower us. We're but bairns after all. But at least his gang will be occupied with us, leaving you to him. Or him to you, in your thinking."

"And what's my plan?"

"He hates you, but he doesn't fear you."

"What of it?"

"He won't just jump out and put a spear through your throat."

"No. He won't."

"He'll want to play with you. Prolong his pleasure. But you, you hate him *and* you fear him. So you'll not hesitate. You intend to make him pay for his mistake."

"Yes. But how?"

"How indeed?" replied Thay. "He's bigger, stronger, wears armour, has weapons a chieftain back home would covet, and he looks like he can use them. I'd say the easiest way for you would be to play his game, let him have his fun, or at least *think* he's having his fun. You could grovel a bit. Make him feel big. Lick his boots and then stick him when you get close."

Thay glanced over his shoulder and actually caught a glimpse of a smile beneath Elkor's hood.

"Your mind has finally thawed. I might indeed just stick him, with a poisonous sting."

"What of Tanat?" Lars asked from the back of the column.

Elkor stopped walking and turned about. Cairn nearly ploughed right over the small Straeling, knocking Elkor back but reflexively catching the falling figure. When Elkor had found his feet again and his curses had subsided, he barked out, "Would someone translate *that* for me? With my pidgin Goatfucker, I thought he asked how I'll deal with a false Goatfucker god. Why the hell would I need to plan for Tanat?"

Lars grinned, "Now who's the idiot? We all know Tanat plays tricks with every plan."

Elkor peered at Lars in silence for a long, tense moment, before turning about and pushing Thay, prompting the tall tawny-haired youth to turn around and resume the march. Lars let loose a hearty chuckle but otherwise refrained from gloating except by adding, "As far as I see it, Tanat has already tricked you; the woman! While you're sticking Korgash, she'll bury a dagger in your back."

"It pains me to concede you're right about plans developing complications but wrong about Oda. She likely *wants* to put a stiletto in my back but won't do it until she feels safe."

"How do you reckon that?" Lars asked before adding, "She wanted you hanged last night."

"No she didn't," Lora countered. "She prevented Korgash from doing so."

Elkor cursed under his breath and snarled, "It pains me to concede *that* as well, but my pain doesn't change what happened. Oda's playing her own dangerous game with Korgash ... and with *Oberherg* Holgarth. She might use her womanly wiles ..." Lora tutted at that. "... to ensorcel that sick scion of scorpions, Korgash, but Holgarth's a different proposition altogether." He fell silent for a while. "It may surprise you to learn that I hate the power and privilege that comes with supposedly *noble* birth..."

"Though not with the power and privilege that comes with *male* birth, it seems," Lora quipped. "Try being overlooked because of your sex. I had to fight to sail with the Sea Wolves."

Another silence fell, though this one was notable for the boys' held breath. Elkor laughed his spiteful, ironic cackle, "Said just like a good Fjordlander! You fought. Would that Fjordland do less fighting." He chuckled once more and then took up his original point, "The *female* has a mind and if I said differently she'd stick me with twelve thumb-lengths of seax! Yes, I do hate the power and privilege that comes with *noble, male* birth…"

Lars interrupted Elkor. "What do you mean by noble birth? Aren't all births something noble?"

Elkor bent double laughing at the question. When finally able to speak he said, "Of course! All you brutes know is chieftains who take their rule one from the other in combat. Well, imagine if you could take it by being born to the previous chieftain."

"That would be stupid," Lars said, aghast.

"Exactly! He thinks after all!" Elkor cried. "You're right. It's not merely stupid, it's bloody stupid." Then Elkor went on to explain the concept of rule through inherited nobility, waxing on about its inherent ridiculousness and injustice. Then he explained, "As much as I hate the nobility, not having been born into it, even I must admit it exists. One must either work to free oneself from it, or, if one's interests align with it, ally oneself to it."

Elkor glanced at Lars and continued, "So, pretty boy, what you need to know is although Holgarth is old and he can't lead a charge against raiders atop his destrier, he's the most important noble in North Straeland."

Lora cut Elkor off, noting, "But Oda steered Korgash away from violence last night, at first by appearing to wish it more than him, and then by getting him to reflect on the consequence of acting."

"You saw through that, did you?" Elkor asked.

Lora said, "Women learn quickly what works, and what doesn't, when dealing with violent men." Then she added, "You three lugs will remember Snorri? Remember when I pretended to piss into his helmet? It could have gone badly for me with him when we first joined the crew of *Rignil*. He was easy to deal with because Kindron liked me. Imagine if he hadn't."

"I'm lost," Lars said.

"*There's* a shock," Elkor quipped.

"It's got to do with the local *herg*, doesn't it?" Thay asked.

Elkor nodded. "Indeed. Harburg's *herg*, that moron Panzler, is loyal to Holgarth. He'd act to bring Korgash and Oda to the old man's court. Yes, Korgash could appeal to the Hag ..."

"Hag?" Lars interrupted.

"Queen, Hag, same thing," Elkor quipped. "He'd lie, rattle his purse, and slither off the hook. That goatfucking fiend is rich enough and has a large following among his idiot peers here in North Straeland that the Hag wouldn't want to up-set things. Oda, though, is vulnerable. Her husband died last spring and she's not allowed to hold title to his demesnes even if they did come to him through her family. There's no heir, so Holgarth is within his right to pick out a husband for her."

Lora jumped in, "That's horrible!"

Elkor nodded, "And there's worse. I told you how nobility works, if she were to marry ..."

Lora finished his thought for him, "She'd lose all her power! It would be her husband who would become powerful, take all the decisions. By Rulla, and I thought I had it hard, fight-ing to become a Sea Wolf! It'd be harder being Oda."

Elkor shook his head. "Don't go all soft on her. The cun-ning truffle-scarfing sow has some few advantages and she's exploited them well. She doesn't just use her pretty face to manipulate the idiots around her, she uses gold and a hon-eyed tongue to build a coterie of allies. She's bought off the local revereds. She's also got a few friendly *hergs* courting her purse ... even if they've backed off since she started travelling around with Korgash. She's got loyal thugs-at-arms and she's reportedly got influence at court, but yes, she doesn't want him to do anything rash that would have her dragged before Holgarth."

"What's she doing riding around with Korgash, then?" Lora asked.

"Back in Stoukton, word had it that *His Goatfuckerness* was to see her safely to Swartskastel up on the Peregrinswater, northeast of Fletcherton. The Hag's idiot brother Prince Kormonez is a puppet commander of the fortress and there were rumours Oda was trying to catch his eye."

"Looked to me that she'd caught Korgash's eye," Thay said.

Elkor nodded. "Yes, but fear of the prince is likely making him behave."

"Because of these loyalties demanded by nobility?" Lars asked.

"Yes, but it's also rumoured the prince is mad as a rabid squirrel. He sends his minions on meaningless quests and he delights in playing the rebab for the unlucky bastards thrown into his dungeon. Korgash won't want to spend a year finding the mythical Sausage of Chaya."

"*Sausage of Chaya?*" Lars said. "I don't understand. What's this got to do with us?"

"*The mythical quest?* Nothing, except that Korgash doesn't want a royal command to go off on one. You could bet your worthless life that if Kormonez issued such a command, Oberherg Holgarth would be quick to jump in and make sure the dangerous Raper of Caprines indeed obeyed the order. But to get back to your long-forgotten point, Lars, Oda won't stick a dagger in my back just yet because she doesn't want to get brought to Holgarth and married off."

"But anyone could kill you," Cairn said. "Why would they blame Oda?"

Elkor laughed again. "Ah! Very good, fat boy. You're finally opening your eyes. The one bit of luck we had was the people of Harburg saw Korgash and her deal with us. It won't matter to Holgarth who does the stabbing, he'll have the reason he needs to get what he wants. He'll marry her off if he has the least reason.

"But the further north we go, the more we come into land where the *hergs* actually like that fucker Korgash. He's been effective in protecting the northern Straels. After all, they suffer more from squabbles with the Polgati across the Peregrinswater, as well as from Thornish raids coming up that great river. And yes, Lars, plenty of longboats pillage Straeland's north, so just you all remember that every step you take increases your danger as well."

"Tell me again, why are we going north?" Cairn asked.

"We'll be much safer once we get to Polgatia. Besides, the best pass over the Boldring Mountains is at the headwaters of the Peregrinswater and the best way to get there is to go north until we meet it. Some winters it does not freeze up entirely. There is a smuggler who hides out in the marshes up there, Mari's her name, who'll be able to get us across. Then we can follow it along the safer, north bank.

"But more importantly," Elkor continued, "you have a man to kill, and *he's* going north."

§

They made the next village by nightfall of that short winter day, but they decided to carry on and camp in the forest, fearful of a repeat of what had happened the previous evening in Harburg. When the first stars came out, they found a nice spot to camp near a frozen stream and under the boughs of large pine trees that had protected the ground from a significant accumulation of snow. Lora got a small fire blazing in no time, Thay lashed a cross-beam for a lean-to between two trees, while Lars and Cairn went off to look for good boughs to form the roof of the shelter. Elkor crouched as close to the fire as he could get and cursed the cold, his company, and a good many other things, which Thay took as a healthy sign.

Lora and Elkor set to work cutting some of their supply of meat into chunks and tossing them into an empty pot for a stew. Thay, as he tied Singrid's burlap to the branches that framed the lean-to, asked, "Tell me about writing and books. You're always going on about how Korgash stole your books, but so what? It seems to me that if I was going to have to lose something to a brigand, better a collection of worthless bits of sheepskin than silver."

Elkor furrowed his brow so far that his nostrils flared and he bared his blackened teeth in a snarl, making him even uglier than usual. "That's the stupidest thing I've ever heard."

Thay smiled as he pulled a cord taut. He lay a branch atop the frame, careful to layer its smaller branches bearing the many pine needles that would provide them cover atop the one he had just finished tying off. "Well then, necromancer, tell me what makes these things valuable?"

Elkor paced about the fire casting his gaze alternately at Thay and Lora. "I would think that you're bloody well goading me into losing my composure ..."

"Except that you've never *had* any composure," Lora quipped.

"... *except*," Elkor continued with a mocking leer, "you young fools are likely so stupid that it's no act. Very likely you really don't bloody well know why writing is so important! Your runic inscriptions - like the ones on your seax, Lora - might help folk remember small, short facts, like who died on what raid, but large slabs of stone or wood take a long time to carve, are difficult to move, and cannot be assembled in one place and stored, for starters. Writing on parchment or vellum can preserve whole bodies of knowledge, which can be assembled in one place or passed across great distances, both of space and time. You don't really write, so you cannot keep your lore intact."

"We have our lore," replied Lora. "We have our stories, our chants, our songs, our sagas."

"Ah, but how do you know that your favourite saga hasn't been partly forgotten, or deliberately altered? You don't, do you?"

"Our bards are masters at what they do," Lora retorted, anger creeping into her voice.

"Ha! Spoken just like Lars, that grand idiot defender of all things done badly over a hundred generations! Well, what if the bard in question has his own bloody perspective on things? What if he doesn't *want* you to know certain things so that *he* can keep what was common knowledge to himself? Suppose one of your fucking bloodthirsty chieftains demands that the bard suppress part of a tale, or worse yet, change it to squeeze out some advantage. You haven't thought of that, have you? I prefer my knowledge to come to me through as few people as possible. No, for me, the best way is to let some scholar write his thoughts in books. Hell, even let that book sit in a hole for a thousand years, and then let me read it. Let me hear his thoughts, his knowledge, directly, without people forgetting, or bards distorting, priests and shamans forbidding, or kings altering. I'll be the wiser for it."

Lora shook her head and chuckled as she tossed some chunks of beef into their pot sitting on the ground. "Well, a thousand year old truth is hardly a truth worth knowing. If our fathers and mothers, or our other forebears before them had no need of it, then I likely don't either."

Elkor burst out laughing at that. "I expect such ignorance from Lars, but I thought you were quicker than that, dear girl. If your pitiful wits haven't figured out why writing's useful yet, then think on this, what do you suppose happened to every useful thing that the people in Jorrumsfjord knew before the Jarlags fell upon them?" Elkor chuckled when he saw the youngsters' reaction to his reference to Jorrumsfjord, "I see you have heard of the Jarlags. I suspected as much, given your accent. Then you likely had family at Jorrumsfjord even if they might have been butchered when you were infants and you never got to know them. So, Lora, aspiring wise woman, or healer, or seer or whatever it is you think you can become, would you not have liked to know what your cousins knew about healing, or beer-brewing?" Lora simply scowled at Elkor, narrowing her eyes and biting her lip.

"Well, you won't ever know, will you? You *can't* know. If I recall correctly, the Jarlags killed every man and woman at Jorrumsfjord for presuming to settle too close to traditional Jarlag fishing grounds. It's part of the reason you folks hate them so much. They took the children and turned them into little Jarlags and filled their little minds with little Jarlag thoughts."

Lora shot to her feet and leapt at Elkor but he dodged away, not daring to strike her and risk her whipping out her seax. Thay stepped forward, but Lora pushed him away and leapt at Elkor again. Such pursuits did not play to Elkor's strengths and Lora soon had him by the hood of his cloak. She pulled him to the left and then punched him in the face with her right fist, sending the deformed man sprawling to the ground and unleashing a wail from him. She pivoted and sent her boot into his gut. Elkor doubled over and cried out again. "Stop!" Elkor croaked before breaking out into a fit of heaving weeping. "Stop. Stop."

The pitiful mewing made her sneer and she moved to kick him again, but Thay wrapped her up in his arms. She made do with hissing out at Elkor, "Shut up! Shut your filthy mouth! Shut up your hatred! Shut up your … your, bile! Shut up!" Then she bent forward, in Thay's arms, spluttered and wheezed; she had clearly not reclaimed all the strength of which her illness had robbed her.

Thay held her tight, hugging her close to him. "Lora," he hissed, "By Sk'van's balls! You've just beaten a near defenceless, crippled man. Does that make you feel like you've defended our honour? Do you feel proud now?"

She shook herself out of Thay's embrace. "Yes, Thay, I do!" she bellowed before storming back to her stew and, with a yell, kicking the pot clear across their camp.

Thay pulled a quivering Elkor upright and patted off the clumps of snow clinging to the odd man's clothes and hair. Elkor shied away from the brushing movements of Thay's hands, but the look in his eyes shifted, transforming from skittish to fiery. Thay clasped Elkor's biceps and whispered, "Not now! Let her work this out."

At length Lora took a deep breath and replied, "No. It doesn't. You're right, Thay. It doesn't make me feel proud."

Thay unclasped Elkor, passed the Straeling the hint of a smile, and then patted the man's upper arm before turning around and saying, "We *have* to listen to him. Our fate depends on it!"

Lora's head snapped up. "Why?" she finally whispered in reply as though not wanting Elkor, only a step beyond Thay, to overhear this intimacy.

"I don't know. We just have to," Thay declared.

Lora's piercing gaze held steady. "It's *her*, isn't it? She who sends you the crimson dreams?"

Thay nodded. "Yes, the winged worm." Then he shook his head and said, "I don't know. Elkor's telling us something important, even if it's lathered in venom. Or perhaps particularly *because* it's lathered in venom." Lora stood still for a long while, before huffing and moving off to retrieve the pot.

Thay said to Elkor. "Go on. Just remember, if you vex her again, she's apt to gut you."

"Oh there's a sweet principle. When it hurts to hear some truth, resort to violence, hey?"

"Aye. That's oft the way of it."

Elkor snorted.

Lora scooped from the snow the vegetables and chunks of beef that were to make their stew. Elkor ventured back to the fire. Thay resumed his work on the lean-to. When Lora finally had her pot dangling above the flames and its contents slowly stewing, she breathed out a long breath and said to Elkor, "I'm truly sorry. I already bought you winter clothes and a cloak, for which I note you never thanked me, but if I can, to prove I'm sorry, I'll buy you a book the first opportunity we get."

Elkor arched his eyebrows and his eyes burned bright, "It would need be a rare book."

Lora shrugged. "Suit yourself."

"It might shock you to learn that you could pay a large sum for a book, nearly as much as a *lifgyld* you would pay back home!" She glared at him but squatted again next to the pot. Elkor seemed chastened. After a while, crouching by the fire, he took an onion in his gnarled hands and chopped it up to add to the stew. "I'll not forget that promise. I can read a half-dozen languages and when I was still allowed into the temples, I had access to perhaps ten score books. I learnt about healing from a master from the Chayan Empire and even managed to read a decade-long debate between a Chayan doctor and a Horothian physician, a debate that distance and warfare would have made impossible if not for the ability to transfer thought to paper. I learnt about navigation from Thrulls, who live on the other side of the world. Did you know that they proved the world is round?"

Lora huffed at that and said more than asked, "*Round?*"

Elkor ignored her. "I've heard of powerful magics of people called the Baranku who can supposedly control animals with their spells. There is an ancient civilization called Laran that is the seat of a powerful church of guardians that its followers believe protects the world from some great evil dragon."

"A what?" Thay asked, taking another pause from his lashing and tilting his head.

"I haven't read much about it, but they seem to think the world will end by some return of a dragon from magical confinement."

"Confinement?" Thay repeated, mimicking the long, unfamiliar Straelish word. "Is that like gaol? Something from which someone would want release, freedom?"

"Just so," Elkor answered, not taking particular notice of Thay's sudden curiosity. "Most religions have beliefs about the end of the world. Your own people believe that a worm will swallow the world whole! My own flock of ignorant sheep believe that a fire will erupt from the belly of the earth without thinking that the nearest volcano is thousands of leagues away. But *I* don't have to be superstitious."

Elkor then paused, and when he resumed, Thay had the impression the Straeling had moved beyond trying to convince Lora and him of the value of books. "It's a sort of freedom, though often exchanged for another sort of bondage. I have oft been subject to the tyranny of envy and irrational fear because of what I have learnt from books. That's why I had to leave."

After hearing him out, Lora observed, "You do not curse when you speak with admiration." Thay thought it another peace offering, an opening for a return to the amity they had before her tantrum.

Later, when Thay finished with the lean-to, and when he finally sat around the campfire with the others to eat his stew amid swirls of falling snowflakes, he wondered at Elkor's words as Lars played a tune on his bone flute, a song about whaling on the freezing northern waters.

§

The next day dawned even crisper and colder than the day before. Very soon the party was trudging through the snow again. It had snowed overnight, leaving a soft layer fresh atop everything. They stamped down tracks in the new snow as they followed the road that took them ever further north.

The youngsters were thankful for the experience of having passed the previous winter on the high pastures and they hummed as they lumbered forward on their snowshoes. Elkor, however, had only limited experience even with Straelish snowshoes, never mind the broader Fjordland kind, and he struggled to keep up.

At midday, while they were taking a rest and having a bite, Lars asked, "How do you mean to kill Korgash?"

At first, Elkor only glowered a reply before kneeling to the catching flames and holding out his hands. Thay passed around some food from his pack and pulled his cloak tighter. After taking a bite of sausage, Elkor said, "Korgash must know what's happening to him. He must look into my face and I must see in his eyes the realization that every pain, every humiliation, every insult has come back upon him! If things go as I hope they do, I will take my time with that pig sticker and I will employ as much creativity as your Sea Wolves have in their store of torture."

The youngsters glanced at each other. Finally Lars replied around a mouthful of sausage, "Torture isn't our way. Killing a man cleanly in duel, facing a horde of enemies in battle so that bards will sing your name for ever after, that is our way. I would not be party to torture, not for a mountain of silver."

Elkor sighed, as though the gush of air explained everything under the winter sun. "Ah yes, the fabled nobility of the Thorn People. I note you spoke of killing a 'man' cleanly. What of the women? What is the Fjordlander way when it comes to them? You might want to ask a few dead Straelish women and see if they were dealt with cleanly when your raids hit."

Lars rolled his eyes and brushed his dangling braid from in front of his face. "So how do a *noble* people wage war, then?"

"That's my point, idiot. A truly noble people *might* wage war, if necessary, but they would measure their greatness differently. Do they have laws that allow people to live their lives safely? Do they permit people to better their lives? Can they survive drought or floods? Do their artisans have the security to un-cover new techniques to fabricate new things of beauty? Do they make their world safe in order to foster *learning* and the quest for knowledge? What do they do with that knowledge? Have they built a civilization that hoards it, like the Chayan Empire, or have they built a land that encourages people to profit from their knowledge by selling it, like Horoth? You've never thought of anything like that, have you Lars?"

"Horoth is not so mighty that we cannot raid it," Lars retorted.

"No, but every year they get more organized in their coastal defences and the raiding gets harder, does it not? *There* is the mark of an advanced people; a grand project of civil works meant to protect its citizens. And any Sea Wolf captain that now spies even a Horothian merchant vessel would steer away from it. In fact, that is a fine example of what I'm ar-guing, though why I'm arguing with people with rocks for brains is beyond me. Take your ships. They are a wonderful embodiment of craft and innovation. Ah, but once the Thorn People figured out how to build fast, sleek, versatile ships that were ocean worthy, what did they do? Did they expand their trade, share their wealth and in so doing create more of it for themselves? No, they used those vessels to share misery. Those ships you build and the quality of the sailors you pro-duce could have made your people giants, instead they made you parasites."

" 'Parasite?' Like a leech? Well this parasite feels like doing some parasiting against your head if you don't keep a civil tongue in your mouth," Lars growled around a chunk of hard bread.

Cairn laughed at that and mimicked, " 'Civil tongue' ? Lars! Who in Hondrig's Holy Name do you think you're speaking to? Come on, get yourselves up. Let's get moving again."

As the others reached for their gear, Thay spoke, "Elkor, you haven't answered Lars' question: how *do* a noble people wage war? Is savagery only a *Fjordlander* trait?" Lars nodded his approval at the unstated accusation in Thay's question while Cairn and Lora looked to Elkor.

The Straeling held an admonishing finger at Thay, "Don't think you've outwitted me, young brat. I was using the *irrealis mood*, that I note you as yet haven't mastered. I didn't actually say the Straels here in the north, the Horothians in the south or Chayans in the east were noble. I admit that perhaps they are less *ignoble*. I will say this: I had the great misfortune of being a slave of your walrus-humping Sea Wolves for five years and at no time were they *not* at war or planning raids against other people. Other nations can be savage, but they can also allow peace to flourish. Polgatia hasn't started a war with its neighbours in over two hundred years. Think on that."

The rest of that they day they trudged along until the track joined another coming in from the east, one that showed signs of recent use by horses and at least one sleigh. Despite struggling to master his snowshoes, Elkor led them through the woods rather than along the snow-bound road. He was obviously used to avoiding well-travelled routes in favour of isolated wilderness tracks. "Less people, less explaining," he said.

At dusk two days later, they reached a walled town that Elkor said was Gearthaeme and that was loyal to the master of the north marches, the old *Oberherg* Holgarth. "I was coming here before that walking ejaculation set upon me the day you found me. The bastard had run me out of Stoukton and I resolved to thwart his plans, knowing his ambitions. Holgarth's seat is in the next valley over the hills to the east. I thought I'd lend the old fool my brains. We'll not find Korgash here."

"Or he you," Lora added.

They managed to get through the town gates without problem and when they came to the square at the heart of the town, they were pleased to see they even had the choice between two inns. They ended up staying at the simpler of the two, but they were happy to escape the freezing night and the inn had a wide sitting room with a large hearth and a modest fire burning in it. Even with the fire, it was cold in the inn but they felt better once they got some warm food into them. To the surprise of the Fjordlanders, after eating, Elkor draped his cloak over his shoulders again and trudged back into the frigid night, leaving them alone but for a pair of locals sitting on a narrow bench by the kitchen and who eyed them with obvious suspicion.

"We are out of our minds travelling with him," Lars declared at the fire.

Cairn shrugged and sang:

> We shook hands on the treaty,
>   we now pull the oars in time.

"I know," Lars muttered. "We have made it blood. It will take blood to get out of it now. I hope we find this Korgash soon so we can be rid of it all."

Elkor returned when the fire had burned down to embers and after the locals had braved the cold wind to get themselves home. Cairn, Lars, and Lora had all withdrawn to their room, but Thay was enjoying a contemplative spell on a cushioned bench by the fire when he saw Elkor scurry in from outdoors. The strange Straeling stamped snow off his boots and shuffled off his cloak, all the while huddled protectively over something in the crook of his arm. Elkor glanced at Thay, looked away, taking a step towards the kitchen, and then turned his stare back to the youngster. They locked eyes - or at least one eye in Elkor's case - across the room. After a long while, an ember cracked in the hearth and broke Elkor's concentration.

"Late night trading?" Thay asked.

Elkor shrugged and replied, "Treasures that would be worthless to your kind. Paper. Some ink. Quills. Wax. The stuff of achievement, not of raping and sacking."

Thay nodded. "The stuff of achievement can only be found in secret on a dark winter's night?"

The small man snorted in disgust and made to carry on into the kitchen, but Thay forestalled him by asking, "What were you doing in Stoukton that got you thrown out of town for necromancy?"

Elkor glowered back at Thay. "I thought Lars was the superstitious one who thought so ill of me."

Thay shook his head. "Korgash and Oda were quick to accuse you of *dead dancing*, necromancy. You were doing *something*, and it involved the bodies of the dead, did it not?"

Elkor did not respond, deigning only to continue glowering.

"You were trying to learn from them, weren't you?"

Elkor huffed and stepped closer. "You figured that out, did you? All by yourself? Well, no, I wasn't *trying* to learn ... I bloody well *was* learning!" Though the words came out in a bile-filled rush, Thay knew that none of the venom in Elkor's voice was directed at him. "And I was documenting my findings. That's why the loss of my books to that vicious goatfucker angers me so! I meant it to be my frigging legacy. A proper tome on anatomy, using precise weights and measures, with diagrams, observations and conclusions! That's all fucking well *gone* now."

Thay nodded at that. "It's still in your head?" Elkor shrugged. "Maybe you can take up your work again ... in Fjordland ... or elsewhere."

Elkor glared down at the young Fjordlander, finally blinking again. "This is the second time you've suggested I could take up my work in your land ... do you *really* know what you mean by that? Have you actually given a moment's thought to what comes out your mouth? No people, anywhere, want their dead cut up."

Thay smiled and nodded. "Yes, I know and I have. I've been thinking more than you realize. I've seen that your necromancy involves more herbs than blood sacrifices of - how did you put it? - deaf, two-headed otters. You're no *dead dancer*.

"I have also come to think that perhaps cutting up a dead person isn't worse than cutting up a live one. If I'm capable of coming to such conclusions, then I'm sure I could convince my folk to do the same."

"Hah!" Elkor exclaimed with a shake of his head. "Don't wager any silver on it; unless the wager's with me and the test case is that idiot pretty boy, Lars. Then, wager lots of silver. Better yet, gold." He sat down on the cushioned bench beside Thay and looked at the blue flames roiling over the embers in the hearth. "You have some empathy, my lad, and you've proven tonight that you're capable of thought. Make sure you've wits enough not to let your empathy cloud your judgement. Many people wouldn't be able to think your thoughts, and most wouldn't want to."

§

Over the next five days they alternated between camping and taking shelter in whatever hamlet lay along their path. Elkor was true to his word, and they never had to spend more than one night in a row camping unless the mood took them. As they travelled, Elkor obliged them to improve their Straelish, making them practice advanced verb tenses. He laughed at their attempts to flip a statement into a supposition, but he would occasionally nod and demand they then convert it into the past tense. That happened with greater and greater frequency, particularly for Lora and Thay, a sign they took to mean growing ability. He also explained to them the broad strokes of the politics of the region. Elkor liked returning to the topic because it was clear that Lars could not get his head around it, giving Elkor an excuse to call Lars an idiot. Thay, though, thought the politics were clear enough. There were seven peoples in the north. The Veneg, in the eastern foothills of the Boldring Mountains, were little more than collections of savage tribes, according to Elkor, and of no account.

"So, to the east of these wild lands there's five proper kingdoms, with all the usual organized tyranny based on supposedly sacred bloodlines derived from the most bloodthirsty of the old warlords. They have their defined territories, lords'n'ladies prancing about while your average serf or peasant works dawn to dusk without a rest and is lucky to see the age of thirty.

"Anyways, as your bloody longboats go along the coast from the mountains, there's the Driga, the Straels and the Moortok before you start hitting the outer provinces of the Chayan Empire, which I note your people don't muster up the courage to attack much. There's also the Polgati and the Catagenians to the north with a big tributary of the Peregrinswater dividing them.

"Just beyond their northern borders lie the Drover lands running from the Worldrim Mountains, what you call the Boldring Mountains, to the Brown Hills. The Drover tribes run their stinking reindeer herds across the wind-blasted northern highlands, except when they come down into the other lands to trade and thieve."

Lars, trudging along ahead of the others, called back over his shoulder in his best Strael, "Reindeer? I thought they are famous for their horses. So how you knew reindeer stink? You'll go to those lands?"

"How! Many! Times! - does a man need to beat the right verb tense into your brain?" cried Elkor. "Yes, I *have been* to those lands. And, pretty boy, use 'I thought' with the right verb tense! Is that dung inside your head so utterly rotten?"

"Were!" corrected Lora, whose mastery of Straelish had always been better than that of Lars. " 'I thought they *were* famous for their horses.' So when *did* you go to the Drover lands?"

"None of your fucking business."

"Right then," she pressed. "Tell us of this Korgash. Where is he from?

"Some pit of hell," Elkor spat. "But he's Straelish."

"Why does he hate you?"

"Everyone loves to hate a freak, though I suspect he doesn't truly hate me or he'd have killed me on the bridge. He's a violent brute, like those who made themselves kings here long ago. He likes to show off his brutality and all the better if he can make a show of protecting the people, or his homeland, or his midden pile, whatever excuse possible. He's a fucking savage."

Thay called up from the back, "Tell us about people you esteem."

Elkor stopped and turned around, " 'Esteem?' Where the hell did you hear *that* word?"

Thay shrugged, "I think I heard it at that inn back in Gearthaeme."

"Who the hell was speaking refined Straelish *there?*"

Thay ignored the question. "So, do you esteem anyone?"

Elkor huffed and trudged off after Cairn. He was silent for so long they thought he would not answer, but he finally said, "I'd esteem the Chayans if they weren't so fucking hierarchical. In the south there are some peoples I might respect, but the Horothians are so artificial, the Hengezo act so submissively with their Lanace masters and so under-handedly with everyone else. No, there is no people that I don't distain in some manner. However, there are individuals I do esteem. There is a surgeon in Horoth who has refined techniques that I find astounding. Can you imagine saving a man from an exploded appendix? Opening the patient, removing the corrupted organ, cleaning the body cavity, closing the incision, and nursing him back to health. Amazing!"

They pondered this in silence, tramping along to the sound of wind whistling in the trees and their snowshoes crunching on the hard-frozen snow. "I can open a man up," Cairn observed.

Lora chuckled, "But you'd be hard pressed to close him up and make him healthy again."

"That's usually not on my mind when I'm opening a man up."

§

Then, on the sixth day out from Gearthaeme a storm blew up when they were high up on the Northwall Hills, driving a fierce wind into their faces and the temperatures into depths as yet unfelt that winter. The travellers were forced to halt their day's march before noon when Elkor led them to a woodsman's cabin in the high forest. The woodsman was evidently wintering elsewhere, for the cabin was closed up against the weather. The cold made the door difficult to shift but it finally gave way after Lars kicked at it.

They were glad of the dry wood laid down in the rudimentary hearth and soon got a fire going to keep them from freezing, though the fire and the shelter were not enough to keep the gnawing cold at bay. They draped their blankets and bearskins over themselves and huddled in front of the fire as best they could. The storm showed no signs of abating as the afternoon wore on and the pile of wood dwindled. Finally Thay got to his feet and grabbed his axe, *Tear Tongue*, "We're not going to last if we don't hew more firewood."

"Don't be daft, Thay, it's too cold out there and you'll lose your nose, or fingers, or worse," Lora implored.

"It'll soon be as cold in here without firewood."

Cairn nodded, "He's right. I've heard of storms like this lasting days up in the mountains. We're going to need fuel." He lumbered to his feet, shrugged off the bearskin and draped it over Lora. "This will go quicker with two."

Lars, too, stood up and added, "Quicker yet with three."

Heads turned to Elkor. "You've got to be fucking jesting! I'm not going back out there."

Lars hauled Elkor to his feet. "Quicker yet with four."

"I can't wield an axe."

Lars smiled, "You can run the faggots back to the cabin. Keep moving, you ken?"

Lora shook her head and said, "I'll help. Elkor, use our stores to make us a broth. You can do that, can't you?" For the first time since meeting the Straeling, an expression of gratitude washed over him, though perhaps it was simple relief. They worked until the gloaming, concentrating on hewing deadwood into logs and lugging them back to the shelter. Cairn found a spade and used it to heap snow against the outer walls of the cabin, building up a layer of insulation against the cold. The physical activity kept them cold, rather than frozen, but by the time night fell, the temperature dropped further and they retreated back inside, though they had amassed a healthy volume of wood. When they bundled themselves back into the cabin, they saw that Elkor had done his best to stack the wood around the outer walls in order to shelter them further from the cold. He also had that hot broth waiting for them. As they slurped greedily at the broth, however, Lars suddenly cried out in agony.

"What?" Lora exclaimed. "Lars, what is it?"

"I don't know! Ahh, my hands hurt. My fingers are killing me!"

"Frostbite," Lora and Elkor said at the same time.

"Cairn, bring me in a helmet-full of snow," Lora ordered. Elkor glanced up and Thay saw a scowl on the man's face. Cairn grabbed his helm and darted out the door. Lora guided Lars in front of the fire, scooped his pale hands in hers, held them close to the flames and began rubbing.

Elkor pushed Thay aside and knelt beside Lora. "That is witch-wife lore!" he chided. "It will do more damage to Lars' fingers."

"Don't play your games now, Elkor. We have been better to you than many others would be in our stead. Stand aside while I deal with this."

"Ahhh!" Lars cried, shaking his hands.

Cairn burst back inside the cabin and handed his helmet to Lora. She set it between her knees, scooped up a handful and rubbed it into Lars' hands. Lars barred his teeth and grunted.

"Stop!" Elkor commanded. "You will maim him badly."

"Leave me to my work!" Lora snapped, applying snow onto Lars' fingers.

With the speed of a serpent, Elkor's gnarled hand shot out and knocked the helmet from Lora's grip. It clattered across the floor, spraying snow about them. Cairn immediately stepped forward, his hand in a fist, but he didn't need to swing as the older man had already skittered back, holding up his palms in submission. "Wait! Listen! This is important. If Lora keeps doing what she's doing, Lars may have to make the choice of losing his fingers or his life." Then he asked Lora, "Tell me true, have you ever treated frostbite before?" Lora, her countenance shifting between anger and perplexity did not respond at once. "Well, have you ever treated frostbite?"

"No," Lora said as Lars cursed from the pain. "But everyone knows this is the way to …"

"No! You think of it as truth, but it's no more than a witch-wife tale. Listen, when those fingers cooled, less blood flowed to the flesh. They might simply be cold, and your cure might not do much damage. They probably *are* just cold because of the pain Lars is in. But if those fingers have actually frozen, then water in the hands will have changed to tiny bits of ice. What happens if you rub rough chunks of ice across the flesh of a fish?" Lora recoiled in surprise at the question. "Well," Elkor commanded, "what happens?"

"You can take the scales off a fish that way," Lars muttered through clenched teeth.

Elkor shot Lars a glance and responded, "That's the smartest thing I've heard you say. You can scale a fish that way, or seriously damage its flesh." Then Elkor took Lars' hands in his own. He studied them, looking closely at the skin and feeling them. "If these fingers were frozen solid, the ice would have expanded and burst the tissue. I am sure this is not the case. That said, the problem with rubbing these fingers is that the ice inside the flesh will cut the tissue to shreds. Holding the hands to the fire will only evaporate the water in the fingers and perhaps cause mummification.

"Just hold Lars' hands against skin. That will be sufficient. The flesh will not lose its moisture. We will look at them once they warm up. If the skin looks normal, then the idiot will be fine. If a large blister forms, then above all we will need to avoid having that tissue refreeze at the risk of complete mortification of the flesh." He yanked up his coat and shirts, revealing the flesh of his stomach. Thay caught a glimpse of scarring across Elkor's belly, as though the man had been whipped repeatedly, but he did not get a good look as Elkor brought Lars' hands against his skin. Elkor gasped but nevertheless pulled down his clothing again to cover Lars' hands.

Later, after they had seen Lars' fingers return mostly to normal, though two fingers showed minor blistering, and after they had finished their broth, after they had stoked the fire and settled down on the floor, after the young lads had dropped off to sleep, Lora glanced across the cabin to Elkor and whispered, "Is all my lore a lie?"

Elkor pursed his lips. "No, just a lot of it."

"So how is one to ken the good from the bad?"

Elkor nodded slowly. "*That* is the question of a woman, not a girl. It's wise to doubt the lore of your ancestors. Put things to tests and measure the results. Don't believe without proof."

Flickering firelight reflected off Lora's face as she smiled in response to Elkor's advice. "After today, I'll not do that."

Elkor snorted, albeit quietly. Then he whispered, "Why then did you believe me?"

"You didn't curse."

"*What?*"

She giggled girlishly and snorted, herself. "Well, you did not use foul language for a start. But I also saw the results, Lars' fingers!" Lora lay down her head. "Good night. Thank you."

Chapter Four

The storm blew out by noon of the subsequent day, although the temperatures remained frigid. Rather than expose themselves to the dangers of being trapped outside in the icy winter, and rather than expose Lars' fingers any further, they elected to stay in the woodcutter's cabin for another two days to wait for the worst of the biting cold to pass. As they waited, nursing their strength and doing their best to keep warm even with the ever-burning fire, Elkor told them that killing temperatures would be more, not less, common.

Cairn passed the time working with the heat of the fire, melting down a few lead nails Lora had bought and using the molten metal to bind other nails into caltrops. Elkor was fascinated by the young man's technique and observed the process closely. The others took turns using their whetstone to restore a biting edge to their axes after all the woodcutting, though occasionally Lars played them Fjordlander tunes on his bone flute.

Finally, on the third morning, the sun came out and they were able to leave the cabin, though Elkor had them restock the wood pile by the hearth for the next person to come along in need of respite from the elements, claiming that it might even be himself. They made the most of their snowshoes on the fresh powder and by mid-morning they had risen above the tree line on the southern slopes of the Northwall Hills. Elkor guided them towards a pass away from the road and the slogging was more difficult, the climb higher and the snows deeper, but nevertheless, by midday they ate a cold, hurried lunch just shy of the summit, sheltering from the north wind behind a large boulder. They crossed over and, given the blasting cold, lurched down the snow-covered northern slopes as fast as their lumbering gait would carry them.

At dusk Elkor guided them across a wind-swept meadow to a shallow cave set in the foot of the hills. He bade them collect dead wood from the forest before scrambling up an incline to the rock face looming above them. At the back of the cave, which was little more than a rocky overhang, there was a narrow fissure that led deeper into the hill. They had to take off their snowshoes and packs to wiggle through, bending down in places. After about a dozen paces they sensed the cave walls fall away from them. All was night-black until a sudden bang accompanied by a plume of light startled the youngsters; at the centre of a cozy, suddenly illuminated chamber, Elkor was crouched over a small fire with a flint and steel in hand. The fire had exploded to life so quickly that Cairn pressed Elkor to reveal how he had done it.

"Dry twigs from my pocket and *huoyow*," Elkor explained.

"*Huoyow*? What's that?" Cairn asked.

"Idiot-proof magic," Elkor retorted.

Cairn gaped at the response, but Thay pressed the point. "Idiot-proof magic would make a man rich. You're not rich."

Elkor huffed and put a few larger pieces of dry wood on the nascent fire. "I suppose that's true enough. *Huoyow* is a word from the Chayan Empire. Some in Polgatia call it dwarf powder. Here they hardly know of it."

The Fjordlanders looked around them. Elkor had started the fire in a shallow hole in the middle of the chamber that had obviously been used as a fire pit in the past. The space was not much bigger than the area for sleeping that they usually enclosed with their lean-tos, roughly three paces by three paces. Above them, the roof of the chamber formed a cone that Elkor said was better than a chimney, for multiple fissures running through the rock dissipated smoke rather than funnelling it into one stream that could be seen from afar. Right enough, soon the space was warm from the fire without filling up with smoke. They jammed their bearskins into the entranceway, blocking the worst of the outside air from bothering them.

Elkor explained that the cave lay at the headwaters of the Arrowsmith River. Though it was but a narrow watercourse, he said, it would lead them directly to Fletcherton. Then he explained that Fletcherton was the last town of any reasonable size before the Peregrinswater, the great river that formed the border between Straeland and Polgatia, the rest simply being hamlets enclosed by palisades. Now they were out of the cold, Lars pulled off the woollen hat Thay always made him wear and shook out his long blonde hair and his iconic braid. He listened to Elkor's explanation, humming to himself. When Elkor finished explaining who all the important *hergs* were beyond the Northwall Hills and why they were all corrupt barbarians, Lars asked, "You know the land well, ugly man. You knew about this cave. You knew about that pass we came over. By Hondrig I'd say you even knew that woodsman's cabin on the other side of the hills was where it was. You knew when to go back to the road so that we could find that town, Gearthaeme. You know some smuggler wench who'll get us across the big river if it's not frozen. You're well travelled."

Elkor shrugged.

"Why?" Lars pressed, flicking his braid over his shoulder.

"Look at me, you great twit. What do you see?" This time it was Lars' turn to shrug. "I'll tell you what you see. You see a monster. Your false Gods be damned, you can't even speak to me without saying, 'ugly man' or some other insult. Yes, your ways are *so* endearing."

"We have treated you well."

"That's the horrible truth, I have to admit it. Now, if your cock has warmed up enough, use the brain in it to think. You see a monster and yet you treat me well enough. So, how about the average superstitious idiot peasant? How do you think such people normally treat someone like me?" Again

Lars shrugged. "You'd travel a lot too, so as not to stay in one place for long.

"If I'd wanted an easier life, I could have joined the priesthood. Usually monasteries don't turn away the ugly or the deformed. But then I'd have had to remove half my brain."

"They cut your head open?" Lars asked, incredulous.

"No! Of course not, though it might make *you* smarter, *pretty boy!*" Elkor spat. Cairn could not help himself and laughed. Elkor added, "As an initiate, I'd have to pretend to believe what the priests told me. Belief without question. Obedience without pause. Tradition without reason. Life without thought. No, I'll risk the road."

"The road took me twice up into Polgatia. In the centre of that country, far from invaders spilling across borders, there is a city called Sar Wielen on the banks of the Strem River. It is a wondrous place, dedicated to learning, full of debating halls and books, rejecting utterly superstition and belief without proofs, indeed it is dedicated to tearing down a world without thought. I went there when news of it reached my ears and I learnt what I could, but I had not the coin to stay long. Years later, when I had come into a bit of money, I went back. I passed this way both times, on the going in and on the coming out, avoiding costs, avoiding people, discovering places such as this."

Cairn finished the pre-dinner conversation by stating, "And sure, you've got that *huoyow* magic!"

Elkor simply rolled his eyes in response.

§

Later, as they stared into the flickering flames of their campfire, Lars took out his bone flute and played them a soaring melody. Then he sang to the same tune, tapping the rhythm with his hands on his thighs:

My land calls from over the mountains,
  my land it lies beyond the Teeth.
    I have not wings
    to take me there.
My land it must bide awhile.

My kin sing a song of remembrance,
  they sing it sat down by the fire.
    I have but legs
    to take me home.
My kin all must bide awhile.

Oh cliffs and sea of the place I love,
  oh kin I cherish so well,
don't look for me on the rising tide,
  for my ship's but a pair of boots.

This land it is rolling and gentle,
  it lies 'twixt great river and sea.
    I have not mind
    to make it home.
My land it still calls to me.

My folk live a life of tradition,
  they live it among the fjords.
    I have a mind
    to build a hearth.
My folk will all take me in.

Oh reach and sward of the place I love,
  your voice, it calls to me,
don't look for me on the rising tide,
  for my ship's but a pair of boots.

Oh cliffs and sea of the place I love,
oh kin I cherish so well,
don't look for me on the rising tide,
for my ship's but a pair of boots.

They sat a long while without saying anything, watching the shadows of their little fire dancing on the cavern walls.

"I miss it," Cairn said in his native tongue, eschewing Elkor's edict to use only Straelish. "I miss our home."

"Our time as Sea Wolves didn't go as planned," Lora noted.

"Little in life goes as planned," Elkor stated, for once deigning to use Fjordlander, "as Lars suggested to me recently." He turned to the young lad and added, "And though I'll grant you've a fair voice, don't think I'm going soft on you. You should work on that last metaphor ... *your ship's but a pair of boots?* Can you not do better than that? And I thought you Fjordlanders liked your songs to rhyme."

"It'll serve," Thay replied, "but what about '*Our ship's but a broken dream?*'"

§

"Is it him?" Cairn asked. He had each of his hands buried deeply within the armpit of the opposing arm trying to keep them warm.

"How the fuck would I know?" Elkor snapped, peering out of the bushes at the side of the road. After having stacked wood for the next travellers who might need it, they had left their warm cave to brave the freezing cold at dawn and had spent the day following the watercourse of the Arrowsmith River, or very often, walking on top of the hard crusted snow that had formed on the ice of the river itself. The last big Straelish town before the Polgati border, Fletcherton, was a league or so north of them, down the road, and they had hoped to sleep inside its walls. To their backs was a sparse wood sitting on a rise between the road, which ran along a shelf above the Arrowsmith, and the river itself, which lay a couple of hundred paces away down at the valley floor. To their front, as they looked out from the underbrush, was a problem.

It was dusk and the light wasn't good, so they couldn't discern whether the fur-clad riders back at the crossroads they had passed but moments ago were Korgash, Oda, and their minions. When they had rejoined the road late that afternoon, they had taken off their snowshoes, thinking to leave less-distinguishable tracks, so they hoped that the riders would not read any particular significance into the passage of five pairs of boots. The men - and perhaps women - seemed simply to be discussing what road to take until one leaned forward over the neck of his giant brown stallion, swung a leg over the saddle, and dropped to the ground.

"Without a shadow of doubt, it is him," Thay said in his by now capable Straelish.

"How the fuck would you know?"

"I'm not blind. Look at how he moves. It's him."

"You've seen him once for less time than it takes to shit and you know how he moves?"

"He's the sort who leaves an impression."

Cairn piped in, "Thay can take a long time shitting."

Thay gave his big friend a slap to the back of the head. "Shut up Cairn," Lora hissed under her breath. "This is dangerous."

"He knows," Thay replied, not taking his eyes off the riders.

"Can you really see him in this gloom?" Elkor asked, incredulity dripping from his tongue. Thay did not deign to respond. At the crossroads, the large figure moved away from the horses, bent down close to the snow-covered ground.

"He's got us," Lora whispered.

"So, what's your plan, ugly man?" Lars asked.

"Use *you* to demonstrate how a marmot can out-think idiotic northerners. Now shut up!" Elkor peered through his furrowed brow at the horsemen. "What are they doing?"

Although Elkor had not specifically directed his question at Thay, they all waited on the young man's response. "The ones on the horses are looking around, so they know the tracks are fresh. Korgash is either in a great deal of pain or grinning with pleasure."

"It'll be the latter," Elkor noted. "Is *she* with them?"

"The two on the left look like women." They watched another rider climb off his horse and also bend down to inspect the snow. Korgash remounted. "It looks like he's put his tracker on our trail." Thay whispered, a new urgency in his voice. "As Lars says, if you've got a plan, now's the time to share it, or we'll be off."

The man they reckoned was a tracker lumbered forward down the road following the trail they had left in the new snow. A shrill bird call echoed through the darkening forest, the screech of an owl. "Well?" demanded Lars. "We can either be on them and take them by surprise, or be on our way, *salich*-like," he said, using the Straelish word for "quickly."

"They know we're here, you idiot," Elkor spat. "There's no fucking surprise."

"Right then … so we go. Into the woods," Thay commanded. The Fjordlanders got to their feet. Elkor hesitated, a snarl flashing across his face. "Come!" Thay ordered in Straelish. Elkor finally got to his feet and followed the youths up the slope. It didn't take long to hear the sounds of pursuit; a loud cry flew through the deepening night.

"Needn't worry about the cold now, it's time to warm up!" Lars said. "It's time to run!"

"No! Wait!" Elkor exclaimed. "If we just go deeper into the forest, we'll leave behind a trail in this snow they'll find no matter how quickly we run. We've got brains, let's use them."

"You use that brain of yours, dead man, I'll use my legs!" Lars declared.

"Look around you, idiot! These woods aren't thick. A man can ride a horse in here, and in this snow, he needn't get down from the horse to track us."

"So what do you suggest?" Lars snapped.

"Put on the snowshoes!" Elkor barked. As he pulled his snowshoes off his pack and tied them to his feet, he said, "We have a sliver of time until they find where we left the road. Hurry!" The force of the order was of such strength that the youths obeyed. "We've got to get to the river. Quick now, follow me." Elkor loped away as rapidly as he could, cresting the rise and heading down the slope. Lora, tying off her first snowshoe, was certain his pace would not be quick enough given how unaccustomed he was to the contraptions. The youths had no trouble catching him up and passing him as they scrambled down the gentle descent, weaving between the sparse oak trees. Another cry behind them signalled that the pursuit had caught the trail they had left from the road.

Lars and Lora encountered the river first. It meandered back and forth between bouldered and thickly wooded banks. Reaching those thicker riverside woods relieved them, knowing that Korgash and his guard could not thunder over them atop galloping horses. They wove between the trees and the largest of the boulders - the smaller ones being covered in snow - and then jogged out onto the ice. They had no fear of crashing through to a watery death for the extent of the recent harsh cold. They stopped in the middle of the channel and turned, waiting anxiously for the others. "Now what?" asked Lars.

Lora quickly looked about. The river wasn't broad; she reckoned perhaps only a score or so of paces across at its narrowest point. The frigid wind blasted them, but it had also scoured most of the snow from the ice leaving just a thumb-deep layer encrusted on top. "Over here!" Lora pointed to the far bank where greater exposure to the wind had left the ice surface clearer. "Scour the snow from the ice beside of that clear patch." They jogged over and Lars set down *Harbinger* to scrape away the encrusted snow with the edge of his shield. Scraping together, they managed to add a patch two paces square to the breadth of clear ice - doubling its width - before they heard the clash of battle joined back the way they had come.

§

When Elkor gave the order to get to the river and shuffled off over the rise, Thay finished arranging his snowshoes and loped after the Straeling. It didn't take long for the young man to realize that whatever plan Elkor had in mind, there was not enough time for them to bring it to fruition; Elkor simply couldn't move quickly enough in the snowshoes and already the chase was on. When Thay drew level to the older man, he looked over his shoulder and, through the trees, glimpsed large, dark shapes of riders on horses cresting the rise behind them at a trot. Thay then glanced ahead to see Lora and Lars, always the quickest, approach the thicker woods at the riverbank. He turned and, as Cairn came lumbering up, he grabbed his friend by the arm and dragged the big youth behind the trunk of a large oak tree. "Elkor'll not make it."

Cairn peeked around the tree back the way they had come. "They're coming quickly, but they don't look like they're being careful. I don't reckon they've seen us."

Thay pointed up the slope to the right where a horse crossed an open space. "*Skeetze!*"

"*Foxt!*" Cairn responded without thought.

"They've put a scout on their left. There's likely one to the right as well."

"Raiding tactics," Cairn agreed, "with probably only a tracker and a scout ahead of 'em." Cairn looked into Thay's eyes.

Thay nodded.

Cairn smiled.

Thay hoisted his shield and readied his axe, *Tear Tongue*. Cairn freed up *Orgor's Awl* rather than his axe and pressed his back to the oak. The first rider, a small man on a filly, wasn't long in coming. Approaching at a trot, looking down at the tracks more than ahead, the tracker didn't see Thay spring from behind the tree. The rider's horse, however, did. Spooked, the filly veered away from Thay's swing. Instead of taking the victim in the gut, *Tear Tongue* sliced into the tracker's thigh. The man let loose a cry of agony as the horse lunged away from the fur-clad attacker, jolting the rider out of the saddle. As the horse careened off, Thay made to follow up his first wild swing but heard the scout following the tracker yell a guttural war cry and spur his horse into a charge. Thay turned and ran.

Just as the scout on his horse pounded past the oak tree, Cairn spun, swinging his maul over the horse's head and directly into the chest of the rider. The force of the impact sent *Orgor's Awl* spinning out of Cairn's grip and into the woods. The scout dropped to the snowy ground while his mount galloped on. Cairn pulled his axe from his belt and sprang forward. He stayed his swing; the scout was clearly in no shape to pursue them. Instead, Cairn stepped forward and dealt the tracker a swift blow to the back of the head.

Shouting sprang up all across the rise, so Cairn spun and bolted after Thay. He weaved through the sporadic trees and spotted Thay and Elkor half way down the slope. Elkor had shed his pack and Thay was lugging it in his left hand. Cairn caught up to them on the lip of a last level patch before a final descent to the valley floor. "Are they coming?" Thay asked, gulping in deep breaths of the frigid air.

In response, the scouts to the left and right came galloping at them. In the deepening dusk, Thay could only see the massive combined shapes of man and horse thumping closer, fountains of snow flying up from the horses' hooves.

"Go!" Thay ordered and Elkor lumbered off towards the trees at the river's edge. The riders ignored the smaller man and bore down on the Fjordlanders. When the scout coming at them from the left closed to within ten paces, Thay swung

Elkor's pack in a wide arc and flung it towards the horse. The rider ducked and the horse veered away. The rider bearing down on Cairn had a spear in his right hand, so Cairn lunged across the path of the horse to get himself on the rider's left side. The rider was experienced, however, whereas Cairn was not. The rider shifted the horse's direction over the final stretch, guiding the horse right on top of the large youth. Cairn gave up any hope of attacking and dove to the ground to his right, but too late. The horse collided with his shield, sending him flailing over the snow down the slope.

After sending Cairn flying, the rider drove his mount at Thay, who spun out of the horse's path and raised his target shield just as the rider shifted his spear at his new target. The steel spear head rang off the iron rim of the shield, sending not only the distinct sound of battle into the deepening dusk, but also a length of broken spear spinning into the air. The rider pulled his mount around, drew his sword and bashed Thay again and again. Thay got his round shield in the way of the blows, but the force of the attack drove the young man down to a crouch. Thay kept his shield above him and sliced horizontally with his axe, nicking a hock of the horse. He didn't hamstring it, but he did send it hopping sideways. The attack gave him an opening. He leapt to the slope and, as he flew through the air, he brought his shield under him, hoping it would serve as a toboggan. He landed with a thud on the encrusted snow and moved no further, the boss of the shield anchoring him firmly in place.

"Skeetze!" he cursed.

Hearing pounding hooves blasting closer, Thay twisted onto his back and saw a big man on a great warhorse bearing down on him, and swinging the beautiful battle axe he had first seen in The Drover's Maid way back in Harburg. Thay kept rolling to the side, barely managing to reach the partial protection of a great oak tree root protruding from the forest floor. All he could do was to pull his shield up to cover his chest and face.

The warhorse trampled right over him.

§

As Lora strung her bow, she heard sword ring off shield, that familiar sound of battle. Lars started forward but Lora grabbed his cloak and held him in place. "Wait!" she ordered. Just then they saw Elkor's black form trundle through the trees and scramble across the rocks at the far bank. He glanced up from his snowshoes, spotted the youths, and shuffled out onto the ice. He hadn't gone a half-dozen paces before Cairn crashed from the trees, leapt the stoney bank, and skidded across the crusted snow atop the ice. He grabbed Elkor by the collar of the cloak as he thundered past, dragging the little man over the ice to where Lora and Lars stood.

"Thay?" Lora barked.

"Buying time for *him*," Cairn panted in reply.

Lars declared, "Brave deed!"

"Let's hope it's not his last," Lora spat.

Elkor got his feet under him and spun back to face the far side of the river. "We'll worry about that later. Now, Cairn, Lars, make a shield wall here," he directed, pointing to the crusted snow beyond the front edge of the patch of ice they had cleared. "Get that smooth patch of ice behind you!"

"Are you mad?" Lars snapped. "Where's the sense in a two-man shield wall? It's stupid!"

"Of course it's stupid, now shut your fucking mouth and do it if we're to have a chance!"

Lars and Cairn looked at Lora.

Lora nodded.

It was neither a difficult nor lengthy process to set up a two-man shield wall. Lora and Elkor had just shifted themselves behind it when an apparition emerged from the trees. The warhorse and its rider congealed from a cloud of exhaled vapour. The rider, furred, helmed, with the axe catching and refracting the last light of the day. Korgash was in no rush and allowed his stallion to pick its way over the rocky bank.

By the time the horse stopped on the ice, eight housecarls had also emerged from the trees. All of them looked formidable; bulky, wearing determined looks on scarred and grim visages. Another rider was the lavishly robed Lady Oda, this time a green skirt flowed from under her ermine coat, sitting atop a dun gelding. Even though the dimming light made her face hard to see, Lora could tell that the woman was studying the ice in front of her.

Korgash, himself, wore a huge grin. "Well, well," he called over the sound of the swirling wind. "What luck! The plague troll spy and his murdering Thorn minions!"

"We've murdered no one!" Elkor yelled back across the ice.

"Tell that to Marlus and Deeter. When we passed them, they looked ready for Galivith's Last Blessing."

"That's what happens to wanking whoresons who attack honest travellers on the Queen's road!"

"Oh, no, no, *no!* You've got it all wrong! I am confronting a band of murderous thieves who have been plaguing these parts. I think the Queen will prefer my version of events. It might even convince her I'd make a better *oberherg* than the one she's got up here. Imagine that! All thanks to a plague troll spawn and its pet Thorns. I might even thank you before I extinguish your pathetic lives."

"I knew you had diarrhoea for brains but I always thought you had balls, even if you usually prefer banging them off goats' arses. If you'd rather debate politics, perhaps you can get your pretty handmaid to serve us tea?" Lora could see the anger building among the henchmen at the insults to their dead comrades as well as the slight against Oda, although she simply smiled and waved. She turned her head and, still smiling, said something to Korgash that they could not hear.

"For once I agree with you, maggot. Lady Oda reminds me that you and I will have time to talk, or even sing, later." Then, turning to his men he yelled, "Spare the beast and the girl."

Elkor hissed to the Fjordlanders, "Be prepared to get back onto the rocks on this bank when they come at us. Then use those damned snowshoes to get around them! Come at them from ..." He didn't get the chance to finish for Korgash launched the attack with a cry of "Straeland and Galivith!"

The horses sprang forward. Lora heard Cairn mutter to himself, "*Foxt!* I've really got to be learning the bow!" Luckily Lora had hers ready. She aimed at the upwind rider and loosed. The wind swept the arrow aside, but Florri manifested Himself, for out of pure good luck it buried itself into the chest of a rider further down the line. She did not have the time to loose another, for the acceleration of the horses over the crusted snow was impressive. In but a moment they had reached a gallop and had pounded past the middle point in the river.

"Now!" Elkor yelled. His feet slid out from under him as he backed across the patch of clear ice but Lora hauled him up and pushed him towards the rocks. Cairn and Lars pivoted away from each other and loped up up the bank.

"Mind the exposed ice!" Oda's voice burst across the river.

The riders spurred their mounts on to a full charge and readied themselves for the leap onto the riverbank. Korgash must either have heard Oda's warning or noticed the patch of clear ice that had been hidden behind the Fjordlander's small shield wall; he hauled on the reins and pulled his warhorse to a skidding halt at the near edge of the clear ice. Perhaps the soldier on the left end of the line also noticed the ice patch, for he managed to steer his horse clear. The next in line pulled his mount to a near stop, though it couldn't halt its full momentum before sliding across the ice, one leg flailing out and the rider pitching himself off. The rider at the far right of the line also managed to divert around the danger, but the horse could barely control its momentum and clambered awkwardly up the riverbank, unable to avoid the burly Fjordlander with the axe leaping from the top of the rise. Cairn swept the weapon, embedding its head deep into the man's chest and hurling the attacker backwards onto the ice. The horse stampeded off into the woods on the far bank of the Arrowsmith.

Lora shut her mind to the frantic screams of the horses: jumping from the river, the back legs of four of them had slipped out from under them. Instead of arcing over the riverbank, they fell, slid, skidded, and crashed into the rocks, throwing their riders into the trees or crushing them underneath thrashing legs and writhing bodies. The horses' screaming overwhelmed the agony-ridden cries of the riders.

The jolt of the blow he had delivered spun Cairn around mid-leap so that he tumbled out onto the ice, limbs flailing around him. Korgash didn't need a second invitation; he hauled his horse around and spurred it upriver at the big Fjordlander. Cairn spotted the huge warhorse coming at him and rolled towards the safety of the patch of cleared ice. Korgash leaned over in his saddle and swung his battle axe. Cairn raised his shield. The axe clove the wood in two and Cairn cried out in agony as the blow wrenched his arm in its shoulder socket.

Lars jumped from the river bank and attacked a henchman sprawling on the ice without a weapon. *Harbinger* came slicing down but the attack called for less slashing and more stabbing because the man had the time to kick out at Lars' leg, sending the swing astray. A spray of snow and ice chips flew into the dusk as the long claymore bit the solid mass of the river. Lars advanced and brought the sword up again in a long arc, but before it could return down on its intended victim, the man dove at Lars' legs, easily getting inside *Harbinger's* effective reach. He tackled Lars, sending the two of them sprawling across the clear ice.

The man spun, whipping out a dagger from his belt and lunging at the youngster. *Harbinger* was a big claymore and Lars wasn't as experienced as he needed to be. He couldn't bring the sword to bear before his enemy was on top of him. All he could do was raise his arms as the dagger flashed towards his throat. He caught the man's wrist and sent the stab high, but the attacker used his knee to pin Lars' right arm to the ice. Lars lashed out with his left fist but missed as the man leaned back, relying on the skill that came with years of fighting, skill the youngling didn't have. Lars didn't even hear his own yelling as he fought.

Horses screaming in agony, the wailing of their pinned riders, the anguished cry of Cairn, and the clash, grunts and yelling of Lars' fight all assaulted Lora's ears. For a moment she felt panic rising in her. But she gritted her teeth, pulled *Íss* from her belt, and ran for Lars.

Again the steel flashed forward and Lars, with no options remaining to him dropped his sword and grasped the man's right arm as the point of the dagger came to within a thumb's width of biting into flesh. Again the attacker drove the dagger at Lars' face, slowed by the northman's resistance but never halted. The blade made for Lars' eye and the youngster twisted his head aside. The blade sliced open flesh, exposing the cheekbone. Lars screamed and drove a head butt at his attacker, but his adversary recoiled before Lars' forehead could connect. The man whipped his dagger back and downwards, catching Lars by surprise and opening a gash down the jaw and across the throat.

Lora dove forward into a spray of Lars' blood, and somehow managed to embed her seax deep into the back of his attacker as she collided with him, knocking him off her friend and sending them both skidding over the clear ice. She rolled to her feet, *Íss* still in her hand. Korgash's man scrambled to his knees, his face twisting in agony, and he threw his right hand over his left shoulder, reflexively clutching at the deep wound. His dagger had slid far out of reach across the patch of exposed ice. Lora stepped forward, the point of her seax held low. The man realized his peril and looked about for his dagger. With a yell, she pounced, stabbing *Íss* forward. The man blocked the blow with his right hand and twisted away. The shock of his defence sent Lora spinning, but she gave herself over to the motion, pivoted wildly, and sliced at the man with a flashing backhand as she past him. By mere luck, the blade took him in the side of the head, slicing temple, eye, cheek and nose. Lora halted her spin in front of the bloody figure holding hands up to his maimed face. She threw herself on the man, pried aside his elbows, and drove *Íss* through the links of his chainmail and deep into his chest. The man gasped and buckled. Lora sat on his chest, sliced off his ear, and then stabbed her weapon deep into his remaining eye.

Lora shoved herself from the dying housecarl and scrambled back to the riverbank. Spying Lady Oda across the river, she snatched up her bow, pulled an arrow from her quiver, aimed, and loosed. This time, Norrgi, not Florri manifested Himself, for the wind pushed the missile right and it whistled past Oda's head. The Straeling noblewoman pulled her dun around and let it pick its way up the riverbank. Lora ventured one last shot. This time Tanat played one of His tricks, for the arrow impaled the gelding's rump and it leapt forward, crashing into the brush on the far bank and charging out of view. Oda did not spill off the horse, though, and as an experienced rider, Lora had to admit that the Straeling noblewoman rode well.

Lora looked around and saw Lars. He had both of his hands clasped to his neck. Blood pulsed between his fingers, forming a large black stain on the chest of his coat. His eyes were wide in shock and his feet were scraping across the ice as he struggled to get up. Lora grabbed his cloak and hauled him to the riverbank where she propped him in a sitting position. "Lars! Listen! I need to see the wound. You're going to take one hand from your neck. One hand!" She didn't notice the warhorse down the river turn about.

Elkor did, though. So too did Cairn, who, even through the agony of his shoulder, saw the sense in moving into the centre of the cleared ice. Korgash prodded his horse forward, appraising the situation. One of his men lay on the ice in the middle of the river, arrow in his chest and his body convulsing, coughing up blood. Two more lay dead on the ice where battle had been joined. Four others were either unconscious, crippled or dead under the mass of writhing horses. Only one other soldier was still on his mount far down river, having managed to divert away from the trap and get his horse's momentum finally under control on the snow-crusted ice. One obviously-hurt Fjordlander stood on the ice, but he was the largest and he looked on the edge of a frothing fury. As Korgash looked about, the big Thorn lifted his axe and swung it back and forth, limbering himself for the fight. The woman he could see attending to the remaining Fjordlander at the riverbank. Korgash cast his eyes about, scanning the woods along the bank. That was when Elkor's voice joined the howl of the wind and shrieking horses.

"If you're done playing with the children, I'm over here."

"Come on you shit!" Cairn screamed, adding to the din. "Come and meet my lover!"

"Now, Lars! Your left hand! Take it away. Now!"

Korgash's eyes shifted back to the slaughter on the ice.

"What are you waiting for?" Elkor called out.

"She'll give you a fucking you've never had before!" Cairn hollered, shaking his axe at the horseman and stepping forward.

"Pressure on the wound, Lars! Right hand! Now!"

"Goat!" Elkor screamed. "Fucker!"

Korgash hauled the reins of his warhorse to the right and spurred it into the woods. Elkor turned and ran.

Cairn yelled in frustration and turned to shout against the bitter wind at the mounted housecarl downriver. The man hesitated, then mirrored Korgash's withdrawal into the woods.

§

Elkor had cursed his luck. The moment when his enemy had finally attacked, he had already lost his pack and all the things in it that he had planned to use. So, while the fight raged on the ice, he had snatched up Lora's pack, undone its ties, pulled open its mouth, and hauled out a rope that he had seen her pack atop her food, clothes, and furs every morning since they had left Harburg. He had dropped the pack, cast his gaze about until he had spied his enemy. At that point, Korgash had been pulling his warhorse about and spurring it towards Cairn. Elkor had bounded along the riverbank as fast as his snowshoes would permit until he had come to a gap in the trees. From here he had been able see out onto the ice without obstruction and he had knelt next to a tree to his right, screening himself from Korgash, who was just pulling his warhorse out of its charge against Cairn. Elkor had tied off the rope, lumbered across the gap between the trees, tied the other end to another tree and hoped that Korgash had not spied him in the dwindling light of dusk. Then he had stood up and scrambled further up the riverbank to the middle of the gap.

Elkor saw that Korgash had wheeled his warhorse and seemed to be preparing another charge at Cairn. Despite the shouting and the screams of injured horses, it wasn't difficult to capture the big Strael's attention; after a moment's hesitation, Korgash pulled his horse around and spurred it up the riverbank towards the gap in the woods.

Elkor turned and ran. He sought deeper snow and glanced over his shoulder to see if his gambit might work. Korgash drove his steed up the bank of the Arrowsmith in a pounding rush. The warhorse launched itself into a gallop at the top of the rise. Whether Korgash saw the trap and guided his horse, or whether the horse itself saw the rope and leapt, Elkor couldn't know. But as he ran he saw the horse fly over the rope tied off across the gap and land without error.

Elkor cursed and then wove through as many trees as he could as he ran, but the woods were no denser on this side of the river than they were on the other slope of the valley. He sought out a deep drift but couldn't spy one. He shot a glance over his shoulder and saw the big warhorse pounding closer, its breath spewing out of its muzzle and sliding away on the wind. He lumbered to the biggest tree he could see, scrambled around its trunk, and pulled out his dagger. He heard the horse thunder closer. From the folds of his cloak he then pulled out a small box and opened it, scooping out a palmful of fine white powder. The horse came pounding past the tree trunk. Elkor saw the flash of steel arching out of the night. Elkor ducked and lunged right, further around the tree trunk. Korgash rode a finely trained beast, however, and it knew what to do; it veered right itself and collided with Elkor, sending the man crashing to the ground.

Sprawled across the snow, Elkor saw the warhorse careen past, hooves and chunks of crusted snow flying as it slowed and turned. He scrambled across the ground towards the safety of the tree trunk. Boots, though, slammed down in front of him, between him and the tree. Elkor was a man of many talents, but one of them wasn't fighting. When Korgash lashed out at him with his boot, Elkor twisted away, but to no avail. Korgash's boot slammed against Elkor's face, snapping his head back and stunning him. He had no means of preventing Korgash from grasping him by his cloak, like a puppy grabbed by the scruff of the neck.

"Got you, again, spawn," Korgash gloated, twisting his arm and bringing Elkor's face close enough to smell his breath.

It was the moment for which Elkor had prayed. He brought his left hand to his mouth, opened it, exposing the white powder, and he blew. The powder exploded towards Korgash's face. But then swirled away as a gust of wind shook the woods. Korgash, momentarily surprised, recoiled, and then smirked as he realized what had happened. "Oh, my twisted fool, my poor, twisted, twisted fool. Don't you know that Galivith, Himself, protects the pure from the likes of you." A puzzled look crossed the man's stoney features and he added, "But the scriptures are quiet on whether He protects twisted plague troll spawn from the pure." Then he smiled. "I imagine that's because he doesn't."

Elkor thrust his dagger forward with his right hand.

Korgash snapped his arm backwards, sending the blow awry. "Another act of Galivith," he purred. Then he slammed his fist into Elkor's face, sending the ugly man into oblivion.

§

"Guliveg be with us," Lora whispered when she saw the wound through the blood welling up like waves on the Andersfjord when a summer storm would send swells landward from the Bight. Lars' wide eyes and gasping breath were her only reply. "Keep pressure on the wound!" she ordered. "Keep it closed. I need my things. Understand?" Lars nodded between rasping breaths, his blonde braid turning red as it sopped up blood running onto his chest. Lora turned to clamber up the riverbank but Lars' left hand grabbed her arm.

He gasped, his voice a wheezing whistle, "Is it … worth … the …?"

"Don't be daft!" Lora snapped. "Of course it is. Pressure!"

Lars nodded and she clambered up the riverbank to retrieve her pack. She realized that Cairn was killing the crippled horses, for the volume of the screaming was diminishing. She did note a pair of the beasts scrambling over the rocks beside her, trying to escape the carnage. She grabbed her pack and pulled it over her shoulder, which motion suddenly spilled its contents about the snow. "What?" she demanded of the woods in angry surprise, kneeling down to scoop up a scarf splayed out on the ground. She dug into her open pack and found her healer's bag. She flung the detritus of her pack on the ground and rushed back to Lars.

He looked very pale. She readied her needle and gut. "This will hurt, all right?"

Lars nodded. Then he wheezed, "Tanat played a trick on me. On us all. Thay's crimson dream … I'll never be …"

"Be quiet now!" Lora ordered.

He nodded again.

She punctured the skin with her needle, Lars grunted in pain, she punctured the skin on the other side of the wound and pulled the gut through it. Blood welled. Her hands and Lars', the needle and thread all turned into a mucky mess. She punctured the skin again. Lars shuddered. Again she pulled.

More blood, though less, spilled over her hands. She made an-other loop. Lars did not grunt or flinch this time. The surges of blood subsided as her blood-soaked hands flew across the wound. She had almost finished closing the entire length of the bloody wound when she heard Cairn whisper, "He's gone."

Lora pulled the gut through the wound. "What? Don't be stupid. He'll be fine."

"Lora!" Cairn barked, snatching her attention from the task at hand. He lowered his voice and added, "He's gone, *Loraling*. Look at him."

Lora pulled her focus back from the end of the wound. Blood no longer swelled from it. She noticed Lars' pale hand lying unmoving on the crusted snow atop the river ice. She glanced up at his face and saw his smile. But his eyes weren't right. "Lars!" she shouted. "Lars, don't you think you can just go! You've got to get us home! You can't leave."

"He already has," Cairn whispered. "He already has."

"No," Lora gasped. "No."

Cairn took her into his arms and hugged her. "He's gone to his Weighing," he said. "Look at his smile. He knew that Hondrig would welcome him. He died a warrior."

§

"Let me look at that shoulder," Lora presently said, her tone flat.

Cairn shook his head. "No, not yet. We don't ken of the fates of two of us. Tend to me after the learning."

Elkor's fate was easy to deduce. They found Lora's rope - Lora untied it and took it with them - followed the snowshoe tracks until they found the site of a short skirmish. Only one set of tracks in the snow led away; hoof prints. Some blood lay on the snow, but not enough to provide certainty about life or death. Without speaking a word, they turned back to the river. They came across one of the horses that had survived the charge on the river - a fine, big warhorse - and they claimed it as part of the *weregyld* owed them for the death of Lars. They loaded their gear on it and led it back across the river and up the far slope. They searched and searched but could find no sign of Thay on the eastern slope of the river valley, so they finally returned to Lars.

The bodies of seven men lay on the ice, most within the mass of crumpled horseflesh at the western riverbank. It was now deep into the night and the sight of the dead looked even more ghastly, lit by the faint green of the northern lights.

Finally Cairn allowed Lora to examine his shoulder. She bade him lie down on the ground beside a tree and sat down perpendicular to him. "Normally this would need someone pulling your other arm. You'll have to pull hard with your right arm, really hard. And it'll hurt like a bugger, but you've got to do it. Now take hold of that tree and get ready." Cairn nodded. She took his left arm, placed her foot against his ribcage and slowly pulled the arm out to the side. As she applied the pressure, she saw Cairn grimace, but only the wind howled, blasting up the river valley from the north and breaking the silence; odd, given that dislocated shoulders caused a great deal of pain. All at once, she felt the shoulder slip back into place and she had Cairn sit back against a tree. Then she took the reins from a dead horse and used them to bind Cairn's arm to his side to keep the shoulder in place. She did her work, but from no sense of duty or loyalty; rather, from the sort of trance she had seen in oarsmen on *Rignil*. When she had finished, she sat back on the river ice. Cairn looked at her; all the thanks he was capable of on such a bleak, cold night.

"Gather stones," she finally ordered. Cairn went about the work one-handed, a task that would have been nigh on impossible without his considerable strength.

Lars' cairn was crafted from the stones of the bank of the Arrowsmith River, and built by his friend who himself carried the name of the thing he built. It took a great deal of hard work, carrying Lars to a place away from the battle site and yet overlooking the river, scraping snow and encrusted ice from the stones, pulling them loose, carrying them and then piling them around Lars' body. They left him his winter clothes and covered him with the blanket that Lora had bought for him back in Harburg with the coin she had earned from selling Monsfried a pair of snowshoes. They disagreed, bitterly, about laying *Harbinger* by his side, but Lora finally won that debate. The claymore, she declared, was part of Krannogberg's future and though Lars might have been its guardian, he had no claim to it in the spirit world. In the end, Cairn strapped it to the back of the horse they had captured, though he felt sullied doing so. In *Harbinger's* place, he laid the axe, *Fjordbird*, so that Lars would not have to go undefended into the afterlife, towards Hondrig's final weighing. Another question was whether to leave Lars his bone flute, but this time Cairn won the argument and kept it as a keepsake.

It was near daybreak by the time Lora sang the chorus of the *Cleaving Rite*, loud, clear and steady despite the wind:

Hondrig,
    Master of the Deciding,
Hondrig,
    to Your shores a soul now sails.
Master,
    when You do the Weighing,
Master,
    let our love touch the scales.
Hondrig,
    as You bid us so we live;
Hondrig,
    waves, reefs, sleet and gales.
Master,
    weights of mercy You can give,
Master,
    let our grief touch the scales.

Chapter Five

Korgash and his remaining man-at-arms met up with Oda in the woods of the near bank. She stood, holding a blood-soaked cloth against the rump of her dun gelding. She had her horse's blood on her cloak and gloves. The spent arrow lay on the ground, blood congealing in the snow. Her brown eyes flicked to Elkor bent unconscious over the withers of Korgash's warhorse and then to the man-at-arms. "Is this all? Are all *three* of my men gone?" she asked. Korgash grunted in acknowledgement. "Well, at least Andrez and Fritzler remained with Jenna. Surely we're in no danger?"

Korgash shook his head, "Only of frostbite, my lady."

She inspected her horse's wound again and muttered, "That'll have to do." She mounted and they walked their horses - the dun gelding limping - back to the road, where they rejoined Oda's worried handmaid and the young men-at-arms. Eager to escape the cold, blasting wind, they rode on to Fletcherton as fast as the injured horse could move. The guards at the town gate at first did not grant them entry; protecting the town against mysterious riders appearing out of the woods after dusk was their role after all. They only relented when Lady Oda pointed out in her well-modulated, high-born tones that the local *herg*, Herg Adolphis, would grow angry if his cousin incurred frostbite on account of guards who couldn't tell a brigand from a guest.

Once through the gate, Korgash waved his man-at-arms forward. "We lost some good, loyal men tonight. I would have us bring their bodies here for Galivith's Last Blessing. We must also round up this plague beast's pet Thorns. Once you have ensured that Lady Oda and her household are well-installed at the inn, the good one mind, go to *Herg* Adolphis' sheriff, make a report, and assist in the mobilization of all available men-at-arms. Make sure we're ready to ride at dawn."

The man bowed his head and moved off. Korgash nodded to Oda and turned his warhorse towards the town smithy. "My dear," Oda called to him, bringing both him and his man-at-arms to a stop. She gestured in front of them with a thrust of her chin, "Are the gaols not *this* way?"

Korgash grinned. "Oh, this plague troll isn't going to the *gaol*! He's *much* too dangerous for that. He might infect the drunks, the thieves or the guards, after all. No, after tonight's bloodletting, I have a *special* plan for him."

"Whatever this plan is, remember, folk rally quicker to a strong, righteous *herg* than a cruel, unjust one."

Korgash forced a smile and replied, "The folk rally quicker yet to a *fair herg* who, by the grace of Galivith, labours strenuously, effectively to protect their families."

" 'Fair' is quite appropriate, but remember also, '*just.*' You must be seen to revere and uphold the Queen's writ!"

"I shall be both fair and just, my lady. It touches my heart that you stay out here in this freezing weather on account of concern over me, but I, too, worry about you. I shall share a glass of Polgati spirits with you in the inn when I arrive. Please go in."

She inclined her head, smiled, and concluded, "I, too, lost good, loyal men this night. I am sure I speak for both Andrez and Fritzler when I say we will ride out with you on the morn." She did not await a response before nudging her wounded gelding after Korgash's man-at-arms. Her reduced household followed.

Korgash removed his prize to the smithy, where, despite the late hour, he quickly secured the owner's cooperation. He found the chains he needed in the workshop and soon had Elkor kneeling on the floor, but held upright, suspended from the rafters by the arms.

By the time Elkor regained consciousness, Korgash had a small fire going in the forge and was feeding coal into it. The big warrior was speaking, although it took Elkor a few moments to register what the man was saying, "... want the fire hot for our little discussion of politics. Although, as Lady Oda suggests, I think we should also discuss law. Perhaps add in a short chat on what social diseases plague our land? That would be nice, wouldn't you agree?" Elkor didn't need the fire to be any hotter for a trickle of sweat to run from his brow and down his nose. It hung there, suspended, for a long moment, during which Korgash approached his dangling victim. He examined Elkor for a long while before shaking his head.

"You stupid, stupid beast," Korgash declared. He let Elkor see the slow, deliberate cocking of his hand before unleashing a backhanded slap to the face. Elkor's head snapped around at the strength of the blow. "Stupid, stupid, stupid beast." The forehand slap snapped his head around the other way. "You consider yourself a fount of knowledge but you haven't figured out that you can't escape the Queen's writ." Korgash punched Elkor straight in the face, pitching the small man as far backwards as the chains would allow. Then he grabbed Elkor by the hair and pulled the small man's head forward. Korgash studied the round, red blotches of skin to either side of Elkor's brow. "Those really *are* horns pushing through your skin! When she sees your head, it will convince the Queen of your guilt. Of course, you'll not get to plead your case for I don't intend to drag your body to Shipton, if you take my meaning." He drove his forehead into his victim's face sending a spout of blood from Elkor's now broken nose.

Korgash walked over to the forge, plucked a poker from the tools hanging on the wall and placed its tip in the roaring fire. Then he returned to stand in front of Elkor. "Eight good men died because of you, spawn. Eight loyal men lost to Lady Oda's household and mine own. Do you know how hard it is to find good loyal men?" He punched Elkor in the stomach, pitching the man's torso and head forward. "Loyal men, yes, one can find loyal men. Usually dim men with undying faith in Galivith and their master, if that master be strong and just, such as *I* am. I have dozens of such men on my estates." Korgash returned to the forge and pulled the poker from the fire. He inspected its glowing length, holding it in front of his face. "As for good men, well, they are common enough as well. The trick is recognizing what each one is good at and devoting the man to that task. Even peasants are usually good at *something*, be it husbandry, or smelting iron into pokers such as this." Korgash moved closer and held the poker in front of Elkor's collection of purple and blue bruises currently passing for a face. "Hmm, I think it could use a little more time, don't you?"

He thrust the poker back into the forge before continuing his discourse, "The problem with good men, *particularly* with good men, you understand, is that they're so rarely loyal. They're always looking out for a better job, a higher station, another plot of land, and so forth." He yanked Elkor's head up again by the hair. "If only they didn't *know* they were good!

"But I, being the leader I am, I managed to find a half-dozen good, loyal men. And because you think you should be able to practice your dark arts to terrorize these lands, five of those good, loyal men are now dead. Lady Oda lost three on top of that! Three of mine had young families! Think on what will happen to them now; their children may *starve*. Their wives may have to sell themselves. All because of you."

Still with his left hand holding up Elkor's head by the hair, Korgash reached over and grabbed the poker. "I think the Queen's justice should be ready by now, don't you?" Elkor's bloodshot right eye, the one not swollen shut, followed the glowing trail of the poker as it arched from the fire and approached his face. He uttered a squeak, and then a loud scream as the blazing point of the poker traced the outline of his face from his left temple, down in front of his ear, and along the line of his jaw. Elkor tried to heave his head away but Korgash's grip was too strong.

The *herg* nodded. "Yes, that actually *improves* your appearance. You'll have to thank me for this." He returned the poker to the forge for it to reclaim its blazing heat. Then he turned back to his victim and tilted his head, considering the pathetic man dangling from the chains, knees and legs hardly supporting the body at all. "Well, I'm waiting." He moved closer to Elkor very slowly, "If you do not show due gratitude to a *herg* of the realm for a boon granted with a generous heart, then it will go ill for you. Galivith teaches that men should be grateful for those who bring order and that the pious should serve such bringers of order devoutly. You can hardly claim that you are respecting His teachings, now can you?"

"Gal … Galivith," Elkor wheezed.

"Yes? Galivith what?"

"… no, cannot … condone …"

Korgash landed a punch on Elkor's face, snapping the smaller man's head around and loosing a scream of agony as well as a pair of teeth. Korgash pulled back his fist and then a grunt exploded from his lungs as he pitched sideways, a huge fur-clad shape colliding into his back. He crashed to the floor, an attacker thumping his head against the smithy's flagstones. He threw himself to his right, aiming to roll onto his attacker, but he couldn't shift the opposing weight. Instead he felt the stab of a dirk catch in the chain mail protecting his abdomen that left him gasping for air even though it didn't pierce his skin. He thrust his right elbow back, felt its impact and heard a grunt, but he could also feel the dirk driving into his abdomen, threatening to spring a link and sink deep into his gut. Korgash then threw his weight to the left to relieve the pressure from the dirk, and he succeeded, rolling underneath his attacker, spinning around and seeing his enemy for the first time. His attacker was the tall, tawny-haired Fjordlander. Korgash yelled in anger; this stubbly-cheeked boy grinned down at him, and no matter how much he heaved, the Thorn's longer limbs provided too much leverage for him to break free.

He felt a rare panic rise inside him as he realized that this *child* was a match for his strength.

Then he felt the dirk bite high into his inner thigh.

§

Thay had rolled to the side, over the root of a great oak tree that protruded from the forest floor. He tugged his shield up to cover his chest and face. The warhorse trampled right over him, as it had been trained to do, Thay supposed. Luckily one edge of his shield had caught on top of the root and although the big stallion's hooves came right down on him, the root supported the bulk of the massive weight slamming down on the shield. Nevertheless, when the warhorse careened off, Thay was in no condition to follow; the impact of the hooves had stunned him and bruised his ribs.

When he could finally sit up, he propped himself against the trunk of the oak tree and, still stunned, could only watch his breath catch the frigid night air in billowing clouds of dispersing vapour. Through the leafless fingers of the canopy above him, he saw the stars gleaming silver, though the sky seemed strange. He turned his gaze to the north and saw glowing green … *northern fire!* The northern lights had come out for the first time that winter! The green even reflected off the snow-covered ground, casting an eerie glimmer among the trees.

And as his gaze traced a path along the glinting green among the trees, he noticed a golden spark flash among the boughs. It darted left and right, and then zipped into the pine needles above him. When he looked up, he saw more of them. In his befuddled state, he wondered if he was seeing sprites.

The uproar from across the valley brought him to his senses; the shrieks of injured horses, the pitched cries of men, the screaming of a close friend … then the yelling of insults further off. He shook his head to clear it of any confusion.

He knew he hadn't been stunned long, but he hoped it hadn't been too long. He realized something later; it was Cairn's bellowing, when Korgash's axe blow dislocated his shoulder, that brought him to full consciousness.

Thay heaved himself to his feet and staggered downhill towards the Arrowsmith River. He tripped and fell, sending another shock through his ribs. He lay there for a long time, trying to regain his breath, before he pulled himself to his feet again, then lumbered awkwardly forward another couple of paces and pitched forward onto the snow once more. He gasped at the pain and rolled onto his back. He sat up again and suddenly realized that he still wore his snowshoes. *Of course!* He had to walk differently. He got to his feet and set off again. The rhythm came back to him immediately and he made his way down the slope, though he noted that the night had grown silent except for the wailing of the bitter north wind howling through the trees: he heard no more screams of horses or men, no challenges barked into the dark, no clash of steel on iron. He cursed the time it had taken to come to his senses as he descended the valley.

As he approached thicker woods, that he presumed marked the edge of the river, out of the corner of his eye he caught the greenish glint of metal reflecting the northern lights and he slipped into cover against a tree. Then he saw two equine shapes pass in the dark, with one of the riders carrying a naked blade. They passed far to the right, a good hundred paces easily. Despite the darkness, Thay's eyes were keen enough to spy a huge warhorse trudging silently up the slope towards the road, a large man spurring it on, a form bundled over its back in front of the rider.

Thay made to follow them, but then caution made him grimace and turn back towards the river. He wove through the close-packed trees and peeked out between those lining the riverbank across the ice. He saw the carnage at the far riverbank; the crumpled bodies of horses and men formed black stains on the icy surface that refracted the blue-green glow overhead. Nothing moved except for a solitary, riderless horse close to him picking its way up the near bank of the river.

He cupped his hands to his mouth to call out over the howling of the wind, but thought the better of it; he had seen that Korgash had one henchman, leaving many another for whom to account. He also pondered the wisdom of crossing the ice and came to the conclusion that he would expose himself dangerously. He watched for a few moments more, but no one emerged from the trees, none of the shapes on the ice budged. The horse plodding its way up the riverbank stopped just a few paces away from him and closed her eyes.

The one thing he knew was that Korgash had a body slung over his horse's withers and had ridden with a housecarl towards the road. From the size of the shape, it couldn't be Cairn, was likely not Lars, but it could very well be Elkor - or Lora. "*Skeetze!*" he cursed under his breath.

He made his decision in an instant. He approached the horse near him. It was not a big warhorse, but rather a filly ... he recalled that it had been the tracker's horse. It snorted a warning and tossed its head but he was able to get hold of its harness. He wasn't as accustomed to animals as was Cairn, but he knew enough to take his time, introducing himself to the animal, letting it snuffle him, speaking softly to it. He looped its reins around a branch while he removed his snowshoes. Then, after a last quick survey of the river, he led the horse back over the way he had taken when running from Korgash. He came across his own pack, as he had hoped, so he dismounted and quickly tied it in place behind the filly's saddle. Before remounting he listened to the night again, but only the wind replied, and so he climbed onto the horse and nudged it into a trot up the hill.

When he got to the top of the rise, he guided the horse north, going slowly over the first stretch to make sure he caught sight of the tracks left by Korgash and his housecarl rejoining the road. He found them easily enough, and as he suspected, when they came to the road, they veered north towards Fletcherton.

Thay followed along the packed snow of the roadway, prodding the filly into a trot, but unaccustomed as he was to riding, he did not venture a quicker pace. Even so, it wasn't long before the woods on both sides of the road opened up, giving way to farmland. He could see no glimmers of light escaping between shutters on windows of isolated farmsteads, but up above him, the northern lights blazed and lent an emerald tinge to everything under their dancing sheen. Smoke from chimneys atop the houses bloomed greenly into the night air before scattering southwards, borne away by the fierce north wind. He pulled his cloak tight about him and bent his head against the cold air.

When he finally saw Fletcherton and its curtain wall, Thay dismounted. He led the horse, flitting behind cover to woods along the Arrowsmith River from which he could study the place where the wall met the frozen river. There were about fifty paces of open space between the last cluster of trees along the banks and the town wall. He tied the horse to a tree nestled in that sheltering grove of firs before draping its blanket over its back, though he left the saddle in place. He rummaged in his pack, sticking the flask of oil in the leather bag he hung from his belt. He pulled out the pouch of caltrops and also tied its laces to his belt. Then he crept down onto the icy river surface. Creeping low to the ice towards the curtain wall, he tried to keep himself under the cover of the riverbank as best he could. He peeked up at the town but what he saw didn't encourage him. The curtain wall carried on along the front of the river, rising as impenetrably as elsewhere. The wall curved back upon itself further along, following a bend in the river, so Thay rose to his feet and jogged along the base of the wall, hoping that on such a cold, blustery night, whatever watchmen there were would be huddled against the wind rather than vigilant.

He heard no cry upon the wind so he carried on to the curve in the wall and saw a stone quay protruding into the ice. He crept forward and spotted an archway where the quay met the wall. He pressed his back to the wall and sidled along it until he could steal a glimpse into the archway. An iron portcullis barred the way, and he caught the flicker of light from a small fire on the stonework of the tunnel that bored through the curtain wall.

Thay said a prayer to Rulla, the Dealer of Fates, and crept to the edge of the archway. He peeked into the tunnel in the curtain wall and saw that after the iron portcullis, there was no other obstruction currently in place along its length and he could see buildings inside Fletcherton. He also saw four guards holding their hands to a broad, deep iron brazier in which a fire burned. They shuffled and stamped, occasionally twisting to bring their backs closer to the warmth. While two stood on the far side of the brazier, they seemed far more intent on the fire than on keeping watch, and so, didn't see Thay peeping around the stonework.

He pulled back out of sight of the guards and studied the portcullis. It dropped down from a gatehouse that sat atop the wall and it appeared firmly anchored in place. It featured a gate - secured with a padlock - so that a person could pass through without the whole structure needing to be hoisted. He glanced across the archway and spied an opening at the bottom of the wall, a culvert passing underneath the stonework and emptying into the river. He considered dashing across the archway so that he could get a better look at the culvert, but it was a good dozen paces across, too wide, he guessed, for him to pass unnoticed.

He studied the stone quay sticking out into the frozen river, an extension of the pathway that passed through the tunnel. Of course it stood at level with the riverbank, but as that riverbank sloped away, the quay's far extremity stood a good three or four feet out of the ice. Thay made his decision.

He crept back along the wall a dozen paces, well out of sight of anyone in the archway, and then shuffled down the bank to the river. Stepping carefully backwards onto the ice, all the while looking up onto the curtain wall to see if anyone stood watch, he moved pace by pace out onto the ice. No guard's helmet came into view through the crenels and no spear poked above the merlons. He ventured another pace backwards, and then another, but still saw no one. He turned and sprinted at an angle towards the end of the quay further out onto the ice. No warning cry flew up from the walls or blasted out of the archway as he dove for cover behind the quay's far end. He pressed himself against its cold stone, which rose a full four feet above the ice and thus screened him from watchers on the walls or in the archway. Although the exertion had been minimal, his heart pounded in his chest, his breath was suddenly ragged, and his sore ribs throbbed anew. One small relief was that there was less of a gale here in the shadow of the stonework.

After a moment, Thay slithered along the ice to the quay's downstream edge and ventured a glance over its lip and down its length back at the curtain wall. He glimpsed no movement atop the wall and, in the archway, he could only see the silhouettes of the four guards huddled around the fire, seemingly oblivious to his presence. Creeping along the quay's downstream edge and using its bulk rising above the ice as cover from the guards in the arch, he closed back in on the curtain wall. When he reached the base of the quay, he crept to the small culvert underneath the wall. Upon crawling inside the narrow space, however, he encountered an iron grating blocking continued progress through the culvert. Tugging and kicking at it revealed that the grating was both well-anchored and strong rather than rusted-through and wobbly.

In exasperation, he cursed, twisted about and leaned his back against the grating, looking out onto the frozen river. "Think!" he hissed at himself under his breath. His anger rose in him as he considered how long he had already dawdled while whoever Korgash held prisoner suffered. Thay's stomach churned at the thought it might be Lora. The north wind blasted past the entrance to the culvert. He suddenly shivered as his inaction caught up to him and his sweat cooled against his skin. In the night air he heard the faint peal of a bell coming from inside the town. That was when a thought came to him.

§

Karel Maggarsfield shivered. He pulled his cloak tighter about him and shuffled closer to the fire. He leaned his left shoulder over the iron brazier. Like his colleagues, he considered the fire a true blessing of Galivith, and he would have faced far worse straits without it, but the problem was that his back froze while his chest burned. He turned and faced out onto the river, and then heard the metallic noise. He twisted his head, trying to catch the noise again over the wind's howl. There it was! - or was it? He stepped away from the fire, close to the portcullis, and cocked his ear again. Yes! He asked, "Martan, do you hear that?"

The grizzled farmer looked up from the fire, "What's that lad? Do I hear what?"

"A noise. Listen."

"Ya," Jarson chimed in. "I hear it. It's like, well, its like ..." He joined Karel at the gate to peer out into the night.

"That's metal on metal. A fight, do ye reckon?"

Karel shrugged. Jarson nodded. "It sounds like it's coming from the other bank."

Martan frowned, "Dunno, sounded like it was comin' from the quay."

"The quay?" Piotor asked.

"Ya," Martan replied. "There! That don't sound like it's on the far bank. It's comin' from the quay, by Galivith." Martan fumbled beneath his cloak for the keys to the lock on the gate set within the portcullis. He brought it forth, unlocked the gate, and pulled it open. "Piotor, you'll keep an eye out." Piotor nodded, though he stayed by the brazier. Martan led Karel and Jarson out of the archway. They stopped at the base of the quay to see if the tunnel beneath the wall had itself played tricks on their impressions about the direction from which the sounds came.

"There!" Karel pointed down the quay.

Martan walked them down the length of the snow-encrusted stonework. They came to end of the pier and saw a helmet bobbling on the air. Martan nodded at Karel and so the young man jumped down onto the ice. He grabbed the helmet, revealing a stick protruding from the ice underneath that had propped the piece of armour in the air. Around the helmet were hanging caltrops, dangling from lengths of gut tied onto the rivets on the underside of the armour. Each length had a pebble tied to the end that caught the wind and guided the strand against the others, bringing the caltrops into contact with each other and with the metal of the helmet itself.

Just then a thudding blast made the three of them spin about. Light blazed from the archway as a gout of flame spilled into the night and then suddenly burned down to a flare pouring up from the iron brazier. They ran back down the quay and filed through the gate. The flare of flame died down and they saw their comrade lying on the ground beyond the brazier, shaking his head. "Piotor!" Martin called. "What's happened?"

Piotor looked up, stunned, and replied, " 'Twas a fire demon. It threw fire!"

§

When the three guards sidled out onto the pier, Thay sent a quick prayer of thanks to Tanat, the Rogue, for his final ploy now only needed to defeat one defender. He pulled the cork from his flask of oil and slipped out from the culvert. Thay leapt past the gate and darted down the tunnel towards the last of the guards warming his hands over the fire in the iron brazier. The guard looked up too late: tossing the flask into the fire was child's play. He dove forward as flames blasted from the brazier. He hit the ground rolling and gasped as his sore ribs felt the impact, but he gritted his teeth, pulled himself to his feet and jogged off.

Once he got in among the buildings, he slowed to a walk to get his bearings. There was no one in the street, everyone huddled indoors against the cold winter night, no doubt. He heard the guards in the tunnel raising a clamour, so he moved into a darkened threshold to consider his next move.

Where would Korgash take a prisoner? Did the town have an equivalent to a roundhouse, where Fjordlanders would hold prisoners? Did the town have the home of a local chieftain or even what the Straelings called a *herg*? If Korgash had Lora, would he take her to an inn rather than a prison of some sort? He only needed to wonder for a few moments when Florri, the God of Good Fortune, intervened. For just an instant, the wind abated, leaving behind a sudden silence only broken by shouting from the gate to the quay. Into that relative silence came the faint echoes of a scream of agony.

"Elkor," Thay exclaimed. He felt searing anger flare up in him. He sprang back onto the street, heading towards the town's south wall. Another wail of agony guided him to a smithy. He pulled out his dirk and crept up to the building. Opening the door a crack to peek inside, he saw his companion on his knees, dangling by chains from low beams that crossed the workspace. Korgash approached Elkor slowly in that tight room, the top of the tall warrior's head only a handspan beneath the beams, and then he unleashed a roundhouse punch to the face. Thay gritted his teeth to hold in his rage, and thus steadied, opened the door quietly and slipped inside. Korgash was twisting to deliver another punch; Elkor was sobbing. Thay launched himself at the big Strael, driving him to the floor.

Holding back a cry of pain from jarring his bruised ribs, Thay drove his dirk into his enemy's abdomen but felt it stick in links of protective chain mail. Korgash struggled under Thay's weight but the young Fjordlander kept driving the dirk, knowing that the mail would spring a gap and then he could stab deep into his opponent's gut. Korgash slammed an elbow back into Thay's stomach, driving a grunt from the young man's lungs. Thay forced his dirk with greater pressure against the resisting armour. Korgash bucked and spun. In response Thay whipped his dirk from the man's side and drove it up from below. He felt the weapon bite deeply.

Korgash yelled in agony, his voice booming off the rafters, but Thay's ears caught other sounds, the creak of the door followed by Elkor's croaking voice wheezing, "Behind!" He spun off Korgash and saw a housecarl brandishing a sword come storming across the room at him. The man swung, and it could have gone ill for the young Fjordlander had not Elkor stuck out a leg from his dangling captivity and tripped up the attacker. The housecarl crashed to the ground and his sword went skidding off to the back of the room. Thay scrambled over to it, shifting dirk-hands, and scooped up the sword. All the while Korgash yelled, "Kill him! Kill him!" When Thay spun around, the housecarl had gotten to his feet and was scrambling towards Korgash's big war axe while the nobleman had risen to his knees, a hand clamped to his groin, blood spilling between reddened fingers.

Thay lunged forward and jabbed the sword at the housecarl, who turned aside from the thrust and managed to get his hand on the axe. Thay thrust again and again the man danced back, this time thumping the haft of the axe against the stabbing sword and knocking it aside. Suddenly the housecarl surged forward, swinging the axe horizontally in the cramped workroom. Shifting backwards, Thay dodged the swing and stamped the heel of his boot into his attacker's hip, toppling him against the huge furnace. The housecarl yelled in pain and whipped his smoking elbow from among the glowing lumps of coke, but he still stood between Thay and Korgash, who was hopping on his good leg to the doorway dragging his left leg behind him.

Thay yelled and lunged forward, jabbing and jabbing again, but his adversary kept using the haft of the axe to parry each thrust. From outside, Thay heard Korgash's voice bellow a call to arms into the night, "Raise the alarm! Ring the bell! Foes among us! Foes!"

Thay bared his teeth and lunged forward with a yell, this time slashing rather than lunging. Once more the housecarl sidestepped and deflected the blow, but he stepped within reach of Elkor and found the prisoner's legs suddenly entwined with his own. He tripped and pitched backwards. Thay darted in and drove his sword into the man's chest.

Thay was tempted to spring after Korgash but he knew time was now his greatest enemy. He quickly unhooked the chains suspending Elkor from a pair of hoops anchored to the overhead beams. He lifted his companion over his shoulder, marvelling at how light Elkor's body was, and dashed to the doorway. Glancing outside to survey the situation, he saw a big man he assumed was the smith pull Korgash through a doorway further along the building. No one else moved on the short street, but he could hear several voices on the bitter wind taking up the call to arms. A coil of rope hanging by the door caught his attention and he grabbed it before dashing out into the night. He jogged towards the south wall, what he hoped would take him closest to the tethered horse waiting outside of town, though he was wary of getting too close to another guarded gate. He spotted what he was looking for quickly enough, turned right between two buildings and bounded to a flight of stone stairs set into the curtain wall.

No guards held the stairs against him, so he sprang up them. Once on the parapet, he set Elkor down and tied one end of the rope around a merlon on the wall. The other end he looped about Elkor, tying it off as securely as he could. "Ready?" he asked, though he didn't wait for a reply and might not have heard it anyway over the blasting of horns that burst into the night. He heaved Elkor over the wall and lowered him down to the ground - about the height of three men. Once the weight came off his arms, Thay let fall the slack in the rope, grabbed hold of it and clambered down hand under hand.

He cut Elkor free with one hard tug of his dirk and again hefted the small man over his shoulder. He spotted the copse screening the horse directly south of him and sprinted for the trees. No one sprang out of the night at him, no one shot arrows into his back, and Elkor did not trip him up, so when he reached the horse, he sent another word of thanks to Tanat. "Can you keep hold of me?" he asked. Elkor managed a nod in reply. Thay then pulled the blanket off the filly and wrapped Elkor in it before setting him in place in front of the saddle. Soon they were on their way, loping south with the frigid wind at their backs.

§

Lora trudged off ahead, her shoulders convulsing as she sobbed silently, while Cairn followed, leading the big warhorse that they had captured. They were exhausted, having spent much of the night looking for Thay and Elkor, and then after having given up their search, having built Lars' burial cairn. Then they had taken what they could from the wreckage of the fight before leaving the site of their fight. They were leaving Lars behind under a pile of cold rocks, a reality suddenly so awful to endure.

Over the back of the warhorse were spread five saddle bags stuffed with the coin, food, and equipment from the fallen that they thought would be useful to them, particularly blankets. They had re-crossed the river and were climbing the slope leading to the road, again looking for any sign of Thay. What tracks they did find were difficult to decipher: many tracks, of horses and of snowshoes, leading downhill; four sets of horse tracks leading back up the slope a hundred paces or so up-river from the two others; two deep imprints of a body halfway down the slope, one on open ground, another nearby next to a huge tree, but no blood and no body to go with them; and, the scattered confusion that Cairn recognized as the site of the original skirmish between Thay, himself, and the scouts. Two bodies lay there, those of the tracker and the scout whose chest Cairn had ruined with his maul. *Orgor's Awl* lay in the snow, its polished oak gleaming in the night's green ghost light. They found Elkor's pack that Thay had hefted at one of the outriders. "Good," Cairn declared, making an effort to sound cheerful. "This'll help us. Ever since Harburg, he's had interesting stuff in this pack. Remember that fire magic?"

Lora muttered a curt reply as she cast her eyes about, looking for Thay, "A pack of trinkets'll not save us."

"It might just, Lora! You never know what else we might have to face and the key to facing it might be right here."

Lora spun on her big friend and shouted, "Cairn! Shut up! Shut up and listen to me!" Tears had traced lines on her face. She panted bursts of breath into the freezing wind. "Don't you see? For Rulla's sake, don't you understand? This has long since ceased being an adventure. Lars is dead! Have you not sussed that out yet? He's dead! He died thinking he had some all powerful *wyrd*, that he'd be the first king of all the Fjordlanders, and that *I* was some sort of seer! Where's that dream now, Cairn? Tell me! What happened to that holy fucking *wyrd* he believed in?" She took a deep breath and spat out, "It's extinguished, so it is! Extinguished!"

Cairn shook his head and breathed out a quiet observation, "You don't know that."

"Yes, Cairn, I do. When Hondrig weighs Lars' deeds against his *wyrd*, I'm sorry, He'll not weigh the deeds of a mighty king of the Fjordlanders! Lars has got no more deeds in him."

"*Loraling*, he died a warrior. Besides, his memory might drive us to great deeds."

"Then they'll be *our* deeds!" she yelled, before letting loose a mighty sob. She took another deep breath and added, "I may not be a seer, like Lars thought, but I can see enough to suggest that our first great deed be to *avoid death*! For all we know Thay might be dead too. We've got to find him. Three of us trying to survive will be harder now than if all four of us were still alive. Pray to Rulla that were *are* still three and not two."

Cairn bit his lip, his eyes teared up, and he said, "We'll get home, Lora. I know it."

Lora suddenly understood that his light-hearted enthusiasm over finding Elkor's pack and his determined optimism were how he tried to find the strength to carry on. She replied more softly, "Helgya was the Darnok seer, Cairn, not you. That fateful *wyrd* that you believe in, that you think means you're destined to have a *harem*, it is meaningless now."

"No, it's not because I think we have some all-important *wyrd* awaiting us. You're right. Lars' death has put the lie to that. I just believe we'll get home. Call it intuition."

"Intuition? Superstition. Premonition. I'm sick of it. I just want to live my life, Cairn. To be honest, I don't care at this point if I go home. I just want to stay alive."

"We'll keep each other alive."

"Like we kept Lars alive?" Lora shook her head, wiped away a tear and dragged her sleeve across her nose. She pointed at the dead tracker and scout. "Now do something useful and see if they had anything of value." As Cairn rifled through the men's clothes, Lora searched for further signs of Thay. In the greying gloom of dawn, the wind shifted its blustery course through the trees and both of them looked up, and then looked at each other. Horns blaring on the wind!

Cairn quickened his search, pulled out a pouch and a dagger, and crossed to Lora. She nodded, giving him the reins of the horse, and they jogged up the rest of the slope. When they reached the road they stopped. "Which way?" he asked.

"It's a north wind. Those horns are blowing to the north of us. We can find no trace of Thay, so something tells me the horns are no happenstance. North, I say."

Cairn nodded and turned north. There wasn't much snow on the road so they walked side by side. They continued hearing horns blasting on the wind and they both wondered what they were getting themselves into. They rounded a curve in the road and saw the track leaving the woods up ahead. Through the gap in the trees they saw a reflection of light from Fletcherton on low clouds that had blown in, more light than would have been normal at the end of a winter night. Then into that gap in the trees through which the road ran, appeared the dark form of a horse plodding and a rider swaying uncertainly. "Thay!" Cairn called out. "Over here!" Cairn tossed the reins of the horse he led to Lora and jogged forward. Lora hurried along behind.

Thay's weary voice floated to them on the wind, "Cairn? You're all right? Rulla be praised! Are Lars and Lora with you?"

"I'm here, Thay!" Lora called back.

"Give me a hand with Elkor, will you?" Thay called out.

Cairn approached and reached up to Elkor. "Careful now," Thay advised, "he's had a rough go of it. Where's Lars?"

Something in the way Thay asked the question told Lora that he knew the answer already. As Cairn lifted Elkor down from the horse one-handed, grimacing at the pain that doing so sent through his shoulder, she replied, "He's gone on by himself."

Thay nodded and clambered off the mount. "We'll speak of it when we can. We need to get on our way ourselves."

Cairn sat Elkor down on a large rock protruding from the snow at the side of the road. When he saw the Straeling's face he gasped, "By Rulla's Hallowed Name! Korgash?"

Elkor nodded his head between rasping breaths. Thay interjected, "Listen, you've surely heard the horns. It might not be long before they come after us. We need to go. Lora, I reckon that horse," he gestured to the big warhorse, "can take the weight of you and Elkor easily enough. We'll shift the gear to the filly. Mount up and we'll heft him up behind you. Elkor, you'll need to hang on for yourself. Lora's a decent enough rider so it should be easier now. Cairn, you and I need to get our snowshoes on. We're going back to the river."

As the remnants of dawn gave way to full daylight, albeit one obscured by wind-driven clouds, Thay and Lora quickly shifted the packs and saddlebags between horses. Then Lora hoisted herself up onto the warhorse's back before Cairn pulled Elkor to his feet and helped him climb up behind her. Cairn, pondering Thay's words, replied, "Sure, if they come after us, Thay, they'll be able to track us well enough on the river."

"I have to bid a friend farewell," Thay declared, "and I want whoever follows us to see the bodies of Korgash's and Oda's dead housecarls. They might think twice about following us on a cold day like this if they see dead men. Also, Tanat has granted me His good fortune through the night. This wind is His, I think, not Norrgi's, and it's still blowing strongly. I will trust in His continued blessing."

Cairn furrowed his brow. "But sure Tanat is the one God that cannot be trusted at all."

"That's why I will trust in Him one last time now. I have amused Him and He'll want me to continue living to do so again in the future. He'll see to our tracks."

Cairn shrugged before turning his attention to attaching his snowshoes. Then he took hold of the reins of the filly and led them all back down to the river. By the time they got to the cairn, the sky had turned to the grey of an overcast day. Thay knelt and prayed. Then he yawned and shook his head to clear it of cobwebs. He collected a rock from the riverbank and set it atop the cairn. He looked up at Elkor on the horse and asked,

"You want me to put one on?"

Elkor managed a shake of his head and grunted. Thay understood the grunt and reached up to help Elkor down from the horse. Elkor limped to the cairn, taking a rock that Lora proffered. Elkor took it in his twisted hand and laid it on top of the pile. It threatened to roll off, so Thay made sure it was solid before helping Elkor back onto the horse.

Then he led them back to the river and turned away from the wailing wind. "Where are we going?" Lora asked, wiping tears from her face with her coat sleeve.

"Someplace we'll not die," Thay replied. "Back south. Into the hills."

Part II

Rites of Passage

Chapter One

Trust in Tanat's continued blessing seemed well-placed, or perhaps Norrgi, the Master of the Winds, granted them succour, for the grey day turned white as the wind shifted to the southwest, bringing heavy snow and warmer air. Thay drove them hard through the grey day, harder than any of them wanted. Elkor suffered from his broken nose, burnt face, and lost teeth. Every jarred step sent a stab of pain through Cairn's shoulder. Lora felt deep exhaustion in her bones, and she worried at Thay's rasping breathing as he walked ahead of the horse. The only respite was a cold lunch huddled beside a thicket. They soon were on their way again, moving back up the river valley. At first they remained quiet, but at length Lora felt that if she didn't talk, her heart would explode from the grief of brooding in silence. "Did you kill Korgash and Oda?"

Thay shook his head. He didn't reply for a long while, but then he heaved a heavy sigh and told them about how he had seen Korgash with a hostage in the woods, how he believed Cairn and Lars, and either Elkor or Lora, must have been dead, his decision to follow Korgash, and how he had managed to get inside Fletcherton. Then they compared their accounts of the fight. Thay wanted to know how Lars had fought and died, about the dead horses and riders, and about how they had missed each other in the aftermath. When Lora pressed him for details about what had happened once he had gotten inside Fletcherton, Thay refused to take the story further, responding simply to their questions with, "We'll have time enough to talk once we're safe."

Thay kept them moving deep into the afternoon. When she could see the land rising ahead of her, Lora said, "I know where you're taking us now."

Cairn nodded, "Aye, 'tis a good place to lie up. We can keep warm. It's easily defended."

Sure enough, as dusk settled on the land, Thay guided them back across that wind-blasted meadow - now lying under deep snow - to the shallow cave set in the foot of the North-wall Hills. They were all, people and horses alike, exhausted to the bone and they had difficulty scrambling up the incline to the rock face. Lora and Thay lowered Elkor off the horse and bundled the injured Straeling into the narrow fissure that led deeper into the hill while Cairn tended to the horses as best he could with his one good arm, taking them back down the slope to the shelter of some trees, removing their saddles and harnesses, and then draping blankets over them.

They were grateful for the store of wood they had laid down the previous day and soon enough Lora had a fire blazing in that cozy chamber where they had last slept, in what seemed like a different lifetime ago, when one of their lives was still being lived. Thay made them a hot meal and Lora examined Elkor's wounds. Their exhaustion ensured that sleep came easily.

A chill in the air finally woke Lora at dawn, after the fire had burned itself down to a pile of ash. She realized that the air in the cave remained a steady cool, not frigid, temperature. She lay there, wrapped in her blanket underneath one of their bearskin cloaks, and thought about home. She missed her kin, even her annoying younger sister Nalane, and she wondered if she would ever see them again. She wondered whether Oda and Korgash hunted them still. She also wondered whether they had long to live. She felt constriction against her chest and her stomach twisted as images of Lars' last moments flashed past her mind's eye. She sobbed silently in that gloomy silence, but then she sat up, shook her head, and took a deep breath.

She cast off her blanket, took up the bearskin cloak, and went outside. After relieving herself, she went to check on the horses, giving them some oats they had found in the gear of Korgash's housecarls. She gathered up more deadwood as fuel for the fire, grateful there was plenty nearby, for the day was a frigid one. The clattering that dropping the wood inside the cave made woke Cairn and Thay, though Elkor slept on in blessed oblivion. When the fire got going again they made themselves a porridge for breakfast and then they sat around the fire staring into its depths, stealing the odd glance at each other. At length Lora ventured a question, "How long do we stay here?"

"As long as the supplies hold out, I reckon," Thay replied.

"Why?" Lora asked.

When Thay didn't answer, Cairn said, "Give Elkor, and me, time to heal. Give them time to think we've gone. Let them drop their guard. Maybe give time for Norrgi to blow the worst of winter away."

Thay nodded and added, "Give us time to think about how we do what we have to do."

" 'How we do what we have to do?' " Lora echoed. "What do you mean by that?"

Thay looked up from the fire. "Lora, you're a great one for solving riddles, but you haven't solved *this* riddle, or perhaps you haven't seen there's a riddle to solve. I'm starting to understand. Everything we've done has been just like we'd figure someone in a saga should do a thing. You're hungry and have a sick friend who also needs to eat; well, steal a sheep. A big man comes along and threatens you, pull out your axe and stand up to him. If his housecarls attack, kill them. It's all very Fjordlander.

"But we need to think like something else. Look at it like this, they have *hergs* here, or Hondrig-knows-what. *They* do the protecting, *they* do the standing up to threats. And what's more, the *hergs* have got to be *seen* doing the protecting and standing up to threats or else people think they're weak. Replaceable. Look at what Oda and Korgash have been doing. They've used us to make Korgash's case for replacing the *oberherg*. We've been playing into their hands from the word go!"

He fell silent again, though neither Lora nor Cairn said anything, sensing something more would come. They were right. Thay said, "I'm starting to think that what we should have done is show the Straelings we're not what they think we are, that we know how to live by their laws. When Korgash showed himself in Harburg, mayhap we should have made our way to the old *Oberherg* Holgarth, or the local *herg* to throw ourselves upon his mercy. Let them solve the problem. A roundhouse full of folk to witness us being meek, polite foreigners making an effort to speak their tongue and follow their laws might have been wiser, no? Instead what have we achieved? Well, we've proven to all folk hereabouts that Thorn People really are the murdering pillagers they always thought we were. How in the pits of Skalagg could we possibly explain what we did near Fletcherton? How could we explain, what? – eight dead men? Maybe nine, and one of *them* some sort of *herg* warlord. How could we explain the fact we have two of their horses and a stash of loot taken from their dead? We can't."

"You killed Korgash?" Cairn asked.

Thay shook his head. "I do not think so. I stabbed my dirk into his inner thigh. It's the sort of wound that can kill a man in heartbeats, if you sink it right. If not, a man can survive it well enough. It depends on how well I got him. He might not be dead. Indeed, he scuttled away quick enough to suggest he'll live. But he won't be climbing that incline out there on foot anytime soon, though he might ride a horse in a week or two."

Lora stared into the fire and asked, "So what are we to do and how are we to do it?"

"I don't know, Lora. But we've killed men here in Straeland now. I don't reckon anyone'll take the time to worry if we did it to defend ourselves. I just figure they'll consider us Thorn People to be killed in turn. We'll see what Elkor has to say when he's more himself, but I reckon once we decide to leave here, we need to spend as little time as we can making our way from here across the Peregrinswater. Once over there, it might just be that trying to get home is the quickest way to getting ourselves killed. Perhaps the only way home is to not go home, but to do what we left home to do."

"Huh?" Cairn asked. "What did we leave home to do?"

Again Thay didn't respond, but Lora was beginning to see where he was going in his thinking and she replied, "To grow up? To become adults?"

Thay nodded. "We assumed the Sea Wolves would do it with their rituals and magic, but that's not the whole of it. Their rituals made us part of them, but their magic is taking young Fjordlanders off to see the world. We were to see how it works, to undertake the duties of adults, to face and over-come the world's perils, often through raiding. I say we don't need the Sea Wolves to do that."

Lora nodded.

He continued, "But there's another thing the Sea Wolves were to have done to us."

"What's that?" Cairn asked.

"Turn you and me into warriors. Things must change for us, Cairn, they become serious. No more games. Lars died because we weren't the warriors we needed to be. From what you tell me we were damned lucky. Elkor figured out a way to give us a fighting chance. We haven't practiced our weapons seriously since our oar mates died. But I'm not going to get myself into a scrape again without knowing I can fight. Lora, I'll want you sparring with me using seax, axe and shield. Cairn, once you can raise your arm, you'll join in. And you, Lora," Thay said, nodding towards Elkor, "you wanted to learn the lore of healing, well there's your master-at-arms for that.

"*Our ship's but a broken dream*," Thay concluded, alluding to the song Lars sang the night before his death. "It's time to leave our childhood behind us."

§

Later, Thay went outside, into the bitter cold that had returned. Despite himself, Cairn followed and they spent the day hard at work with the horses, hauling tree trunks and branches up the hill, and chopping the dry wood into faggots. It was agony for Cairn, and he wasn't of much use because Lora had bound his left arm to his chest, but he couldn't abide sitting doing nothing in the cavern where Lars had spent his last night on earth. By the end of the day, they had built a rustic shelter for the horses in the bowl of the cliff face that held the fissure leading into their den; a windbreak of tree trunks, bark, and moss, all packed with snow on the outward face. The enclosure seemed bitterly cold to Thay, but Cairn said that the horses' coats would grow still thicker and their manes shaggier with the advancing winter. Indeed, by that nightfall, the horses seemed well-enough contented.

When they returned to the cave with the firewood, they saw that Lora had rifled through the rest of the supplies of the housecarls who had attacked them and had found smoked sausage, apples, bread, and cheese. Cairn supervised Thay in feeding the horses again after the day of labour, and on their way back into the cave, he said, "They'll need more oats than we have after a few days."

Thay nodded: that problem could wait for the moment.

Elkor overcame a difficult first two days and then showed signs of recuperation. The swelling in his face receded and his left eye, that had swollen shut, opened a crack, allowing him to see better. The line of burning leading from his left temple down in front of his ear and along his jaw remained raw with blisters, but he seemed to Lora to whimper less from the pain of it. His breathing grew less laboured and he regained the capacity to breathe through his nose. Lora took it as a good sign, then, when he started cursing her lack of knowledge of treating wounds such as his. So began her schooling, and she soon learnt how to pack a broken nose with wadding and cover it with a hard, protective piece of material like the nose guard of a helmet - or bark off a tree in Elkor's case, held in place by twine taken from the dead housecarls back by Fletcherton. She also learnt - from the contents of Elkor's pack that Cairn had retrieved - about pain-relieving ointments and opiates, substances Elkor had her administer to him during the first days of his recovery, though after a phase of the moon had passed, he had her cease abruptly, after which he turned grouchier than usual.

Once the first two days had passed, there came a break in the bitter cold. Cairn and Lora, the better riders, ventured from the hideout, leaving Elkor in Thay's care. It was a sunny day, but they stuck to the cover of the woods as much as they could, making their way east during the morning to the road that ran north - south across the Northwall Hills from Fletcherton to Gearthaeme. They found the highway and rode down from the heights until they came to a hamlet where they might buy supplies, particularly feed for the horses. One thing they weren't short of was coin, as one of their fallen adversaries seemed to have been some sort of quartermaster whose equipment included two hefty pouches of money. Although Lora did the talking, they had no doubt that the Straelings with whom they dealt noted their strangeness. They took care to approach and depart the hamlet along the road and they only left the highway again when they thought they had gone far enough to throw off any possible pursuit. Cairn, more experienced in dealing with the snows of the plateau back home, took time to cover their tracks. When he re-joined Lora, he found her sitting on a fallen log staring at her filly's reins in her hands. Cairn could see she had been crying. The horse stood in front of her with ears tucked back listening. The other horse, the big one, was tied to a tree nearby. Lora looked up at Cairn's approach, red eyed and sighing. "Ho there, *Loraling*, what is the matter?" Cairn asked.

"I failed him, Cairn," she wept, fresh tears welling up.

"We all failed him," Cairn replied.

"But I might have saved him, either afterwards with healing skill, or by killing that man an instant earlier. Just an instant, Cairn. It's all I needed. One spark of time. He believed in me, in my visions, and I couldn't even see enough to save *one spark of time*! How can I truly be a seer if I can't see something so important as Lars losing his life?" Her body heaved as a fit of sobbing grabbed her.

Cairn sat down beside her and draped his big right arm about her. He held her for a long time, until the sobbing had subsided. "I miss him," Cairn said.

Lora snuffled and dragged her sleeve across her face. "I do too. His songs keep coming back to me."

"Kyre's songs," Cairn pointed out.

"Yes, he spent so much time with Kyre, but he had started coming up with his own ballads. I failed him Cairn."

"Failing him would have been in the not trying. You killed his killer. He'd not name that failure. I saw him go while you were tending to him. At the end he had a smile on his face."

"One spark," Lora repeated. "One moment."

"A moment of regret joined to the end of years of fellowship. I don't know how we're to deal with death," Cairn murmured, "but it seems right to think on the years and not the moment."

§

That day when Lora and Cairn were gone, Thay forced Elkor to venture out into the light of the sun. He used the excuse of needing to gather firewood, but once through the fissure, Elkor took one look at the piles of faggots stacked outside and saw through the lie. Even so, the angry man had to admit that breathing fresh, cold air again and feeling the sun on his face was an unexpected joy. They walked in silence down the slope into the woods but finally Elkor spat out a harsh, "What do you want?" Thay turned and stared at the other man. Elkor's voice had changed either from the broken nose or the missing teeth, or both. "Well? *Lifgyld* for having saved me?"

Thay shrugged and turned around again, walking deeper into the woods. "I didn't go get you so you could pay me," he replied. "I went for you because you might have been Lora."

"I should have known," Elkor muttered.

Thay spun back to Elkor and retorted, "But there's more truth than that. I knew it was you and not Lora once I was in the town. When I heard you scream I didn't hesitate or you might have ended up in worse shape. You might be just as dead as Lars. Or worse yet, maybe still alive and in Korgash's clutches. The ugly truth *I'm* trying to come to terms with is that I didn't hesitate. You might scorn me for thinking it, but it seems you're an oar mate to me now."

"How touching."

Thay shook his head, but then finally gave an ironic smile and said, "There are others I'd sacrifice myself for, though you forget I lost one of them that very night. I lost him because of some grudge *you* fostered in someone. So, I can't say if it's touching or not that you're an oar mate but now you can't complain about the entire world hating you. There's at least one fool, though I reckon it's three, who'd sacrifice themselves for you. Only you can say whether it's touching."

They stared at each other for a long time - Thay always wondering which of Elkor's eyes to stare at - like they had done in the inn in Gearthaeme, when Elkor returned late at night with a box under his arm and found Thay by the fire. Finally Elkor broke the stare, as he had done that night, and muttered, "Well, you have my thanks."

On their way back to the cave, they gathered up some firewood and Thay asked, "Can you teach me to see the meaning of books?"

"I'm not a fucking miracle worker," Elkor replied. "Explaining things to you lot makes my bloody brain hurt."

"Well, looking at you makes my eyes hurt!"

Elkor snapped off a dead twig from a nearby tree and flung it at Thay, who caught it against his chest. Elkor snapped off another twig. "Well, you're perhaps the least thick of the three of you. Observe." he ordered, marking a straight vertical line in the snow. He added a loop to the right side of the line, ending up with a: þ

"That letter," Elkor declared, "is what the Straels call a *thorn*, appropriately enough. It represents the 'th' sound. This is an *ash*: æ That represents the 'a' sound. Last is the 'eee' is *yough*, like so." ʒ "Now do it. Scratch a thorn followed by an ash and then by a yough. Go on, do it."

Thay made the three symbols in the snow. þæʒ

"There, that's your name. Thay. 'þæʒ' You see, in Strael, or Polgati, each symbol represents a sound. Chayan is different … each symbol is more complex and represents a whole word. I doubt I could beat Chayan into your useless brain with a warhammer."

"I wouldn't go threatening *me* with a warhammer."

"You're right. I'll threaten you with plain Straelish. That should work well enough to beat you into submission. Now this mark here …"

§

They stayed in the cavern for a fortnight, nursing Elkor back to health, giving Cairn's shoulder time to support the weight of a shield and waiting out another bitter cold spell. Each day, Thay took Lora down to the woods, but the gathering and chopping of firewood became a simple warm up for sparring. Working with seax, spear, and shield was nothing new to her, but the intensity of this sparring was different from anything she had endured before. Thay went at her and went at her, again and again, until she thought her shield arm would simply fall off; indeed, at times she *wanted* it to fall off so she could escape the throbbing agony of working it so hard. Lora had always been quick with *Íss*, and she used that advantage over Thay to push him in fighting without his axe. They went at each other mercilessly, each driven by thoughts of what had happened to their departed friend. Lars gave speed and force to Thay's attacks. Lars forced Lora to move more quickly than she ever had before and dulled the pain of Thay's punishing blows crashing against the shield she held. Lars kept them at their sparring when they would normally have returned to the cavern. Towards the end of the fortnight, Cairn joined in the sparring, though he did so without using his left arm to hoist a shield and had to rely on his axe rather than *Orgor's Awl*, that needed two hands to wield.

They held no illusions about making themselves much better, except at fighting against each other, but they noticed their conditioning improve. Elkor would come outside and heap scorn on their efforts, but they soon realized from his critiques that though the Straeling couldn't wield a weapon, he had seen capable warriors spar often and could instruct them on their style. Elkor relished the opportunity to coach them; it gave him an opportunity to berate and laugh at them as they tried out the new attacks and defences. Lora had the impression that her blade-work improved as the days went by because, over time, she managed to oblige Thay to pause more often in his attacks, forcing him to come at her less frequently and less directly.

One evening in the cave after their exertions, and after a session of Elkor scraping Straelish letters into the dirt, Thay asked the Straeling, "You have been in Polgatia before and you know some smuggler who can get us across the big river, but do you know anyone who could train us in weapons, if we were to get there?"

Elkor sniffed. He answered first by referring to a Straelish verb tense: "That's an adequate usage of the *irrealis mood*. Your Straelish is getting tolerable." Then the small man fell into silence for a long while. Something about his bearing stayed the others from pressing for an answer to Thay's question, and then he finally heaved a great sigh. "One man I studied with in Polgatia, the son of a merchant woman and a bastard, bigot of a father ..." A pause. Then, "He is the only person who never persecuted me. Indeed, we grew close."

"Close?" Cairn asked. "To *you?*"

"Yes!" Elkor snapped. "Very close."

It was Lora who laid a hand on Elkor's knee and asked, "*How* close?"

Elkor knocked Lora's hand aside. "None of your damned business."

Thay observed, not unkindly, "Close enough you learnt his father was a bastard bigot."

Elkor retorted with a "Pah!" though he did not gainsay Thay's comment. Rather, he returned to his answer to Thay's question, "We have maintained a correspondence. I understand he's become a formidable trader in his own right, one who ventures either close to Polgatia's borders, or at times beyond them. That's a dangerous proposition: the Drovers are nothing if not incorrigible thieves; the barbaric Catagenians are nearly as bloodthirsty as your kind, who *do* come up the Peregrinswater to raid every few years; and, you've already met the brute with the pretension of becoming the Guardian of the North, the *Oberherg* of North Straeland, a bastard so fixated on his brutishness that he's delegated his thinking to that cunning sow, Oda. My friend had to recruit guards to protect his caravans. He's never done anything in half-measures, so I wasn't surprised when he informed me that he'd hired the champion duelist from the capital, Sar Danskaya. I'm sure, *were the request to come* from me, he would let his champion instruct you." Then he turned to Cairn, "You see, that's how you construct a hypothetical statement in the *ir-realis mood*."

Something about considering a future beyond the Peregrinswater helped the three youngsters deal with their grief and their fear.

§

"So what do we do when we leave here?" Cairn asked.

This was the question in all their minds. They sat around the fire eating a meal of beef, carrots, onions, and turnips; the fruits of Lora and Cairn's restocking expedition. Elkor's missing teeth gave him so much trouble with the meat that Lora cut the beef up for him. He grunted, forestalling an answer from anyone else. He chewed and chewed for a while before finally breaking the silence with a question of his own, "Have you forgotten your promise to me?"

Lora shook her head. "No, but Korgash might already be dead."

Still chewing his first bite, Elkor declared, "So then we have to go and find out."

"I reckon he's still alive," Thay said. "Sure I wounded him right enough, but I don't think I stuck him so well that he bled to death. He looked injured, but alive, when I last saw him."

"Well then, we're going back to Fletcherton and we're going to make sure he's dead."

Cairn said, "I doubt they'll give you a lavish welcome."

"I don't care. Korgash must die." He furrowed his brow and looked at the three youths. He swallowed the bit of meat and asked, "Why are you all so hesitant now? It's because of Korgash that Lars is dead. Don't you want to exact your rightful revenge?"

"I just want to live," Lora said, sadness evident in her voice.

"What a noble ambition! I am sure Lars would be proud of you."

Cairn's voice rumbled in menace, "I'm sure Lars'd thump your head off your shoulders if you presumed to know what'd make him proud, least of all something that bothered Lora."

"Fine. I'll preserve the dignity of your friend's memory," Elkor replied, rummaging around on his plate for a mushy carrot and avoiding the beef. "Yet I seem to recall him thinking yours was a noble people who respected their oaths."

Again Lora shook her head. "You profess to be a knowledgable man," she declared, "but I think I've sussed out something you've not."

"Oh? And what's that *Wise Woman?*" Elkor let the Fjordlander title drip off his tongue.

Lora blinked at Elkor, then smiled. "Thank you, that title pleases me. I shall carry it now with your blessing. You know much but for all your learning you've not a measure of wisdom."

"Do I not?"

"No. In your mind you know most folk must realize they'll not achieve their dreams. Few folk do, after all. But you still haven't sussed out that you're the same as them. Why do you believe that you're so special that you'll achieve your ambitions when others won't?"

"I am *so* grateful you have deigned to share your wisdom with me, girl. You'll forgive me if I decide not to adopt the philosophy of a teenager." He popped a piece of carrot into his mouth.

"Scorn her all you like," Thay interrupted, dropping another faggot on the fire, "but even I have figured out what her words mean in the here and now. Look at yourself. Since I have known you, Korgash has nearly killed you twice, villagers in Harburg had to save you another time, and you have singularly failed to kill *him*. Sk'van be damned, I came closest!

"You're always telling us to open our eyes," he continued, "well then, open yours. You're not going to kill Korgash. You're *never* going to become some sort of counsellor to *Oberherg* Holgarth. You'll never find a home that will accept you here in Straeland.

Korgash has branded you a brigand and a murderer, and you'll never persuade anyone to believe you rather than him. You'll be lucky to escape with your life. This is the moment *you* get to realize you'll not achieve your dreams. You're just like everyone else. You're the slave who believes that with hard work his master will free him. You're the tenant farmer who believes that just one run of good growing seasons will allow him to give up renting and buy his own plot of land. Well, the master has just arrived with the whip after years of loyal service. The jarl has just asked for the rent. Pay up."

Elkor brooded without responding. Cairn sighed, "You can still come with us.

> We shook hands on the treaty,
> we now pull the oars in time.

"We *will* honour our pledge." he added. We may even come to nurse a certain love for you by the time you get us home."

Thay added, "And you might find Krannogberg more agreeable than you think."

"I *will* kill Korgash."

Cairn couldn't help but retort, "If you do, it'll be by accident."

Elkor huffed and leaned back against the wall of the cavern. The fire crackled and cast dancing light around the chamber.

At length Lora observed, "Nevertheless, the question still lies before us. What are we going to do?"

Thay poked at the fire and said, "We stay well clear of Fletcherton and make our way out of Straeland as quickly as possible. I remember you speaking about a place called Sar Klella, Elkor, across the Peregrinswater. It was our destination. It still is."

"And once we're there?" Cairn asked.

"We find work. Perhaps with Elkor's ... *friend.*"

Elkor huffed again. He set aside his plate. Then, muttering under his breath, he curled up on his blanket and pulled his cloak around him, seeking the solace of sleep.

Chapter Two

They left their hideout at dawn on the first warm day in two moons. They loaded up the two horses with all their equipment - Cairn named the warhorse Odir and Lora named the filly Frya - leaving their backpacks light. Then they strapped on their snowshoes and walked down the incline into the forest. Snowmelt, glinting in the shafts of sunlight, dripped all through the forest. Snow remained underfoot, though its top layer slowly softened to a slushy mush and they gave renewed thanks to their snowshoes for keeping their feet above the worst of it. Elkor guided them to the northwest instead of to the northeast where the road to Fletcherton lay. Despite the bright sunlight, their mood was gloomy. For the Fjordlanders, their departure represented the first epoch in their lives without Lars. Elkor didn't share the reasons for his own despondency, but Cairn guessed that the Straeling was still angry about not pursuing Korgash.

They left the line of the Northwall Hills because Elkor told them that the hills marched southwest before turning north and that they could cut across the lowlands. They dropped down from the heights over the course of the morning and they could feel the temperature rising. By the time they paused in a meadow for their lunch, only Elkor still wore his cloak. They carried on through the forest, but as they descended, they saw signs of human activity; a trapper's hut, a stack of fallen trees waiting their turn to get hauled off to some lumber yard, and then finally a meadow well-bounded by hedges that would no doubt be a summer pasture for a nearby farmer.

"How settled is this land?" Thay asked Elkor after seeing the hedges around the meadow.

"I don't know," Elkor replied. "I have never come west of Fletcherton."

"Then how do you know that we're taking a short cut to meet up with the hills again?" Cairn asked over his shoulder as they walked along in single file.

"That's a question so stupid that even Lars would be proud of it," Elkor snapped.

Cairn turned around and punched Elkor in the stomach. As the Straeling gasped for breath lying on the snow, Cairn leaned over him and advised, "Be careful how you speak about the Dead."

"Goatfucker!" Elkor gasped in reply. "I ... I ... was insulting ... *you* ... not Lars."

Thay came and looked down on Elkor as well. "We'd best not be insulting each other. Ever. We're oar mates now. Got it?" Elkor, still gulping air into his lungs, stared up at the young man for a long moment before nodding. Thay held out a hand and hauled Elkor to his feet.

"No ... insults," Elkor wheezed. "What ... what about violence?"

Thay nodded and turned to Cairn, "He's got a point. No punching." Cairn rolled his eyes. "Good, that's settled." After he had nudged Cairn on his way again, Thay added, "Maps."

"Maps?"

"Yes, maps. That's how he knows about the hills."

They carried on, but proceeded cautiously in light of the signs of people in the area. They came to a wide, slushy brook and followed it, as Elkor said it flowed into the wide basin of the Peregrinswater. As day gave way to twilight, they came upon a log cabin in a snow-bound clearing. A wooden fence surrounded the cabin and separated the clearing into two small paddocks on either side of a cart track leading away to the north. There was a shed by the woods behind the cabin and a small barn opened into the western paddock. Two big horses, what folk back home called dock-draggers, stood in the paddock munching on loose hay that had been put into a wooden trough set on four legs to raise it well above the height of the surrounding snow. A curl of smoke rose from the cabin's chimney and trailed off into the dusk. The dock-draggers either saw or caught wind of the horses that Cairn and Lora led and whinnied loudly.

A broad, balding man of about forty winters stepped out of the cabin in response to the whinnying and looked about. He spotted the group of strangers, called over his shoulder and two young men joined him on the porch, pulling on cloaks against the dusk chill. Elkor called out, "May we approach?" The older man nodded and stepped off the porch onto the ground. He drew closer but they saw he took pains to maintain a certain distance.

"Three men and a woman," he stated, "loaded up for travel. And one of the men hiding his face. The other two looking like young bears. The woman young too. And handsome. Two of them leading quality horseflesh. A man doesn't see such things often in these parts. Travellers always keep to the road. Pass through Fletcherton. Travel's easier, safer. There's more towns with their inns that weary travellers can sleep in. There's more folk on the road, making the travelling safer."

Elkor nodded and replied, "Perhaps. We have come down from the hills because we're making for," he gave only the very slightest of pauses before continuing, "Smyrton. Fletcherton is some distance out of our way."

The man nodded. "True," he conceded, "but likely quicker, especially at the fag end of winter. Travel's a slog and you've got the cliffs to contend with comin' this way."

Thay chimed in, "There are brigands harassing folk on the road between the hills and Fletcherton. We've no want to expose ourselves to any of that."

Again the man nodded. "I suppose not. Yes, I heard about trouble in Fletcherton. Sounds like the town itself was attacked by a fire demon. Burned half the place down." He brought his clasped hands to his lips and closed his eyes, evidently sending a quick prayer to Galivith seeking protection from such horrors. He opened his eyes, lowered his hands, and carried on, "*Herg* Lethar went to help round up the summoner what summoned the apparition and his band of henchmen. They've been gone now for couple a weeks."

Lora replied, "We heard. Didn't exactly give us heart to go near Fletcherton. Demons and summoners. We prefer quiet even if it's harder. Besides, Galivith values hard work."

The man nodded. "Right enough. Well, just so as you know, my sons and I keep a good watch out, as do our hired hands. There's never been a problem round hereabouts that we've not been able to solve. If you've a few coppers, you're welcome to sleep in the barn. There's no space inside the cabin, with the hands and all. If you've a few coppers more, we'll bring you hot food, for you should know I don't allow no fire in the stable, got it?"

Thay looked at Elkor and arched an eyebrow.

Elkor returned the look for a few moments before nodding.

Thay pulled out the small coins he had in his pocket. He counted out ten copper pennies and handed them over to the man. "Here," he said, "There's a copper for each of us for the night, another copper for the hot food, and two more for the hay and oats that the horses will eat."

The man took the coins and replied, "Settle yourselves in. We'll bring out the food when it's ready." He retreated into the cabin, the two big lads following him.

They led the horses into the barn, took off their bridles and gave them hay to eat. Cairn stood behind the doorway and kept an eye on the cabin. "Well?" Lora asked.

"He didn't haggle," Elkor warned.

Lora nodded and asked, "Why haggle if you're going to rob folk anyway?"

Elkor added, "Indeed. Rob and take prisoner. He's well aware of what his local *herg* is doing. I suppose news like ours travels quickly."

"Quicker than we've travelled anyways, after laying up for so long," Lora agreed. "They've surely been warned to keep a look out."

It was Thay's turn to nod, "They'll come at us when they're 'serving' us our dinner."

"So what do we do? Jump them before they jump us?" Cairn asked from the doorway without taking his eyes off the cabin.

Thay shook his head, "That's Fjordlander thinking. I doubt he's as many hands as he says he's got. That was to prevent us from having a go at the cottage. But there *might* be a few more than we've seen. The horses haven't had a good feed in a while. I say we get on our way as soon as they get some food into them."

And so they did just that. While the horses munched on hay, they rummaged around until they found some sacks of oats and they slung one up onto Odir's back. Then they slipped back off into the dusk-shrouded trees, circling around until they came to the cart track leading away to the northwest. They hurried along it, walking until deep into the night. They finally veered into the woods again where a flat, rocky outcrop cut across their path and offered an opportunity to leave the cart track without leaving an obvious trail. Cairn put on his snowshoes and carried on along the road, laying a false trail. The others were able to follow the outcrop up onto a low ridge that ran to the north for several hundred paces. They found a knoll at the end of the outcrop where they made a cold, uncomfortable camp, fearing that a fire would reveal them too easily to any pursuit. Cairn joined them a while later and volunteered for the first watch. The others, exhausted by their long day, fell into an uneasy slumber.

§

Hounds baying in the chill morning air woke them. Lora sprang to her feet and shook the others into full consciousness. "Who fell asleep on his watch?" she snapped. "Get up! On your feet!"

Cairn shook his head and hauled himself up. "Sorry!" he gasped. "What's going on?"

"Dogs," Lora barked, pulling a saddle over to Frya.

"*Skeetze,*" Thay mumbled as he blinked in the dazzling morning light.

"*Foxt,*" Cairn replied, reflexively, picking up Odir's saddle.

Elkor scrambled to roll up the blanket and bear skin that had formed his bed for the night. Cairn threw the saddle on Odir's back and set about securing it. The wail of a horn joined the hounds' baleful baying.

They were soon on their way, heading north, away from the chase, crashing through the grasping branches of the forest underbrush. The going was difficult owing to the denseness of the thickets. Slender branches scratched their faces, they tripped over hidden roots, and the horses had to be hauled through the worst of the underbrush. All the while they heard the horns and the barking of the dogs drawing nearer. Suddenly they burst from the woods and emerged onto a high, bare shelf overlooking a vista of scattered farmlands amidst thick copses and winding streams. In the middle of the vista, they could see a squat castle brooding over the surrounding lands, a half-dozen thin lines of wood smoke from chimneys emerging from it. Far off to the north they could see a line of glimmering light that Elkor said was the Peregrinswater.

The cliff in front of them fell away dramatically, only reaching the ground some two hundred paces beneath them. Between them and the trees of the forest floor far below at the foot of the precipice was a vertical rock face unbroken by anything as practical as a path or a stair or a series of outcroppings that could have given them hope of making a descent. The cliff carried on as far as they could see to the left, forming not only a formidable escarpment, but a very real barrier to their escape. Looking right they saw that the cliff top gently descended towards the Peregrinswater flood plain. There was no need for debate; the geography made their choice for them. They turned right, even though it meant heading east rather than west.

The level ground atop the cliff was open for a half-dozen paces between the forest edge and the lip of the precipice, with only the odd bush pushing through the rocky shelf. They were able to move much more quickly given that they had no need to barge their way through underbrush and clawing branches. The only danger was slipping on a patch of ice or tripping over a protrusion of the rock surface. They kept close to the edge of the forest, in the shade of the trees, so that they could see better against the morning sun and thus avoid the hazards. They jogged along at a pace as quick as Cairn could manage, Lora up front urging them on, but the faint baying of hounds and the odd horn blast were their real motivation.

About a hundred paces ahead of them, a wolf-sized dog sprang from the forest, tail curled high above its back, its nose lifted to the air. A man atop a horse followed. The dog's tail and ears dropped, and it scuttled sideways to keep some distance between itself and the larger animal. The rider halted the horse, a nimble palfrey, from the looks of it, pivoted it east, facing away from them and giving them a moment to dart under the eaves of the woods. The man had a fur-lined cloak draped over his shoulders, a large sword across his back, and gloved hands. Lora peeked around a tree trunk and said, "He's shielding his eyes from the sunlight. He's not looked this way yet. I think he's haranguing his dog." Sure enough, the dog skulked around and only regained its pep when it again got ahead of rider and beast.

Elkor, breathing nearly as hard as Cairn from the jogging, wheezed, "Likely making sure … we haven't gotten … past him … before coming this way to look … look for our tracks."

Lora nodded, "Makes sense. He's pulling his horse around to come this way. Aye, that's what he's doing, right enough. He's coming this way slowly and looking at the ground."

"Let's get hidden, and somebody hold the horses' mouths in case they're in a greeting mood," Cairn said, before leading

Odir into the woods at a place where the underbrush was thin. The others followed him, first Elkor, then Lora leading Frya, and Thay following behind. They went about a score of paces into the forest and hid in a gap screened from the cliff top. They tied Frya and Odir's reins to stout trees and Lora and Elkor held their hands over the horses' noses. Then Cairn and Thay readied their weapons. "What's the plan?" Cairn asked.

Thay bit his lower lip, turned to Elkor, and said with a shrug, "Sometimes the Fjordlander way is the right way."

Elkor nodded. Cairn took *Harbinger* from its sheath and studied it, contemplating its first use in anger since Lars' passing. He didn't have long for such thoughts, though, because not long thereafter they glimpsed the horse through the gaps in the bushes. Thay crept closer to the opening they had followed into the woods. Then he spotted the dog. It halted in front of their opening, lifted its nose and sniffed, its head swivelling here and there to catch the scents in the air. Lora saw it clearly through a narrow gap in the underbrush. It wasn't a hound, as she would have thought. Rather, it had the shape and the erect, pointed ears of a wolf, though unlike its lupine cousins, it was varicoloured, with a black muzzle, back, and top of the tail, to go with beige legs and stomach, though the black back and top of the tail was also streaked with the same beige. It had a rusty hue to the ears and top of the head. Two thin lines of black reached from the back around the chest and neck, and another crept forward from the crown of the head to end between and above the golden eyes. The tail was arched into the air, with the tip curving back over the hindquarters, and it showed that the dog was poised, ready for either the chase or a pitched flight. Just then it gave a start as something fell at its feet.

Lora turned her head and looked at Cairn; the big lad was breaking off another piece of hardened beef jerky that he promptly tossed at the dog. The dog itself was slowly wagging its tail and sniffing at the first chunk that Cairn had thrown. It gobbled the first bit down and then ventured a step closer, and then another, slowly making its way over to the second bit of jerky, wasting no time snapping it up. It chewed contentedly as it looked into the woods at Cairn, wagging its tail heartily now, its eyes bright. It was so spritely that Lora didn't think she - it was female - could be more than a year old. Cairn tossed another chunk, even closer this time, and the dog dutifully sprang across a fallen branch and into the forest to get it. Another chunk brought it closer yet. It looked up at Cairn and wagged its tail, a partly-open mouth allowing a thick pink tongue to loll out the side.

"Dog!" yelled the rider's voice from further along the cliff top. "Dog! Come!" The dog's ears swivelled towards the voice but its tail drooped and it looked worried, its head lowering and eyes losing their brightness. "Dog, dammit! Come!" The voice was closer. Cairn held out the remainder of the length of jerky and the dog skulked forward, taking the meat and then seeking Cairn's hand. Cairn stroked the dog but also took hold of its rope collar.

"Dog! I'll whip you senseless!"

That was their signal, though a completely unplanned one.

Lora and Thay sprang through the aperture in the underbrush, Elkor clambering along behind them. The rider had come close to the opening into the trees, but from an angle that screened his vision. He had no time to react as Lora snatched the bridle and Thay swung *Tear Tongue* in a high arc. The man tugged on the reins, but Lora controlled the horse's head, preventing it from carrying its rider away. At the last instant the man ducked under the swooping axe blow but the shaft knocked him askew in the saddle. It was a simple matter for Elkor to grab hold of the rider's extended leg and thrust the man over onto the rocky cliff top. The man yelled a loud "Ahh!" before slamming onto the rocks, the "Ahh!" transforming into an exhaled "Oof!" He clutched his sides and rolled slowly over onto his stomach. The blunt back of the Thay's axehead to the back of the man's skull was enough to send him into oblivion.

They dragged the man - a young man - into the opening into the woods. "He's just unconscious," Elkor said. "He might come to shortly or at some time over the course of the day."

The Fjordlanders all understood Elkor's unstated question.

Cairn responded, "He was prepared to whip a dog he hadn't even bothered naming."

"That doesn't mean he has to die," Thay replied. He glanced up at Elkor, "Can you make sure he comes to more towards the end of the day?" Elkor nodded. "Right then," Thay continued, "we'll take whatever he's got of value, but let us leave him his life … and some food."

Elkor got to work mixing a potion with Lora looking on. The lads liberated a coin pouch, two gold rings and a silver brooch in the shape of a bull. "This must be some *hergling*," Cairn said. "Sure he must be no older'n us and he's wearing gold and silver!"

Elkor gave a scornful snort and said, "The Bold Bull, that's the local *herg's* informal title. You're likely right, for once, Cairn. It's probably the Bold Bull's by-blow." That last earned a matching snort from Thay.

Thay opened the money pouch and found a pair of gold coins among silver and the much more common Straelish pennies. There was wine in the man's water jug, and its content was not the sour stuff they had tasted now and again back home and with the Sea Wolves, but rather a robust and delicious vintage. The man's sword was finely made, an elegant length of steel that curved back upon itself, a design the lads had never seen before but that Elkor said was better for attacking from horseback. The palfrey the man was riding was a fine horse, nimble and quick rather than big-boned and strong; more appropriate for hunting down fugitives than charging into battle. Lora claimed the sword and the man's winter coat, which was a well-crafted, warm piece of clothing even though it was long for her. Elkor likewise switched boots and Cairn switched cloaks. They switched food with him as well, leaving some of their hard tack and jerky in a bag beside him, although the dog showed enthusiastic interest in liberating the bag.

When they were ready to continue their flight, Thay asked Elkor, "Should we bring him with us, as a hostage? It could give us an advantage if he's the son of that *Herg* Lethar."

"Perhaps," Elkor replied, "though he would slow us down, he could also give us away, and we'd always have to keep close watch on him. If we're confronted over the course of the day, offering where we've hidden him in exchange for leaving us alone might serve just as well as keeping him a hostage." Thay nodded and they were soon on their way with Lora leading their new horse. It was no surprise when the bitch followed along with them.

Cairn named her Fylgja. Later, during a short pause when the others weren't listening, he scratched her behind her ears and whispered to her, "Welcome to the Flight, our current saga, such as it is. I wish you better luck than my last friend."

§

They wanted to escape the scene of the assault as quickly as possible, so Cairn mounted Odir and Lora on Frya, while Thay helped Elkor get up on the *hergling's* palfrey. Thay and the dog, Fylgja, jogged alongside the horses. The cliff top slowly dropped towards the floor of the floodplain. The baying of the hounds faded and as the sun rose into the sky they only heard the faint echoes of the odd horn blast. When they stopped during the pleasantly warm midday, the shelf on which they descended was no more than a score of paces above the tops of the tallest trees and they could no longer see the river off to the north. For lunch they enjoyed the spoils of their attack that morning, eating venison and cheese on fresh bread. As delicious as the food was, Cairn made sure Fylgja got the bread crusts, any fat on the meat, and even a small piece of cheese, using her new name at every opportunity.

Not long after they set off again, they came upon a spur of rock protruding from the cliff and offering them a way to scramble down onto the floodplain. Getting down was difficult; snowmelt drained down the slope, making the rocks slippery. They made their way cautiously and reached the forest floor without incident. Then they struck due north among the groves of pine trees, a direction that would allow them to avoid the lands close to the castle they had seen when they had first emerged from the woods atop the cliff. No trouble raised its head for the remainder of the afternoon, although they proceeded more cautiously as the woods grew thinner and as they came across pastureland. By nightfall they made camp in a dell in the middle of a copse from the edge of which they could just descry a quiet, nondescript hamlet with a temple rising from its middle and surrounded by a wooden palisade. The dell itself had a small clearing at its centre and was protected from the direction of the hamlet by a fallen tree, its trunk providing them a two foot high barrier to anyone who might come at them.

Although the day had been gloriously warm, as soon as the shadows lengthened the air turned cool, and then cold as day gave way to night. Even with the woods screening them, they didn't dare light a fire for fear that it might be seen by anyone pursuing them from atop the escarpment. Despite their exhaustion, Thay, Lora, and Elkor turned their attention to building a lean-to for shelter from the worst of the freezing temperatures. Cairn tethered the horses, took off their saddles and harnesses, draped blankets over their backs and gave them a good feed of oats. For her part, Fylgja curled up and fell asleep amid all the activity.

Lora and Thay made as comfortable a nest as they could in the lean-to, stacking their packs around the walls, positioning the saddles to act as headrests, placing the bear skins on the ground, and spreading their blankets overtop it all. Elkor prepared them trenchers of the remaining bread, venison, and other treasures from the *hergling's* saddlebags, slices of onion and a hard-boiled egg. Fylgja had woken the instant Elkor began preparing the meal and so Cairn fed her a dinner of biscuits and venison gristle. The young dog had evidently recuperated some of her youthful energy and brought Cairn an endless series of sticks to throw among the woods. She was so demanding that Cairn lost out on the better places in the lean-to, consigned to the upwind position rather than one of the much sought-after inner places or the downwind slot. As they settled down to sleep, though, Fylgja crawled down to the bottom of the shelter and settled against the big youth's feet, providing more than enough compensation with her own body heat … until Cairn woke early in the night to discover the treacherous cur spread-eagled on her back in the middle of the blanket between him and Lora so that he only had a few thumb-lengths on the outer edge.

Thay dreamt a crimson dream. He was in a great stone hall with a marble floor and arches reaching up to impossible heights. The giant worm lay coiled about a throne in the middle of the hall, her vast ruby wings folded back on themselves and lying flush against her side. Her great tail trailed off into the darkness at one side of the vast chamber. A figure approached the worm; too thin to be a man, too tall to be a woman, and accompanied by a half-dozen darting birds that swirled, swooped, and buzzed about its head. The worm's voice spoke in his mind, "Fie! Villainous deceit hath bound our wings and tip't the scales. Canst thou rebalance the weights?" The voice was deep, like the thunder that had blasted through the Demon Teeth, but also sibilant like the north wind that had blown on the night Lars died. "Canst *thou* touch thy bairn and cure it of its illnesses? Thou canst not, for *others* sucketh miracles' marrow and mindeth not at all for the cost. But art thou willing to pay a cost? Wouldst thou free us and right a wrong?" Then he woke.

He usually woke from the crimson dreams warm and re-freshed, but this time he felt cold and weary. Thay shivered as he opened his groggy eyes a crack and looked around. Fingers of mist crept among the tree trunks and faint moonlight fell through the skeletal branches. Odir stamped the ground and he guessed that the horse had woken him. He heard Fylgja whimper as she suffered some sort of canine nightmare but he otherwise only heard the settled breathing of his compan-ions and of the horses. He saw nothing in the woods as he shifted his cloak from his back to over his shoulder and down his side. He shuffled into his blanket and flopped his head down onto the spare tunic he used as a pillow.

His head shot up. Had he seen something before his head met his tunic? He peered into the woods. He could feel his heart pounding in his chest, and then it felt like it had leapt into his throat.

At the far side of their tiny dell, the moonlight gave a silver sheen to the mist seeping through the trees. But when the line of mist touched upon the fallen tree, and came to a point where a knot in the wood protruded from the trunk, the va-pour turned to a golden shimmer as though illuminated by a torch from below, before floating onwards and turning back to silver. Thay stared, transfixed, as the flaxen mist blossomed from a line into a roundish shape a little larger than a fist. Within that golden vapour, he thought he could see a pair of shining points of light, small glimmers of gold amid the fainter cloud. Thay screwed his eyes shut and drove his head into his jacket. He willed the lights to go away and prayed to Tanat the Rogue to take mercy on him and stop playing tricks on a poor, humble mortal.

He concentrated on his breathing, willing his thumping heart to calm itself. His heart, however, had no intention of being brought under control and Thay realized that his arms were shaking in terror. His ears only heard his laboured breathing; even Fylgja had seemed to settle out of her nightmare. Thay swallowed and raised his head, though his courage failed him and he could not will his eyes to open. He took two deep breaths and whispered another prayer, this time to Hondrig. Finally, he pried his eyes open and looked.

He saw no golden mist or glowing eyes; the silver fingers of mist drifted among the trees and shafts of moonlight dropped into the grove from on high. Thay shifted his blanket onto the sleeping Elkor and clambered through the lean-to's narrow opening. Fylgja also emerged from their shelter, ears pricked and pivoting. Thay crossed to the fallen tree and looked around, though he could see nothing in the woods. The light of the moon wasn't strong enough to allow him to search the ground for tracks, so instead he crept through the trees, Fylgja following along behind. As he neared the edge of the woods, the dog suddenly bounded forward, her hackles rising, her tail arched into the air, her head swivelling to catch scents on the night air. Thay caught her up, took her in his arms and, when she made to bark, closed his hand gently over her muzzle, whispering a "shh!" Then he released his grip, made a *tutting* sound to have her follow him. He slipped behind a large tree and looked out at the quiet hamlet across the expanse of snow-bound fields.

Only the hamlet wasn't so quiet.

Light from torches lit the pre-dawn air above the settlement and reflected off the houses. At the edge of his hearing, he could just pick out the sound of dogs barking, what had, no doubt, triggered Fylgja's reaction. A party of riders - Thay couldn't tell how many, though he guessed between six and eight - had clustered before a gate and he watched as that gate opened, allowing them entry. Thay turned and crashed back through the copse to their campsite. He shook his companions awake, saying, "Wake up! Get up! We've got to go. Now!"

Lora was the first out of the lean-to, hauling Frya's saddle behind her. Elkor had to kick Cairn into full consciousness, though Thay thought Elkor viewed the task as an opportunity rather than an obligation. As Thay heaved a saddle onto Odir's back, he hurriedly told them what he had seen. Lora quickly moved off to the edge of the wood to keep an eye on the settlement. Cairn, stuffing blankets and bear skins into their packs and readying the horses's saddlebags, asked, "So what do we do?"

Elkor pulled the remaining saddle from the lean-to and muttered, "I don't know … yet."

"What would a Straeling do?" asked Thay.

Elkor hefted the saddle to Cairn, who set about fastening it to their new horse. Then the ugly man replied, "You mean, what would a Strael fugitive do? Well, one who was guilty would likely do as we've been doing, simply flee."

"What would innocent Straelings do?" Thay pressed.

"The stupid ones or the smart ones?"

"I said 'innocent,' but let's assume I said, 'smart and innocent.' What would *they* do?"

"They'd bloody well flee."

"Would they live?"

"The odd one might. Ones with supplies and horses."

"Like us," Cairn interrupted.

"Except we don't have a horse for each of us now do we?" Thay had the impression Elkor nearly added something like, "he of deep thought and little insight," but the ban on insults seemed to be holding. Elkor continued, "Ones with horses might just make the border."

"Right," Thay declared before asking, "What about the stupid ones?"

"They'd throw themselves on the mercy of the local *herg*. They'd spout gibberish in their own defence before being flogged or hanged. The ones who got flogged would be sentenced to serfdom, likely on the lands of the noble who accused them. The irony is that life wouldn't be so much worse than what they knew before." Elkor finished stowing away the last of their gear into a pack and he passed it to Cairn. He stood and looked into Thay's left eye, and a place over his left shoulder, "The absurdly stupid ones might just be so pathetic they'd escape the flogging."

"Absurdly stupid?" Cairn asked, fastening the last pack onto Odir's back. "What about the absurdly smart ones?"

"Good question," Elkor observed. He pondered for a while as the Fjordlander lads tightened the straps about the horses' girths. Cairn and Thay took hold of the horses' reins to lead them from the grove when Elkor answered, "The smart thing to do, the really smart thing to do, would be to take advantage of this fucking mess."

"How?" Cairn pressed.

Elkor shrugged.

Thay interjected, "I suppose the thing to do would be to use a weapon against which they are ill equipped to defend themselves." Elkor nodded. "Not many people know their letters, do they?"

Elkor cracked his sickly smirk and observed, "Now that is no Fjordlander question."

Just then Lora came darting back through the trees hissing, "A large party of riders with torches and dogs just rode out of the hamlet, heading southeast." Then she caught the looks passing between Elkor and Thay. "What?" she asked.

Chapter Three

With all the able-bodied men-folk gone, there were no proper guards on the gate. Instead there were three townsfolk; an old man, an adolescent girl, and the girl's young brother. The man, Heinroch Mergel, sitting atop a platform overlooking the fields, lifted his head and scrunched his face, trying to focus his aged eyes on the woman urgently yelling from beyond the palisade. "Whaddya see?" he asked young Prina. "Who's that calling out?"

Prina stood on her tip-toes and peered into the dark. "I can't see nobody. Wait! There! It's a woman."

"Of course it's a woman, lass, I can hear her as well as you. Who *is* she?"

Unsure, the young girl didn't answer. Her brother joined her and tried to get a look over the hewn tree trunks that formed the palisade, "It don't sound like *Frouw* Wandy do it?"

"No, it don't," Heinroch replied. Then he repeated, "Whaddya *see?*"

The boy said, "There's a horse coming over the field."

Heinroch furrowed his brow. "*Over the field?*"

"Jarro's right," Prina agreed. "It looks like a woman and she's riding quick."

The woman's voice carried to them again through the night. This time they could make out the words, "Brigands! Brigands in the woods!"

"Is she alone?" Heinroch queried.

"Ya," Jarro replied.

"Anyone chasing her?" the man asked.

"I can't see anyone," Prina replied.

The woman crossed the last furlong of snow-encrusted field and allowed her horse to scramble up the embankment to the track that led off southeast. Then she spurred her mount down the track as quickly as it would take her towards the hamlet.

"That's no shaggy hill pony she's riding," Prina declared, "it's a fine palfrey."

The woman brought the horse to a scrambling halt in front of the palisade gate. "Let me in!" she called. "I carry orders from *Oberherg* Holgarth and there are bandits pursuing me!"

Heinroch could see the woman now. "Hey! Ho there! Who are you, young *frouw*? What are you doing out in the night? Where's your husband?"

"I am Singrid Madrington," she called up to the defenders on the platform. "I have no husband. I am a messenger from the *oberherg*. Please let me in."

"She talks funny," Jarro whispered to Prina.

Just then Prina yelled, pointing across the fields, "More riders!"

"That's them!" the woman gasped. "Please, please good sir. Let me in!"

"More riders?" Heinroch asked. "Where?"

"Coming just like she did. There's two. One's huge. I can see axes!"

"*Axes!* No one fights with axes."

"These are Thorn People!" the woman exclaimed.

"*Thorn People!* Galivith protect us! That'll be them! Jarro, let the *frouw* in," Heinroch ordered. Jarro darted down the rickety wooden steps of the ladder, followed by his sister. Together they heaved up the heavy wooden beam from the iron brackets set in each half of the gate. They swung one half back, allowing the woman entry into the hamlet. The woman jumped off her horse and grabbed the beam, heaving it back up and into place on the brackets. "Thank you," she gasped once the beam was securely in place. "What did you mean by '*That'll be them*'?"

"There's a troop of Thornish bastards ranging the lands un- der the thrall of some fire-demon summoner or of some necromancer, or both. The *herg* himself has ridden off to round 'em up, but they was spotted atop the cliffs comin' this way the day before yesterday. You'll have been lucky to escape them! Galivith Himself only knows what they'd have done to you."

"That's why I have been sent!" the woman gasped. She breathed deeply and then said, "They caught my escort, Galivith bless their souls. I have a message for your *revered* before carrying on to *Herg* Lethar's castle and its steward."

"Prina!" the old farmer yelled down from the platform. "Get back up here! Tell me what them savages are doing. Jarro, take the *frouw* to the temple." Prina clambered up the wooden steps.

"Thank you, good sir," the woman called up to the old farmer. He grunted in reply.

As the woman lead her horse off after Jarro, she heard the girl say from atop the platform, "They're turning about. They're going back into the woods."

Jarro led the towering, determined-looking woman, Singrid, to the middle of the hamlet, a small open space dominated by the stonework of the facade of a temple at one end and against which the wooden, tile-roofed houses appeared as nothing. There was a post to which the young woman could tie her horse. After she had done so, she unstrapped the saddlebags and draped the horse's blanket over its back to protect it from the cold pre-dawn air. She slung the saddlebags over her shoulder and then the lad took her up two broad stone steps, tapped on the thick oak doors before setting his weight against them and pushing them open. The inside of the temple was an open, circular space, illuminated by a pair of torches and a fire burning in a hearth in the wall opposite the doors. Four circles of benches in various states of disrepair radiated out from a central altar raised upon a dais. Dried sheaves of wheat and a sword lay atop the altar. Beneath it, kneeling on the floor, was a man dressed in rough-spun breaches and a thick wool tunic. He also had a red cloak slung over his shoulders, trimmed with black and upon which was embroidered a sheaf of wheat in yellow thread.

The priest took note of their arrival and rose to his feet. He was a middle-aged man of medium build, and like many a Straeling, he had blue-grey eyes and straw-coloured hair, rather like Thay. "Jarro, my boy, you bring a worshipper in the dead of night?" he asked.

"I do, Revered Krugar. She rode in with Thorn People after her."

"Did she indeed?" the man asked. "Well, thank you for your courtesy. Galivith teaches us to offer hospice to those who need it. This night you offer courtesy to this *frouw*, but sometime in the future she might offer it to you. Now, run back to *Herr* Mergel. He'll need your sharp eyes on the palisade." Jarro made to turn, paused for a moment, and considered the stern look in the revered's eyes. He turned and dashed off, pulling the heavy oak doors closed behind him.

"Now child, what hospice can I offer you?"

The woman, holding her saddlebags in one hand, stepped forward and brandished a scroll in the other.

Revered Krugar looked down at the scroll for a long while before slowly holding out his own hand. The woman thrust the scroll into his grasp and said, "With your permission, revered, I'll warm my hands in front of the fire." She didn't wait for a response and simply strode off to the hearth in the temple's far wall.

She didn't have much time for her hands to warm up before the priest came up behind her and said, "Child. I do not read well. Does this say what I think it says?"

The woman turned around, keeping her back to the warmth. She looked at the opened scroll from his hand, a bit of wax falling to the floor from the seal. "I can't read, revered," she replied. "But I know what it says. I have given such scrolls in three villages since crossing the Arrowsmith. It orders the village to give me two horses, a day's worth of food and a waterskin. I would also ask for lodging after spending this cold night riding if the *oberherg's* mission wasn't so pressing. I must be on my way as soon as possible for I lost time, companions, and a horse with the brigands chasing me. I carry an urgent message to *Herg* Lethar's steward. I was told to have it in his hands by noon of this day that dawns."

"You'll have a hard ride, then, especially if the day is warm and turns the road to mud. What can be so important for old Warrik?" The woman suddenly looked nervous. She swallowed and the priest stepped closer - over his years of service, he had found doing so exerted his authority. "What is it child? Tell me!"

She swallowed again and held up another scroll sealed with wax. "*Herg* Lethar has ridden on to Fletcherton with his men. I have orders for the steward, in his place, to light the beacon fires and raise all the levies. The brigands our *hergs* have been chasing are but a diversion. The Catagenians have invaded across the Peregrinswater downriver from where the Northwater joins it; the east of our land is overrun!"

§

The priest left at once to arrange horses, food, and a waterskin. When he had closed the great oaken doors of the temple, Lora sprang into action. Elkor had told her where she would be most likely to find what she needed. She crossed to a door beside the hearth and let loose a breath of relief as she found it unbarred. She passed through the doorway but kept the door open behind her to cast light into the darkened room beyond, a narrow space that served as vestry, bedroom, and kitchen. Two windows looked out over a pair of cottages, the palisade beyond, and the first hints of daybreak in the pre-dawn sky. Beneath one window was a wooden counter with all the accoutrements of a kitchen, from cutting boards and knives to wooden bowls and spoons. Across from the window and the counter was another hearth - a cooking hearth, though darkened - that backed onto the stone chimney of the larger fireplace on the other side of the wall. Beneath the second window, on the other side of a door leading outside was a rumpled bed, perhaps the product of an eventful night with bands of riders arriving and departing. There were two stools and a low square table sitting in between.

To the left of the doorway where she stood was what she was told to find, a *klydershank*. She had never seen such a thing before; a box of polished wood standing upright on four low, stout legs. It had two doors set in it set with silver knobs. When she pulled open the doors, they revealed a space where the priest stored his clothes. She studied its contents, taking care not to disturb the order of the shirts, tunics, jackets, breeches, and small clothes. She extracted the only red cloak she found along with both grey robes sitting on the bottom shelf. She stuffed the clothes into her saddlebag, closed the wardrobe, and left the room.

§

Revered Krugar returned to find the *frouw* praying in front of the altar. While he was hesitant to disturb her, the safety of the province depended on her mission. He cleared his throat, and when she looked up, he beckoned her outside. She emerged into the grey dawn light looking tired but warmed, with her saddlebag hanging heavily over her shoulder. She looked about at the cluster of villagers - most of the women folk, old Heinroch Mergel from the platform above the gate, and a younger man missing a hand - who had come to witness the spectacle of a messenger from the *oberherg* leaving on a mission to rouse the land for war.

The revered swept his hand in an arc to present her the horses he had found. The men of the village had taken the sturdiest horses, leaving only a few fillies, more suited the task of running than pounding over battle lines, which of course made them perfect. "Here you have two mounts that can carry you quickly over the land. Each has a blanket and saddle-bags with oats and barley. *Herr* Mergel has transferred your saddle and he will take care of your horse until your return."

"'Tis a fine beast, if I may say so, girl," the old man remarked.

The woman nodded, "As it should be. It comes from … a noble stable. Take good care of it, the *oberberg* wants it back!"

Revered Krugar said, "The day looks to be dawning bright and clear. Once the sun warms up the road, the frozen mud will go from solid to soggy. You'd best be off and ride hard as you can for as long as possible before the mud slows you down. We will send you off with all our prayers that Galivith speed you on your way."

The young woman looked up and replied with a simple, "Thank you."

They watched her pass through the hamlet's northern gate moments later, riding one horse and leading the other. Young Jarro followed her progress with his eyes from the platform as she rode off and he whispered a question to his sister, "You didn't think she spoke funny?"

§

Straight north they rode over fields and between copses, directly towards the Peregrinswater, even though it would not take them much further from Fletcherton, which Elkor said now lay directly to the east of them. They rode as hard as Thay and Elkor could manage; neither was an experienced rider and neither was a natural, so they could only handle a trot with difficulty. But with the extra horse Lora had procured for them, they each had a mount and at least a trot was quicker than having one of their number jog.

Once the sun had risen above the trees, they judged that they had put the hamlet far enough behind them to take a short pause. Lora took the clothing out of her saddlebags, tossing the red cloak to Elkor, and a grey robe each to Cairn and Thay. "Why does he get the red cloak?" Cairn asked.

"Because the fucking revereds do all the talking and the ordering," Elkor answered. "Acolytes are expected to keep their mouths shut. Got it?"

Cairn drew the biggest of the two grey robes over his head. As though swimming through honey, he flailed his arms around and wiggled his torso, trying to squeeze into the tube of cloth. Thay, his own grey robe snugly in place, ordered Cairn to "stop your grunting," grabbed the hem of the cloak up near the big lad's shoulders and tugged down. Despite the best efforts of both young men, which as it happened involved a lot of grunting, Cairn couldn't squeeze through. Fylgja started barking at the strange apparition that had suddenly swallowed her new master and that was twisting and thrashing among them. For the first time since that fateful night on the Arrowsmith River they heard Lora laugh at their exertions. It was a sound that brought all their thrashing to an immediate standstill. Fylgja shifted her attention to the usually dour girl and gave a tentative wag of her tail. Even Elkor, despite his usual lack of compassion for any misery but his own, shifted his bi-focussed gaze at the young woman briefly before looking back to the unfolding spectacle.

"Well," Lora said with a giggle, "it looks like I get to become a *priestling* and the many-talented Cairn here some sort of body-guard, for he'll never be a dancer in spite of his efforts."

"As long as he's a bloody *mute* body-guard," Elkor declared.

"He could be a court jester," Thay chimed in.

Cairn, two-thirds of the robe dangling off his head, offered an angry, muffled retort, "You're one to talk, Thay Sorig. A jester needs his barking lap dog and you've done your bit to get me into this mess. Now do something useful and pull this damned thing off me!"

Thay grabbed the dangling robe and gave a heave, triggering a welcoming leap as Fylgja saw her master regurgitated from the grey monster. She knocked the big man onto the hard-packed snow, loosing a final winded grunt from Cairn as he thudded onto the ground, her paws planted firmly on his chest and her tongue lashing his face. He, too, laughed, for the first time in what seemed a long time for a lad well used to seeing the amusing in life. Smiling, Thay tossed Lora his cloak, taking the larger one from Cairn as his own, and said, "*Priest-ess-ling.*"

Soon they had Cairn looking as Straelish as they could; clean shaven, hair trimmed, his usual Fjordlander travelling clothes replaced by the Straelish garb they had bought back in Harburg, his axe, *Orgor's Awl* and *Harbinger* stowed away among their gear, and, the *hergling's* curved sword that Lora had claimed the previous morning hung over his shoulder. He also put on some gear they had taken from the dead housecarls that night by Fletcherton including a pair of leather arm grieves and an iron brooch engraved with Korgash's sigil, the flames. As they worked their transformative magic on the big lad, Elkor briefed them on who they were and their mission. Soon they were on their way again, pleasantly warm in the sunny, pre-spring day, though perhaps as warmed by the levity that had dispelled for the moment their grief over losing Lars as by any physical touch of the sun's rays upon them.

§

Their pace diminished as the day grew warmer. Where there were fields - they spotted the odd farm house along their path - the sun had turned the snow cover slushy, which itself turned the fields into a sucking mess. Where there was rough, untilled countryside, the going was easier, but such terrain was petering out among settlements and agricultural land. Only Fylgja seemed to have no trouble passing over the terrain, though she had turned herself into a mucky abomination. She loped alongside the horses, darting off into the occasional copse they passed by, only to emerge from it ahead of them, dutifully waiting for them to catch up. They soon came to a track crossing their path and leading northwest. They could see a hamlet in the distance, more or less in the direction that the track led. Cairn reined in Odir and allowed the others to catch him up. "Well?" he asked.

"Lay on as we have been, Cairn," Lora replied. "Keep cutting across the fields and skirting these villages."

Elkor struggled for control of one of the new horses - one that obviously hated him - but managed to voice his own counsel, "No. Priests don't skirt villages, they bloody well terrorize them. Any chance to exert their control and extract silver, not to mention a free meal. If we want to avoid suspicion, we're best sticking to the tracks now, passing through the towns and acting like we own the world. We'll be able to move more quickly than on the stinking bogs these peasants call fields."

"Where are we?" Thay asked.

"I'm not fully certain," Elkor replied. "Based on where I think we came down off the escarpment and how we've been moving ever since, I would say that we're getting close to the river. We're likely just south of Smyrton, a town that sits on the Peregrinswater. If we can get there before our pursuers, I should be able to get word of Mari and her gang."

"Who's Mari?"

"The smuggler. We'll need her help if there's open water on the river." He turned to Lora and Thay and ordered, "Pull those cowls up and, Lora, don't reveal yourself no matter what happens. Women might accidentally find themselves crowned queen, but they *don't* become acolytes."

They turned onto the track and rode for the village. Sure enough, the horses still had to ply through mud, but their pace nevertheless quickened again on the harder-packed trail. After a short while they came upon the hamlet, the gates of its palisade open during the daylight hours. Some youths, both girls and boys, stood watch upon the wall. There was a lot of activity in the small settlement as they entered; children beat the dust of winter out of rugs hung from clotheslines, old men on rooftops mended tiles cracked by frost, grizzled traders bartered goods in groups around women drawing water from the town well, periodic clanging filled the air around the smithy, young lads loaded up a wagon with wooden beams in front of a lumber yard, chickens rooted around in the earth until Fylgja came chasing after them, and a revered stood erect in his red cloak, hood cast back revealing a full head of brown hair streaked with grey. The priest, the only man of an age to take up arms that they could see, observed with an imperial air the goings-on from the steps of the town's temple.

"Uh oh," observed Cairn as the revered turned his gaze on the newcomers riding into the centre of the hamlet, and especially on the vari-coloured dog causing a ruckus among the poultry. Cairn whistled to his dog, calling her to heel before she caused any bloodshed. They slowed their horses to a walk and crossed the square, by-passing the staring traders and the women at the well. Elkor knocked his heels against his horse's flanks but it steadfastly refused to pass Odir, perhaps afraid of the bigger beast. Cairn had the good sense to pass the steps of the temple and wheel Odir around as though surveying the scene for threats, allowing Elkor space to rein in to a halt in front of the priest.

"Good morning, Revered … Revered whom?" Elkor greeted the man from the depths of his hood.

"I'll ask the questions here," the priest replied in a deep, stern voice. The man's brown eyes seemed like rusted iron. "Who are you?"

"Revered Wilham," Elkor replied without hesitation. "May the peace of Galivith be with you. Would you be so kind, revered, to tell us in what village we find ourselves."

"Revered Wilham," the priest repeated, almost as though tasting the name and finding it sour on his palette. "Of where?"

"Of Shipton," Elkor responded.

"Of Shipton? Is that so?"

"It is, honoured revered," Elkor confirmed. "I come from our grand new basilica that the Queen is building to the greater glory of Galivith."

The man frowned. "His glory is beyond question; it needs no Queen's construction."

"No doubt you are right, good brother. Such debates are far above my station, though our Holy Council joined its will to the Queen's in this. It has ordered every effort be made to finish the work this year before the autumn winds blow. But I do not wish to trouble you with such things, revered, and please forgive my intrusion. We are making our way to Smyrton. Are we on the right track?"

"Who told you to come this way to get to Smyrton?" the priest growled.

"Revered Krugar of the last village we passed suggested we come this way."

"I might have known. The man's an idiot. He's brought you far out of your way if you're travelling to Smyrton from Shipton." The man's ruddy eyes narrow and he added, "Though you were already a good ways out of your way if you were speaking with Revered Krugar."

"Alas, geography features not among my strengths," Elkor said, holding up arthritic hands in supplication to Galivith for understanding. Cairn, already marvelling at Elkor's politeness, took note of the priest's surprise at seeing the state of Elkor's ruined hands. Elkor continued without pause, "By nature I am best at undertaking whatever duties my superiors set upon my shoulders. At the moment, I have been ordered to deliver these two acolytes safely to Smyrton."

"What's in Smyrton that needs two acolytes?" the man demanded. "Bringing Galivith's word to the marsh smugglers?"

"Are the smugglers along the Peregrinswater heathens? Well, I know not why Smyrton needs two acolytes. What I do know is that a good revered must follow the Holy Council's directives. I beg you, my brother, please point us in the direction of Smyrton."

The man snorted and said, "You have two options. You can return the way you came, ride for about half a league, cross the Smyrra River, and then make north along its east bank until you come near the Peregrinswater. That will be a muddy ride, though I note from your cloak and robes that you are well-used to mud."

Elkor cast an accusing glance at the priest's own robes that showed evident signs of use and replied, "Yea, I lament it. Galivith teaches that cleanliness is a virtue placed high above others, does He not? And yet, perhaps He will understand that some of us do His work under harsh conditions, whereas others but bask in the sun."

The priest's iron eyes narrowed into a menacing glare, "And He teaches that a civil tongue is placed very highly indeed."

"Indeed He does, revered, indeed He does. So when I report back to the Holy Council of those who have helped me achieve my mission, and of others who may have hindered me. You might pray that my tongue become most civil indeed."

Cairn didn't know if he should barf or laugh.

The priest stared at Elkor through those ruddy eyes for a long time. Although he could see nothing, Cairn imagined a smirk of triumph break across the ugly man's features. "The *other* way, would be to carry along this path until you come to the Perigrinswood, and then simply ride along its eastern eaves. Also muddy, but there is a track that will lead you into Smyrton from the southwest. It's a longer trail, but a quicker one."

"Brother," Elkor hissed, "you have earned my eternal amity."

§

"That bastard revered knows," Elkor declared the moment they were through the gates of the hamlet's palisade.

"You think so?" Cairn asked. "I thought you were convincing. You never even swore."

"I know so. The fucker wouldn't even give me his name. It's a courtesy he would certainly have extended had he thought we were who I said we were. You keep a watch out behind you and you'll see a signal of some sort. Or a rider on a fast horse. I'm not sure what arrangements our friendly local *herg* might have put in place."

"If he was so certain, as you say, then why didn't he just call on the villagers to kill us?"

"Are you bl …" Elkor paused, stifling the insult that surely was to follow, perhaps mindful of Thay's ban on antagonizing each other. At length the man simply sighed and replied, "Didn't you see them, Cairn? Yes, they were numerous, but they were women armed with frigging brooms and buckets, old men armed with roof tiles and hammers, and some lads armed with muscle and stupidity. Whereas you are armed with a freaking steel sword, you're mounted on a warhorse, and your friends there could have anything under those cloaks including armour and weapons, which I note they *do* have. That bastard is a genuine fucker, but a cunning one. He didn't want trouble. Instead, he'll be satisfied simply to cause it for us."

And so they rode as quickly as they could, keeping to the track heading north by northwest towards the Peregrinswood and a hoped-for encounter with some smugglers. They prayed to Guliveg, who nurtures all life, that their head start on any chase would be sufficient that they could maximize the distance they could travel on the firmer footing offered by the track. But again, Thay and Elkor slowed them down and before noon they spotted a lone rider across a wide field who, upon seeing the party of horsemen, raised a horn to his lips and blew three loud blasts that reverberated in their ears. Fylgja barked in reply and made a charge part way down the field, but the rider simply retreated into the woods. More horn blasts sounded in the air.

They pressed on, Lora urging the two laggards to a canter. They followed the track into a forest and slowed to a trot, keeping an eye out for any hidden traps. At length they rounded a turn and discovered a narrow tributary of the Peregrinswater in front of them, traversing the woods from southwest to northeast. It was still frozen over but the ice showed clear signs of softening, with patches of slush and areas of pooling water on top of it. On the other bank of the river, however, was a more serious problem; six men were dismounting from horses. One of the men wore a breastplate and his helmet gleamed in the afternoon sunlight peeking through the trees' leafless branches.

Cairn pulled on Odir's reins, hauling the warhorse to a halt on the near bank. The others came to a stop behind him. The horses whinnied greetings to each other across the narrow river and the men on the far bank looked up at the sound, surprised at seeing their quarry suddenly close to them. "My *herg!*" someone cried. One man, a groom, hauled five of the horses away towards the woods, the armoured man swung his leg back over his horse's back and pulled out his sword. The remaining four men grabbed bows and bounded to cover at the edge of the woods, fumbling for their bowstrings. That the track emerged from the far side of the slushy mess in front of him was enough to convince Cairn to spur Odir down the bank and through the soup atop the river ice. Fylgja leapt after them, barking madly. Lora instinctively spurred her own mount forward. Elkor and Thay simply hung on for dear life as their horses dashed after Odir and Frya.

Cairn's guess that a ford would lie under the slush was an astute one; the ice exploded apart under Odir's hooves, but only because the river flowed over a shallows of gravel and the ice was therefore thin. Odir blasted across the ford and sprang up the far bank. The *herg* atop his horse had only just managed to pull his sword from its scabbard when Odir pounded past. The man swung, but his horse recoiled from a snap of Odir's teeth and the sword only sliced air. Cairn let loose a war cry as he carried on down the track. He easily caught up to the groom, who by now struggled to keep control over the other, panicked, horses. Despite the man's best efforts, the horses bolted forward to escape the mounted banshee chasing after them, pulling their reins from his hand. The groom only managed to keep hold of one horse, its nostrils flaring, twisted around and rearing, screaming in the face of the approaching menace. Cairn flew past yelling and laughing at the top of his lungs.

Lora came through right behind Cairn. Odir's snap had sent the *herg's* mount recoiling off the track and the man had to duck to avoid the thick branch of a nearby tree. He presented no threat to Lora as she swept past. The thrill of chasing after its herd-mates was enough to drive Elkor's horse quickly through the ford and past the enemy. Thay though, coming along behind and struggling to maintain his own balance, saw two of the men on foot spring onto the path, lunging for his horse's reins. He kicked out uselessly, forgetting he had a stirrup on his foot. One man missed his grapple for the bridle, but the other made no mistake, grasping hold of the bridle and letting his weight twist the horse's head around. Thay slipped his boot from the stirrup and stamped on the back of the man's head, sending his victim flying to the mud of the track.

His horse, though, had lost much of its momentum and suddenly found itself flank to flank with another mount. Thay caught a glimpse of the gleaming breastplate. Realizing his danger in the nick of time, he ducked the man's backhand swing, the force of which would have taken off his head. He drove his heels against his horse's hind quarters and it sprang forward again, but not before the man sliced his sword down, biting into Thay's left shoulder. With an anguished cry, Thay bent over and clutched at his horse's neck as it galloped off.

Chapter Four

It was dark. They sat inside a fisherman's summer hut; four walls, one shuttered window, a draughty door, a peaked roof, a rudimentary hearth, and a dirt floor. They had a fire going in the hearth to cast light on Elkor's work.

The hut itself was hidden under the eaves of a wood that overlooked the white, wide frozen river. They had finally reached the banks of the Peregrinswater at dusk and looked around, taking in their bearings. Only a stroke of good luck had allowed them to spot the hovel in the woods. Cairn had explored the copse and discovered that the setting sun shone upon the its narrow chimney that was painted red and that stood out among the relative starkness of the trees in winter.

Having crossed all the lands and tributaries leading to the Peregrinswater, they now sat close to the safety of Polgatia, provided they could get across the great river. They had left the track, letting the horses walk, and skirted a wood before coming to the riverbank.

"This'll hurt," Elkor advised Thay, "but it won't kill you."

"It already hurts," Thay grunted in reply through gritted teeth.

"Well, it's going to hurt more," he declared.

Through the pain, Thay cursed himself for having taken the wound. His reactions may have saved him losing his head but his poor horsemanship had cost him a debilitating injury, one that could yet kill him. What's more, had he been a better warrior, he could have ridden with Tear Tongue in his hand and he would have used the axe to deflect the damaging blow. He thought back to Lars, who had died because he wasn't a good enough warrior, and as he clenched his teeth in agony, he knew he had fallen afoul of the same thing. He needed to make himself better. A better warrior, a more-able horseman, a more-worthy chosen one for the winged worm's crimson dreams. As in a haze, flashes of the events after the injury passed before his eyes.

The horse had charged after the rest of the herd. Never having been comfortable on the beasts, he had clung on as best he could but his left arm had become useless and he bounced from the saddle, pitching onto the track with a jarring impact. The others had cleared the forest and he could no longer see them. There was nothing for it but to get up and run after them as best he could. Fear had risen in him as he ran. Injured, horseless, companionless, he had become more vulnerable than he'd ever been.

It had been Lora who had come riding back to find him. Just as he had finally neared the eaves of the forest, she appeared on Frya leading the horse that had thrown him earlier.

"Thay!" she had called, leaping from Frya's back. "What's happened to you?"

Thay had staggered to a halt, in pain, wheezing. All he could muster as an explanation had been, "I've never been good on either horses or the sharp ends of swords. Thanks for coming back. Help me up, will you?"

Lora had first glance at his wound. "I can't see much," she had said. "We must hope your mail prevented the sword from biting deep. There's not much blood, so that's a good sign." She had hoisted Thay back onto his horse and then tied its reins to her saddle. During the jolting ride back to join the others, he had felt as though he were in the grips of Sk'van, the Twisted. The feeling of being tortured did not diminish as the party continued their flight.

During their ride along the track they had passed in and out of copses, and had woven their way around fields and pasturelands. Once, they had found themselves in the open between fields when from up ahead they saw a party of three riders emerging from a copse and come galloping down the track towards them. Cairn had reached for *Harbinger* but Elkor called out "Cairn, no!" and Thay's big friend forestalled his movement. When the riders had come close they slowed their mounts to a trot, then a walk. Elkor had taken the initiative, "My sons!" he had called out from the depths of the cowl of his hood as they neared, "You are needed at the ford! Make haste!"

The lead rider had glanced at his companions and then back to Elkor. "Will you not join us, revered? We could use the protection of Galivith from summoners."

"We have an urgent mission that we cannot set aside, my son. But fear not, you will ride with Galivith's blessing upon you." Elkor had held up a gnarled hand and murmured words that Thay had not been able to make out. Then he had ordered his compatriots, "Ride hard my sons. Go!" And they had gone, riding off as quickly as their mounts would take them and not even taking notice of Thay's pained efforts to sit straight on his horse.

When they had finally come to the banks of the Peregrinswater, Thay had been in so much agony that he had felt no elation, no excitement, nothing but the burning pain in his shoulder.

Now, safe for the moment in the fisherman's hut, Thay cried out as Elkor extracted the chain mail links and cloth underneath that were embedded in his wound. "Look girl," Elkor said, pointing. "Now we can see the fracture. In some ways it's a good wound. The collarbone - what people here call the *withybein*, given that it's a bone that has the tough flexibility of a willow branch - tends to protect important veins lying beneath."

"So, how do you set a broken collarbone?" Elkor asked, inspecting the wound in the light emerging from the small hearth.

"You can't," Lora replied.

"Hmmm," Elkor observed. "I'm not sure about '*can't*.' Someone somewhere may know a technique that I do not. I would say, '*you don't*.' The best approach I know of is simply to put the arm in a sling, advise the patient to be careful - a useless prescription in this case, given the patient - and then hope for the best. Pain will be an issue. Does the injury cause you any worries?"

"Yes! It causes me worries, right enough," Thay grunted.

"No one asked you," Elkor chided.

"No worries," Lora replied. "Beyond wanting to do a good job stitching up the wound."

Elkor glanced at Lora and arched an eyebrow accusingly. "No worries? Well it causes *me* a few. First of all, although the bones aren't smashed and I see only one clean fracture, the blow nevertheless opened a wound and drove both cloth and metal links *into* it. There is a possibility of infection and fever. If the patient survives …"

"*Survives?*" the patient exclaimed.

"Quiet," ordered Elkor, "… then my second worry is the arm's mobility. There is more than damage to a bone. The blow may have cut muscle and the cords that hold our body intact."

"So what will you do?" Lora asked.

"I do not know *how* it works, but I have observed that wounds suffered in the winter seem to do better. I believe applying ice or snow to the wound will diminish the possibility of infection and counter-balance the heat that the poisons from the wound will generate. As for the muscle and ribbons, I have read a text that suggests applying dung of cattle spewed under a full moon. *That*, however, strikes me as a witchwife tale and the text offered no details on how many times this remedy was applied, in what quantities, and how much success it achieved. Therefore, I recommend doing nothing for fear of doing harm. I would encourage the patient, *if he survives*, to exercise regularly, work the arm a bit like the patient himself forced upon Cairn after …" Elkor did not complete the thought. He didn't need to. They all thought of Lars' death.

Lora nodded and murmured, "Look at us! Lars is dead, Thay is hurt badly, Cairn is still recovering from a separated shoulder, me ... I am terrified ... and you?"

Elkor shrugged, "I am as hateful as ever, I suppose. Or, how did you put it? - refusing to contemplate the possibility that we won't kill Korgash. Didn't you chide me about that once?"

"That was me," Thay snarled through clenched teeth.

A silence fell on the cabin that even Fylgja sensed and respected. "We should clean the wound and stitch him up," Lora finally declared.

"Indeed we should. Set your needle in the fire for a while. Then bring in a helmet-full of snow to put on the wound. We'll use the cold to numb the pain a bit." Lora set about doing as much. Elkor slapped Thay on the back a little too hard for Thay's comfort and observed, "As I said, this is going to hurt."

§

Cairn went outside in the pre-dawn darkness. Any hope of leaving the others undisturbed was undermined by Fylgja as she followed behind, wagging tail banging against the wall of the hut as she waited for her master to open the door. Once outside, she bounded off into the woods, intent on doing her business. Cairn followed to do his. When he finished, he found Fylgja peering at him, crouched and ready to pounce, tail wagging furiously. Cairn looked down. The dog's tail came to a sudden stop and she crouched lower. At his feet was a round, frozen horse turd. "Euch," he said, kicking the turd away. Fylgja pounced, leaping through the air and landing front paws on the turd, sending it skittering further along the ground, triggering a second lunge.

He looked out over the Peregrinswater. It looked big, about as wide as the Andersfjord was back home, though it didn't have dramatic valley walls, sitting in a broad flood plain as it did. It flowed east, down out of the Boldring Mountains, according to Elkor, and carried on for some forty leagues before it was joined by the Northwater, another broad river that Fjordlanders knew flowed down from the northeast. Cairn had heard talk among the Sea Wolves who had sailed it that the Lower Peregrinswater flowed south by southeast seventy leagues, the full length of Straeland, from the confluence of the two big rivers to the Peregrinsmouth. The Peregrinsmouth, where a mere seven moons ago Kindron had put Thay and Lora ashore on a mission while he and Lars had stewed in envy on board *Rignil*. Kindron, *Rignil*, and Lars were gone now. Lost in the past.

Fylgja bounced over to him, dropped the turd again at his feet, backed up a half-dozen paces, and crouched into chase position. Cairn couldn't help but smile. He snapped off a branch from a dead tree and waved the stick in front of the dog. Fylgja ignored the stick and kept her gaze fixed on the dung. Finally Cairn gave up and kicked the turd across the frozen ground. Fylgja again leapt through the air and pounced on her victim.

Cairn looked out over the river again. It was hard to tell in the half-light, but the full expanse of the surface appeared frozen. There was a bitter, driving wind, and Norrgi, in His wisdom, had blown in clouds overnight. Cairn doubted the snow and ice on the river would do any thawing that day. Elkor wouldn't be happy, he guessed, for the Straeling's plan was to find a smuggler who could row them across in a boat of some sort, obviously expecting the river ice to have broken up. He wondered what the alternate plan would be. His thoughts were interrupted by a sharp, urgent bark from Fylgja. Cairn glanced around and, sure enough, found the turd back at his feet and the dog ready to pounce again.

Cairn moved directly in front of the expectant dog, whose posture changed, more erect with the bushy tail wagging. He knelt and ruffled the scruff of her neck and said, "Why are you so cheerful, girl?" Despite himself, he smiled at the look in her sparkling eyes. "I miss a friend very much. You would have liked him. He knew all the old stories. He'd know a story about a band of raiders needing to cross a vast, perilous river, and it'd inspire him to a plan, so it would." Fylgja hopped up and licked the end of his nose. Cairn smiled at that. "I hope Thay's all right," he said before shaking his head and going to check on the horses tethered deeper in the woods.

§

Thay showed no signs of fever upon waking; but as Elkor had predicted, the wound pained him greatly. He did enjoy the balm of hot porridge prepared in the hut's hearth; ever since leaving the cave in the Northwall Hills, they had not dared light a fire. Cairn reported that the river appeared completely frozen-over and they debated what to do. "Go straight over," Cairn said. "It's cold out, it's been a cold winter, that river looks frozen solid."

"The Peregrinswater is a big frigging river," Elkor retorted, "It usually doesn't freeze entirely. If we expose ourselves out on the ice, visible up and down the river banks, and find open water in front of us, we're fucked. The only question would be how many times Lora'd be raped before joining us in death."

"Charming," Lora observed.

"It's a real danger, girl."

Lora whipped out *Íss*. "So's this! So's the point of my new sword. So are every single one of my arrows. Men seem to have trouble raping me when they've an arrow stuck in their eye."

Elkor leaned back and looked, for a fleeting moment, afraid.

Lora concluded, "Exactly."

Silence reigned for a time. "I'll go have a look," Lora offered finally. "I run the least risk of going through thin ice. My snowshoes'll spread my weight. If people see one woman out there, they might not think it's the band of demonic raiders."

"I wouldn't take that wager," Cairn replied.

"For once he uses his br ..." Elkor began before changing his tack, "For once I agree with Cairn. The risk is too high."

"All right then, we stay here for the day and I do it tonight," Lora countered.

Elkor shook his head, "The longer we wait, the greater the chance the pursuit catches us."

That was when they heard their horses whinnying.

Lora leapt to her feet and pried open the shutter on the window a fraction. She saw horses thundering past the hut, pounding their way along the riverbank. The riders were heavily armed and were hauling hard on their horses' reins in response to the whinnying, hoping to slow their own horses down.

"Riders!" Lora exclaimed. The young Fjordlanders sprang for their weapons, Thay with an audible grunt of pain, while Elkor snatched up his and Lora's packs. They burst from the hut, Fylgja flying past everyone to get into the vanguard. She darted forward barking in a savage staccato that included a guttural, menacing growl. The sight before them was unexpected and completely confused. A score of armoured riders yanked on reins, willing their mounts to a sudden halt in the morning light. Horses heaved and surged, heads flung back and nostrils flared, struggling against control, neighing wildly. For some reason, the mounts recoiled, or jumped, or shook their heads, as though a swarm of angry wasps had gotten among them. Adding to the chaos, Cairn's big multihued dog flew among the horses, leaping to nip at withers and shoulders, driving them further upriver against the will of their riders. Legs flew into the air as a man lost balance with the sudden surge forward of his steed. Another flew sideways from his horse.

Cairn knew for a certainty that the world held things he didn't and couldn't understand. He accepted the fact that the horses resisted their riders without thinking, much quicker than Elkor, for example, who stood a-gawk with his hands, still clutching the backpacks, dangling at his side. While Elkor stood, stunned, Cairn simply sprang at the nearest rider, a young man he recognized as the *hergling* and former master of Fylgja, an urgent anger suddenly roaring inside him. That roar bellowed into the air, likely heard clear across the river in Polgatia. Thay knew that roar, though he would have sworn on Hondrig's Holy Name that the voice belonged to Knab, their clan chieftain. Cairn flew at the young rider who was kicking and cursing at his horse as he struggled to haul it around. The *hergling* didn't have a shield. Cairn had *Orgor's Awl*. The blow caught the *hergling* full in the ribs and threw him off his mount, though his right foot caught in the horse's stirrup. The beast bolted, dragging its hapless rider away with it, the *hergling's* head bouncing off the ground.

Thay could hardly help himself. Without thought for his wound, he lunged at another rider with *Tear Tongue*. This one saw the overhead blow coming at him, but none of them had been expecting such an immediate fight and his shield was still slung across his back, so he tried to pivot his horse away from the attack. The tactic worked in so far as Thay's blow bit into his leg rather than sunk itself into his head. With a yell of pain, he spurred his horse forward, allowing it to stampede off, as it clearly wanted to do anyway. Thay sprinted to the next rider but found Cairn before him, swinging *Orgor's Awl* and spewing spittle as he roared.

From somewhere off towards the woods, Thay heard Lora call his name and he looked around. In the confusion of the mêlée, a giant warhorse thundered counter-current against the flailing beasts. Thay recognized the warhorse and dove out of the way. A massive steel battle axe swept through the air where he had stood half an instant before and a new roaring joined Cairn's. This roaring, however, Thay could understand as cursing in Straelish. "Galivith-bedamned worm! Get up! Fight me!"

Thay twisted away from the warhorse's stamping hooves. He couldn't put any weight on his left shoulder, already sending spasms of agony through him, and he couldn't roll away as he would have liked. The hooves flashed closer, slamming into the ground next to his head and showering his face with encrusted snow. "You fucking, coward!" the voice roared from above. "Worm!" Thay gave another lunge away from the hooves, knowing it wasn't enough. That was when Fylgja struck. The warhorse did not resist its rider's commands like many of the other horses, but it would not ignore a dog's snapping teeth. Fylgja raked a front shoulder and sent the beast surging forward, away, putting Thay out of danger. The roaring continued, however, joining the screams of terrorized horses and uncomprehending yells of their riders.

Elkor, too, recognized that big warhorse and its rider. The confusion had found a focus in Cairn; the big youth spun, *Orgor's Awl* flying in all directions. Since the eye of the storm had yet to approach Elkor, he dropped to a knee, threw open the flap of his pack and drew forth a wooden case, almost drooling at the prospect of his deepest dream coming true. He felt a twinge of regret, but also a surge of joyous anticipation when Korgash spurred the big warhorse towards Thay. As Elkor opened the case, Korgash swung his axe, though thankfully Thay dove aside. Elkor extracted one of three long darts with dark-stained tips and dropped the case to the ground. The rider roared a challenge and Thay struggled to roll away from the horse's stamping hooves. Elkor stepped forward and flung the dart at Korgash.

But Fylgja struck and the warhorse lunged forward, taking Korgash out of danger. Elkor yelled in frustration and spun to snatch up another dart. His yell, though, caught the ear of Korgash. The big warrior spun his warhorse around and spurred it forward. When Elkor stood up with his second dart in his hand, he looked around only to see the beast thundering directly at him. He flung the dart wildly. Wildly wide. He wanted then to fling himself out of the way of the warhorse, but it was too late. Two bits of luck were on his side: the warhorse hadn't had much space to accelerate, and, the hut was close behind him, preventing the horse from throwing its full momentum at Elkor and simply pounding through his target and onwards. The stallion collided with Elkor and sent him hurtling among the trees.

"Plague troll spawn!" Korgash bellowed. The big man leaned forward and deliberately, slowly swung his right leg over the back of the warhorse. Elkor, gasping for breath and clutching his ribs, rolled onto his back. He saw Korgash lower himself gently, hesitantly, to the ground before turning towards him. Elkor groped in his voluminous cloak for his dagger, pulled it out and hefted himself to his knees. Korgash moved with a pronounced limp and wasn't closing the distance quickly, so Elkor heaved a deep breath and rose unsteadily to his feet. "I've got you now, demon worshipper!" Korgash roared, limping closer.

Elkor charged. He drew on the fire of his hatred - every bitter humiliation, the torture that he had suffered, the pain that he had endured - and he lunged at the warrior. But Elkor was no warrior; Korgash knocked aside the stabbing dagger with the head of his axe before driving its butt into Elkor's stomach. Elkor doubled over from the blow, only to have Korgash's knee driven into his face, re-breaking his nose and sending him flying backwards again. Korgash grinned and limped forward. Elkor twisted to his hands and knees and scrambled deeper into the woods, his legs flailing to find purchase in the snow-encrusted ground. Korgash hurried his limping gait, closing to within a pair of paces, but not without grimacing in pain. Elkor's foot slipped out from under him and he fell flat on his face.

Korgash was on him in an instant, grabbing his trailing leg by the ankle and hauling him backwards. The big warrior clasped the hood of the revered's red cloak that Elkor still wore, tugging it half off and yelling, "*You* might sully Holy Cloth, but *I* won't." Elkor flailed and writhed but Korgash's grip was strong and the clasp of the cloak had caught around his neck, preventing him from slithering free. A fist crashed into his face and he screamed from the pain of it. The shock dislodged the clasp and Korgash pulled the red cloak from his victim. "You're a *dead* plague troll now," Korgash breathed into Elkor's ear. "The Queen's justice has a long arm, especially when that arm is *me*."

"My *herg*!" cried a voice. "Behind you!"

Korgash snapped his head around and dropped his shoulder, pivoting Elkor around to face whatever threat was coming at him. In the event it was Thay.

§

Lora wasn't one for standing back and watching, especially after having failed Lars. When they had first heard the horses, she had grabbed her weapons and burst from the hut with Cairn and Thay. Amid the stunning confusion of the horses, the roaring of the men, the barking of Fylgja, and the sortie of her friends, she willed herself to control her instinct to attack and, like her mother would have done, assess the tactical situation. The scene was confused, thus her advantage lay in control. She strung her bow. Two riders fell from their panicked horses, so she began her bloody work there, dispatching both quickly with arrows to the chest before they came to their senses. Another rider had pulled his horse around despite its fear and had it on the cusp of obedience, so she grasped another arrow and used it to stab the horse's rear end, sending the steed pounding off along the riverbank. She pulled back to the edge of the woods when she saw Korgash approach on his massive warhorse, bearing down on Thay. She yelled out to her friend, saw Thay turn his head, recognize the danger, and leap aside.

A rider jumped from his mount and came at her. She put an arrow in his face. Another unhorsed attacker ran at her before she could notch a fourth arrow. She dropped her bow, pulled out *Íss*, and rolled away from the man's stabbing sword. She scrambled to her knees but felt a hand grasp her initiate's cloak.

She twisted, reaching for the clasp on the cloak to free herself, but then all the force drained from the man's hand. She shuffled off the cloak and took in the sight of a stupefied man, wide eyed and open mouthed, slowly pitching forward onto the ground, and Cairn spinning away from him.

She grabbed her shield, got to her feet and looked around. Cairn now spun in a fury, forcing three mounted Straelings away from Thay splayed out on the ground. Out of the corner of her eye, for an instant, she thought she glimpsed golden sparks darting between the ears of the horses, but when she looked, she only saw the animals shaking their heads and bucking without apparent cause. Their riders tugged at reins and dug in their spurs, snarls etched on their faces. Korgash's warhorse, less the big warrior, stamped about, tossing its head. That's when she saw them: a dozen golden sparks alighted upon Thay.

§

Thay felt an uncontrollable surge of energy course through him and the pain of his left shoulder suddenly dulled. He looked across towards the hut and saw Lora staring at him, her mouth agape. He had no time to figure that out, for he saw that Elkor was in trouble; Korgash had grabbed hold of his ankle and was hauling the little man backwards.

Thay snatched up *Tear Tongue* and surged to his feet. He took note of a leader of the remaining riders off to his right marshalling men, readying a charge, but he ignored them, charging, himself, across the riverbank. He heard a cry, "My *herg*! Behind you!" Ahead, Korgash shifted around, hauling Elkor about, using the smaller man like a shield, though Thay saw the man's movement wasn't fluid. Thay had just a splinter of time to make a decision: he knew about Korgash's wound that he, himself, had delivered; and he knew it was hard to wield a battle axe one-handed while dragging around dead weight. Thay lunged.

He dove low inside Korgash's half-strength blow, trusting to his mail to protect him. Luck then played a role, for the Straelish *herg's* axe twisted in his hand mid-swing and the cutting edge didn't bite properly. Even so the strength of the blow was rib-shaking as Korgash drove the axe into Thay's left side. Thay kept driving his legs and his good shoulder collided with the big warrior's gut. Thay leveraged himself up, taking Korgash off his feet and pitching the Straeling *herg* to the ground. Elkor had enough of his wits about him that he seized the opportunity to drive his elbow into Korgash's gut, but chain mail over boiled leather armour meant that only Elkor cried out in pain.

Thay put his boot into Korgash's inner thigh, unleashing a howl of agony from the warrior. When Korgash cried out, his lieutenant signalled to four of his comrades and yelled, "Ride!" The soldier spurred his horse forward, the others followed, all of them thundering to the rescue of their liege *herg*. Thay knew he had little time: he shifted *Tear Tongue* to his useless left hand, grabbed Elkor with his right, and thrust the hunchbacked man towards the woods behind the hut. "Ready the horses," he ordered. Then he spun and faced Korgash, transferring the axe back to his good hand. The Straelish *herg* had hauled himself to his feet. Thay stepped forward but Korgash limped backwards, anguish written on his face. Thay prowled in an arc, appearing to seek an opening, and so the Straeling kept limping backwards, turning to prevent Thay from getting behind him. Thus Thay herded the big warrior into the path of the oncoming riders.

The prospect of trampling their leader slowed the Straelings' charge and allowed Fylgja to get back into the fray, grabbing one of the horses by the nose and hauling its head down. Cairn flew at the attackers from the flank, swinging *Orgor's Awl*. One of the riders leaned over in the saddle and clasped Korgash by the arm. The Strael noble needed no second invitation to heave himself up onto the horse, as the other riders spurred their mounts forward and thundered away.

Thay called to Lora, "Help Elkor with the horses!" and then leapt to restrain Cairn from chasing after the riders. Cairn bucked and yelled, and the jolts sent stabs of pain through Thay's shoulder. "Cairn!" Thay bellowed. "Fylgja's chasing them! Call her back! They might turn and kill her." Cairn stopped. Thay draped an arm over his friend's back. Cairn shook his head and said, "*Skeetze!*"

"*Foxt!*"

"I'm here."

"Good."

"Fylgja!" Cairn yelled, before whistling.

Lora brought the horses to the hut - Elkor, panicked, stunned, and again injured, was of no use and even unsettled the beasts - and she hefted up saddles and equipment. As she did so, Elkor finally said something coherent, though his voice was thick and mumbling from his newly re-broken nose as he said it, "They'll regroub. They'll be bag soon. Korgash'll muster them quigly."

"You're the one who's supposed to know where we are and where to go," Cairn panted while helping Thay mount one of the horses.

Elkor looked about. In a strained voice laden by fear and pain, he said, "Thay, do you see open wader on the river?" Thay nodded, triggering a curse from the Straeling. Elkor twisted around and looked upriver. "We've no frigging choice! Upriver only taigs us to where the current flows rapidly. It'll have *more* oben wader, not less. Without a bloody boat, thad'll get us nowhere. Downriver's broader, slower, and there are marshes, where I have heard Mari subtimes camps. Downriver it mus be."

Thus they rode downriver, oddly, following their pursuers.

Chapter Five

The day had begun overcast and dim, but the Godspace brightened as the morning progressed, though a low mist hung over the northern banks of the Peregrinswater, over Polgatia, over safety. To Thay's great relief, they kept their pace gentle at first. The open riverbank provided good ground for riding, though they did have to navigate around copses of trees and thickets lining creek beds that crossed their path. They passed the odd farmstead; normally a long, snow-clad field reaching down to the great river from a cottage, barn, and granary. Only once did they encounter buildings on the riverbank and they blew past them without seeing a single soul abroad on the cold, blustery morning.

That changed when they came to a confluence of the Peregrinswater with one of its lesser tributaries, an iced-over river roughly twenty paces wide. Lora was in the lead when they pulled up to halt at the riverbank. She looked around and then pointed south; not far up the smaller river they could see three riders at the far end of a stone bridge that spanned the watercourse. Two riders appeared much like the others they had battled at daybreak, but the other was distinct: long, chestnut-coloured hair framing a narrow face, sable cloak overtop a coat of ermine, white skirts flowing across the body of a black stallion. Lady Oda took note of them and turned her horse up-river, nudging it into a languid walk, towards them. The housecarls followed her.

They looked at the ice of unknown thickness of the tributary and then up at the approaching horses. Lora pulled her bow off her back. The movement didn't go unnoticed, and, as she strung her bow, Thay said, "She's signalling to us. I think she wants to talk." Sure enough, Oda had pulled out a blue handkerchief and waved it at them as she approached. Lora nocked an arrow, though she waited before loosing, no matter how great the urge to shoot. At length Oda drew level with them across the frozen river.

"These fine men are Andrez and Fritlzer," the noblewoman called out in her patrician tones, her gloved hand motioning towards her housecarls. "I would *rather* prefer you not kill them, though I have no doubt they'd feel honoured to die in my service. Please lower that bow of yours so we can talk like civilized people. You *are* capable of civilized discourse, are you not?"

Elkor spat at that. "Whad do you wand?" he snapped, his voice still sounding half like it was coming through a blanket.

"Oh dear. I can hear you've had a rough go of it. Perhaps I can help. You see, I seek a mutually beneficial arrangement," Oda replied.

Cairn laughed and asked in Fjordlander, "Did she say she wanted to bargain with us? Why in Skalagg would she do that?"

"She's playing her own game, remember," Lora replied. "She saved us back in Harburg."

Elkor responded for them, calling out "Whad do you propose?"

Oda leaned forward in her saddle and gestured at Thay with her chin. "I saw that boy there back in Fletcherton, though I doubt he caught sight of *me*. He was a bit busy, carrying you over his shoulder and running across a frozen landscape. Very impressive, I must say."

"She's delaying us," Cairn declared, again in Straelish.

Oda called out again, "You are dangerous people, as this morning's muddle proves to anyone who cares to look. You don't trust me, that's completely understandable. As a gesture of my goodwill, I can tell you something of Korgash's plan. There is a hamlet just up the road; he's regrouping, sending messengers to his allies ..." Then, catching the look that crossed Cairn's face, "... oh yes, there *are* allies out and about, scouring the lands. Rather a great number of them. He'll be bringing them all here now. He will soon ride back this way, scouring the riverbank and driving you upriver until he catches up with you."

"And how did *you* come to be here, enmeshed in all this?" Lora demanded.

Oda smiled at that. "Oh, I think I've come to understand something of how you think. It might suit Korgash to bellow at his peers that you're necromancers and raiders who summon fire demons, and he might even believe it, but I know you're just looking to escape. You've made a direct enough line from Harburg to the edge of our realm and you didn't even once disturb any graveyards on your way ... except of course to put eight men into Fletcherton's, and a few more this morning, I don't doubt. I also know you can't escape by going upriver. The local *herg*, *Herg* Diepmar, briefed Korgash on the ice conditions beyond the next village ... a great deal of quick-flowing open water, I'm afraid. No escape that way. But if you go down by the marshes, I'm told that the ice there remains intact."

Elkor, a hand on the bridge of his nose, yelled, "Hounds don't bargain with the hare. You have your idiodig, tyrant goons and you've god us pressed against a river we can'd cross, but you wand some sort of *arrangement*? I am no idiod born yesderday!"

"Listen to me!" Oda yelled, anger or frustration creeping into her voice. "You have no time for this! The arrangement is based on the fact that there's another person as well as Andrez and Fritzler I would prefer you not kill. He *is* rather heedless of his own safety. It is Korgash. He has men with him and they'll kill you all. But on you," she pointed at Thay, "he'll want his revenge. He will fight you one-on-one. Normally I would wager on him. But he is not healthy ... and I see danger in you. I need him for the moment and I cannot risk losing him to either a lucky blow by any of you or an ill-shot arrow from an amateur who does not know how to use a bow when a breeze is blowing. Cross now and you all live, and so will he."

"You'll call thad drooling goadfugger, Korgash, to heel?" Elkor asked, incredulity spilling from his tongue.

Oda wrinkled her long nose in distain of Elkor's insult and shook her head. "Oh no. I'm afraid we're far beyond that now, your boy there rather took Korgash out from under my influence back in Fletcherton. What he did may have been impressive, but it put your destiny into Galivith's hands. No, listen. Although I cannot call Korgash to heel, as you so eloquently put it, I *can* divert him. It would help you, and keep him alive. He accepted my offer to keep watch on this bridge confident that my men-at-arms would keep me safe. Cross it now, quickly, and go around those woods behind me. Watch if you like, though I would keep riding were I you. When he comes, I will say that you have not crossed. He will carry on. That might give you the time you need."

Elkor exchanged glances with the youngsters. Thay nodded and said, "I'm in no shape for a fight. We're better off avoiding one."

"Can we trust her?" Cairn asked.

"Of course we can't," Lora replied. "But what does it matter? We'd be across the bridge."

"Across the bridge and trapped, if Korgash is hiding in those woods," Cairn pressed.

"Yes, she's a fugging viper," Elkor wheezed, "and cerdinly playing her own game, but hiding behind her petticoat isn'd like that ocdopus-fugging perverd. I say we go."

And so they went. Oda and her housecarls withdrew a safe distance up the track that crossed the bridge. They crossed the river and split up, Cairn, Thay, and Elkor carrying on, Lora remaining behind in the woods, as Oda suggested she could do, to watch. She looked on as Oda's housecarls went about confusing the tracks in the snow. They had just finished when Korgash's posse thundered down the track and, after a quick pause to confer with Oda, carried on over the bridge. Lora saw that it had grown. From the cover of the deep woods, she counted two squadrons of about a dozen riders each, all heavily armed and armoured. She saw a big, middle-aged man riding alongside Korgash. She also recognized the surviving housecarl from the fight on the river the night Lars died. The first squadron rode behind a banner-man holding a long spear, from the end of which fluttered a pennant of blue showing crossed swords beside the same sheaf of wheat that appeared on the red cloaks of the priests of Galivith. They rode on good horses, in good order, and under their billowing cloaks, she saw tunics of the same blue hue. The second squadron straggled along behind in a disorganized cluster.

Lora rapidly guided Frya to the edge of the copse, mounted, and spurred to catch up to the others. The filly was fleet of foot, so catching up to any group of riders would not have been difficult, and it proved even less so given that her group included Elkor and an injured Thay. On they rode, blowing past a quiet hamlet - presumably where Korgash had mustered his new posse - where all the women had their children huddled by firesides and where no one dared venture outdoors for terror of the necromancer and his minions. Lora and Frya were their rearguard and Lora dared hope that they had left pursuit far behind for, after the hamlet, she saw no one following.

At length they came upon a broad bay, an indent on the southern bank of the Peregrinswater. A forest of dried out cattails rose from the bay, a sure sign of shallow water. Looking left across the breadth of the great river, the wispy mist had lifted perhaps three fathoms into the air, revealing a tall riverbank of broken stone, though its crest remained hidden in the cloud. In front of the far riverbank they could see more marshland, a twin bay of cattails to the one in front of them. Between both sets of dried out cattail stalks, however, lay a broad expanse of ice of unknown thickness covered with crusted white-grey snow.

A real forest, one of pine trees, encircled the far side of the bay. They had seen it looming closer as they rode, a dark green band stretching from the river far to the south. "Here," Elkor called out to Cairn up front and they reined in their horses. "I have read of these marshes near Sbyrdon."

"Smyrton?" Thay asked.

Elkor nodded. "The wader under the ice should be slow-moving here if anywhere."

They rode around the bay to the woods, Elkor looking ahead seeking cover from which they could plan their next move, the young Fjordlanders looking to Polgatia, their hearts pounding as the mist lifted some more, revealing a forest of birch trees awaiting spring's arrival. In the distance there was also a spire that rose beyond the trees, perhaps from a temple of some description. Elkor stopped them when they came to a hillock from which they could see any pursuit behind them. They dismounted and Cairn and Thay tethered the horses while Lora looked at Elkor's nose. She shook her head and said, "It's swelling. It'll need tending to once we're safe."

They reopened the debate on how to get across the ice. "I say we try with the horses," Lora declared, looking out across the river at the birch trees standing atop the tall stony banks, all under the hanging mist.

"They're a heavy weight," Cairn replied.

"Of course they're a heavy weight, Cairn, they're *horses*. It's just that they could give us a big advantage on the other side. Sure, they're good horses and those we don't keep would fetch us fair coin, which might be useful to us. Also, *being a heavy weight*, Cairn, they could test the strength of the ice for us. And I've become as attached to Frya as you are to that dog ..."

"Fylgja," Cairn corrected.

"... Fylgja, then. Well, I'm sure you don't want to leave her behind."

"Right enough."

"Well then, neither do I want to abandon Frya." Cairn nodded.

They debated the plan as they lightened the load for their steeds, pulling off saddles and saddlebags, working quickly for fear that the pursuit would catch them up. They had begun their preparations when Fylgja growled at the trees deeper into the pine forest. They turned around and drew their weapons, peering into the gloom. Just then, six men stepped from behind a ragged line of thicker fir trees about twenty paces away. Four had their heads in misshapen woollen caps, but they all had long, shaggy whiskers that blossomed from their faces, and they wore layers of furs draped over homespun clothing. They also had bows bent and arrows nocked. One tall woman stood at their centre, dressed much the same. They had likely wanted to come closer before revealing themselves but Fylgja had forced their hand. "Lay down your weapons!" the woman yelled.

However the Fjordlanders and Elkor might have wished to react, Fylgja lunged forward, barking like mad and rushing at the closest, a red-nosed man in tattered breeches beneath the layers of fur. Her attack distracted the assailants as they tracked her charge with their bows, and the red-nosed man loosed his arrow at the dog, but it slammed into the forest floor behind her as she darted forward. The Fjordlanders themselves surged forward at the distraction, veering left together to put more trees between them and those to the far side of the woman. Cairn saw the blur of an arrow streak past in front of his face as he charged through the brush and among the trees. He heard another strike a tree somewhere to his right, heard the crashing of his friends through the woods, heard a man's cry of pain and Fylgja's barking turn into a savage growl, but over it all he heard Elkor yelling, "Mari! We're freds! We're freds! Hold! Hold! Cairn, hold!"

Cairn didn't hold.

As he charged forward between fir trees he caught a glimpse of a man flailing on his back with Fylgja pulling at a leg. Cairn burst around a final large fir and fell upon another man as he was fixing arrow to bow, crushing the weapon between them. Cairn was now a big man and he easily overwhelmed his opponent, pinning the bowman in a vice-like grip in front of him, screening himself from any other arrows. Lora, meanwhile, had fallen upon the man on the ground, Íss at his throat. Thay, catching sight of at least two assailants training their bows on him, darted behind a large tree next to Cairn, throwing his back against its trunk, and heard three arrows whistle into the forest where he had been standing.

Íss held to the neck of the man kicking at Fylgja silenced his wailing, though Cairn could still hear the dog's growling attack. Cairn also heard Elkor yell, "Thay! No! Hold! Peace, freds! Peace!" When he looked up, he saw the small, hunchbacked man limping forward, arms held high in the air.

From somewhere ahead of him, screened by trees, he heard the woman call out, "Call off the dog and we'll not skewer ye!"

"Cairn!" Elkor cried. "Call off Fylgja!"

"They can put down their bows first!" Cairn yelled back.

Elkor, arms extended in supplication for peace, spun to the woman and twisted his hands, palm to the sky, as elegant a manner of expressing, "Well?" as any. The woman, nearly as tall as Lora, heavy-built and with a mop of messy black hair, nodded twice sharply. Then she loosened the tension on the bow and lowered it, a fraction. Her companions followed her lead.

"Fylgja, no!" Cairn ordered. The dog, jaws clamped around the man's ankle, pivoted her ears in response to her master's voice. She stopped growling but didn't release her grip. "Fylgja!" repeated Cairn more forcefully, "Come!" Fylgja reluctantly released the man and crept backwards towards Cairn, ready to pounce back on her victim if necessary. "What's the game, Elkor?" Cairn called out.

"These folk aren't our edebies. They're our freds."

Cairn shouted back, "You're not telling me that now our *friends* are out to kill us?"

"This is the woban sbuggler I told you aboud!"

"Why be we your friends?" the woman asked, her brown eyes shifting from Fylgja to Elkor and her bow still showing tension. "I don't know you."

"Ah, bud you *do*, Bari," Elkor replied, thrusting back the hood of his black cloak.

The woman's eyebrows shot up in surprise. "Aye, well that be a face a woman can't forget," was all she said.

"Cairn, Lora, these are the Barigold Sbugglers."

Mari cocked her head at that, "*What?*"

"Thad's what they're calling you. After all, you're Bari, and it's said you like gold."

The woman laughed, her bow slipped lower and she released tension further on it. "*Marigold* be it? Well, I'll be." Then, suddenly serious again, she asked, "And weren't you close - too close - to that merchant, Marrakus? I had to get you across the river with some haste, if I recall. And who be *them?*"

"Have you heard aboud trouble in Fletcherdon?"

"Ya," was all she said.

"That was us. We've kigged the hornets' nest. Every *herg* above the Northwall is hunting us. The worsd of the sadisdig whoreson basdards might not be far behind us and could be here soon with a big party of men, two squadrons of cabalry. Soon your *real* edebies will be swarbig over this riverbang."

"All the more reason to deal with you quickly," one of the smugglers said.

"Agreed," Elkor replied. "Listen, we can't fight each other with our common edeby closing in on us. You can helb us and come out of it ahead."

"How?" barked another man.

Elkor pointed at the tethered horses. "We give you two of those horses and you have two of your men ride them towards Sbyrdon."

"Why don't we just take all four?" the first man called.

"Then you'll have two dead freds and it might go ill for the rest of you," Elkor snapped. "Listen, there's no time for this!" He stepped closer to the woman. She pulled on her bowstring and raised her bow a fraction. "Bari, these are good beasts we're offering. Just ride for few hundred paces and then take them into the woods. We'll be across the river and out of your way. You do us a favour and you come out ahead."

"With riders on our ass," Mari observed.

"Don't you always have the local sheriff hunting you? What's one *herg* more?"

"It be the 'on our ass' part that be worrin' me," she countered.

"Two good beasts. It's a tidy sum of horseflesh."

Thay called out from behind the tree, "Elkor, this is taking too long!"

Mari bit her lip. Then she said, "You'll never get the horses across the river. You'd be best off giving us the lot."

"Why is dat?" Elkor asked.

"The ice is breaking up."

"I didn't see any open channels."

"There are some further downriver. And upriver, too, for that matter. I wouldn't trust it."

Elkor looked at Lora. She shook her head. "Fine, taig all the horses."

"No!" Lora and Cairn yelled, as one.

Elkor held up a gnarled hand to forestall any further words. "Come spring, we'll be bag for the filly and the biggest. They'd best be in good shabe. You can keep the other two."

Mari nodded. "Done. As long as you be bringin' a pair'o casks of Polgati spirits with you. Now call the big lad and the girl, and the dog off my men."

Cairn rose from the man under him and stormed towards Mari. Elkor stepped in front of the young Fjordlander, who stopped, but he nevertheless declared, "You take good care of those horses! They're *good* horses, and not just because they are worth much money. They're good, honest beasts and I will beat anyone who harms them."

"You mustn't be havin' 'em long if you says they be *honest*. You see, I don't be likin' Thorn People much." Cairn leaned forward, as though to brush past Elkor, but Mari added, "But I *do* like animals. Will ye pay for feed?"

Elkor almost fainted from the extended negotiations, but Cairn surprised him by agreeing readily, offering to pay whatever good feed cost upon again receiving Odir in good shape. Mari concluded, "Well then, as long as they don't bite me, I'll be takin' good care of 'em."

§

Later, after Mari and her men had departed, laying down a false trail for any pursuers, they ventured out among the dried-out cattail stalks poking through the ice of the bay. The going was not quick as they wore their snowshoes to spread their weight over a larger surface of ice. They kept low, beneath the tops of the cattails, but soon enough they emerged from the bay and needed to risk being seen out in the open. They unslung their packs and tied them to Lora's rope so that they could drag the burden behind them and be lighter themselves. The final element of their plan, to Elkor's disgust, was to say a prayer to Florri begging Him for good luck before carrying on.

Lora did indeed go first out onto the open ice to test the way, with the other end of her rope tied about her waist. The ice didn't groan, pop and break apart, so Elkor followed a dozen paces behind, Thay another dozen behind him, and finally Cairn. The big lad had refused to take any chances with Fylgja's fate, especially after the forced separation with Odir, so he had taken another length of rope from Mari and made a harness for the dog, loping its end around his wrist. Each man held onto the rope that led from Lora ahead of them to the packs behind. Although she was tempted to make for the nearest extension of the far bank, she kept her bearing towards the forest of cattails poking from within a deeper recess, hoping that with its width there would be less current flowing underneath the ice there. She slid one snowshoe-clad foot slowly in front of the other, yearning to be already clambering up the tall riverbank on the far side. Despite the blustering, frigid north wind, she felt sweat dampening her brow and her heart pounding in her breast. She kept her eyes down at her feet, focussing on the ice, assessing it for fissures or movement.

That was when she did, indeed, hear a popping crack radiating out from her position, echoing off to the right. She stopped.

"What is id?" she heard Elkor call from behind her.

"It cracked. Underneath me," she turned her head and called back over her shoulder. Looking behind her at Elkor, she was suddenly surprised to see how far they had come; they were right in the middle of the broad river. Then her eyes caught movement on the riverbank behind them. "*Skeetze. Foxt,*" she gasped. "Riders!" Then, spotting the blue pennant among the lead horsemen, she yelled, "It's *them!*" She looked about her, seeking any sign of where thin ice might sit and feeling panic rising in her. "What do I do? Do I move backwards?"

She heard Elkor's voice, calm, determined, "Cragging is normal. Id habbens because ice is thig and expanding, forcing idself against idself until sobthing gives way, shifts up or moves sideways. It's colder today than it has been. Don't worry. Just keeb moving."

She nodded. "Right then. I'll be on my way, right, feet? Start moving!" She took a deep breath, felt a trickle of sweat slip from her brow down her cheek, and shuffled her feet forward again. Just when she thought she might have her heart back under control, a horn blast from the riverbank behind her made her jump in fright.

"Let's get a move on!" she heard Cairn shout from the back. She shuffled her feet more quickly. Her eyes flicked up to the birch trees atop the tall riverbank, to where she desperately hoped they could be safe. Over the pulsing of the blood through her ears, her panting, and the scrape of the snowshoes across the crusted snow atop the ice, she wasn't sure if she heard more cracking. She *thought* she did but couldn't be sure. She did feel the rope tied to her become taut and she looked back over her shoulder to see that she had outpaced the others, using all the slack in the rope. She saw Cairn, the last, dragging the packs across a patch of rough ice, Fylgja obstinately playing tug-of-war against her master. "Fylgja, no!" Cairn yelled. "Stop it!"

Behind Cairn, though, she saw the pursuit. About a half-dozen blue-cloaked riders had spread out and were trotting forwards across the ice. The others were coming along further back, in a wide line. She snapped her head around and looked to the far bank, although it was now the near bank. A hundred paces or so, she guessed, would take her to the thicket of dried-out cattails, though only about forty lay between her and the nearest spur of rocks and boulders sticking out into the river. She again looked behind her to size up the speed of the pursuit and took her decision, veering towards the spur of land. Despite her mind yelling at her not to do so, she began a jog, her footfalls colliding with greater force onto the ice. Again, she *thought* she heard the ice cracking. She ignored it and felt herself speeding up even more, until a tug on the rope halted her in her tracks.

She nearly screamed in panic and frustration. She was close, now, to the spit of rocks and boulders, perhaps only a dozen paces and she wanted to get to the safety of the tall riverbank with its sanctuary of birch trees. She spun around and saw Thay hauling on the rope between him and Cairn, and her big friend oddly shuffling forward. She saw that Cairn's left snowshoe had gone through the ice, for it was dripping wet and when he stepped on the ice, snow became encrusted upon it, clinging and resisting his movements. Behind him now lay an oval-shaped patch of water with small chunks of ice bobbing in it.

Behind that, Lora recognized the leading horseman. A grinning, black-shrouded avenger standing in the stirrups atop his massive warhorse, his right arm pulled back, that oversized war-axe raised and ready to deliver death to Cairn.

The warhorse galloped closer, ahead of the followers, already approaching their packs only a score of paces behind her big friend. Fylgja had given up on the game of tug-of-war and now barked madly at the approaching menace as Cairn dragged her backwards.

Spouts of water burst from around Korgash's big warhorse, which pitched from view, swallowed up by chunks of ice exploding in a fountain from the river. Shock waves shot out from the breach in the ice. Though the other riders reined in, a lateral fissure passed close to one leading horse and the surface pitched, one side heaving high into the air and the other collapsing under the equine weight. The sound of the ice erupting was like thunder booming off the fjords back home. Korgash's warhorse came to the surface screaming amid the large, floating pans of disconnected ice. It slid downriver in the shockingly strong current. Its front hooves pounded on the edge of the ice, knocking loose further chunks and sending plumes of water shooting into the air. Lora saw no sign of Korgash in the channel of frothing water that had suddenly opened behind Cairn.

She was so stunned from the horror unfolding in front of her that she forgot her panicked need for solid ground. Cairn came loping forward tugging Fylgja by the tether, her baying making it clear she wanted to jump into the frothing river. Thay, his teeth gritted from the pain in his left shoulder, pulled the packs one-handed across the last swath of ice. Elkor, looking triumphant, hurried past her and she grabbed him by his arm. "You lied!" she snarled.

"You needed courage," he snapped back. "You owe me your thags!"

"I don't owe you my thanks. I owe you nothing!"

"You owe me a boog!"

A thought overcame her shock, "If I promise you *another* book, can I kick the snot out of you again?"

Elkor actually laughed. "We're nod safe yed! Get a fugging move on!"

They scrambled up the rocky river bank. Thay and Cairn followed, hauling the dog and their packs respectively. Cairn and Thay kept spouting, "*Foxt! Skeetze!*" though the dog's barking drowned them out. Lora could see that Cairn's left snowshoe was encrusted with ice and his boot was wet. She helped him up onto the spur of land. Then they clambered as quickly as they could across the rocky spit to the tall river-bank and found a steep path they could climb to get in among the birch trees atop the slope.

The opening of the channel deterred any attempt by the riders to circle around and find an alternate ice bridge to the Polgati side of the Peregrinswater. As the Fjordlanders and Elkor took off their snowshoes atop the riverbank, fixed them to their packs, and slung those packs on their backs, they witnessed an act of bravery when the remaining riders managed a rescue of the second horse from the channel. They saw nothing of Korgash's warhorse, nor of the Straelish *herg*, nor the other rider.

"Will they try to find another place to come across?" Lora asked of Elkor.

Elkor shook his head. "In numbers like dat, they could trigger a war. They've ligely been seen already. *We* ligely've been seen too. We should go."

Further back beyond the channel and behind the rescue efforts, on the safer ice, a noblewoman sat atop a black stallion. She brushed a strand of her long, chestnut-coloured hair from in front of her as she watched the fugitives evaporate into the mass of Polgati birch trees.

Epilogue

Across the Peregrinswater, just as the sun touched the western horizon, Elder Adrean, Priest of the Light, lumbered through his Temple of the Guiding Stars, trudging past the rows of empty benches that awaited the arrival of worshippers on the morrow. The banging on the wooden doors echoed in the small temple, in response to which he shook his grey-haired head and waved a hand in useless chastisement - no one was in the temple to see the gesture and those banging on the door certainly wouldn't know of it. He took a breath and croaked out as loudly as he could manage, "I am coming, I am coming. Have a bit of patience." He reached the door, took hold of the iron loop anchored to it, and heaved it open. Then he looked out at the person - the people - causing the racket. "Oh dear," he observed. His rational mind told him he should feel afraid, but he couldn't muster it. "May I help you?"

The ominous, hunchbacked shape in the black cloak replied, "We have fled persegution across the river. By de Lighd, we require hosbice, for we are colt and hunry."

"Pardon me?" His old eyes could just see enough of the face inside the cowl to note a piece of bark attached to the man's nose and wadding of some description hanging from the nostrils. That explained the *"Light"* coming out sounding like *"lied."*

"We need help," said the tall, auburn-haired woman in Straelish.

The priest bobbed his grey-capped head. "I can see that now. And hear it in your voices. Come in, do come in. The Light will not turn away those seeking refuge in a holy hall such as this." He stepped back to give entry to the temple to the young woman and the three men - two he could see were young and he supposed the one in the cloak would be as well. To Elder Adrean, everyone now seemed young. They streamed past him peaceably enough, though he gave a start when a big herding dog also crossed the threshold. "Oh my! Does ... he or she?"

"She," said the biggest of the young men ... the word was the same word in both Straelish and Polgati, but the cadence led Adrean to believe the man, too, spoke Straelish.

"Does she require hospice as well?" He placed an arthritic hand on the dog's neck and ruffled her fur. "That is quite all right. I like dogs. She, too, is welcome." Then he put his shoulder against the heavy door to close it against the cold evening air.

He turned about and beheld his *guests* standing meekly, waiting for him to lead the way. First, he placed a hand to his chest and said, "I am Elder Adrean. You are welcome here. And you are?"

None of the three youngsters spoke. Instead, they cast their eyes to the hooded figure, a gesture that led his old mind to think that their Straelish was decent ... it was similar to Polgati. The hooded figure replied, "You bay call me Barragor. Dis is Lora, Cairn, and Thay. Dat is Fylgja."

Elder Adrean nodded. "Fylgja, is it? That's an odd name. I suspect there's an odd story to go along with it. Pleased to make your acquaintance. Follow me, my children." He lumbered back around the benches, heading towards the door to the rectory. "Persecution across the river, you say? Well, that hardly surprises me."

He heard the one named Barragor snap, "Whad is *thad* subbosed to bean?"

Elder Adrean chuckled. "My ears are not yet so deaf that they cannot hear that you speak Polgati well, if not with some difficulty at the moment. It means just what it should, my son."

"Thad just de loog of us beans we deserve do fall vigdim to bersegution?"

"Oh no, no, indeed not," he replied. He nodded respectfully to the altar and then led them to the rectory door. "Come through here, we'll sit you in front of a fire and see about getting you something to eat." He opened the door and allowed them to file through, though now he could see, despite his poor sight, fire burning in the eyes of the cowled man. "Take off your cloaks and stand by the fire. No, I said nothing of *deserving* persecution. It's just that two of you at least, these young boys here, and likely this tall young girl from the looks of her, are obviously Wicked Westmen, what some call Wickeders in these parts.

"Let me get you some tea."

"Dea?" Barragor asked, incredulity touching his tone.

"Oh yes, I know. Tea is quite the proof that the Chayans have an advanced civilization! A trader I know receives shipments of it from the Empire and he always saves me a modest pouch." He moved from the sitting room, through the open space to the kitchen, took a kettle, checked it had enough water already in it, and then came tottering back. As he went about he said, "I have never had the honour of meeting your kind, though I have had to tend to some of your victims."

Barragor shook his head, "I ab Sdraelish. Dese ones are nod."

Elder Adrean nodded. He tottered to the hearth and hung the pot over the flames. "Well then, that *is* something. You are welcome, as long as you are not fleeing something ghastly. No right-thinking person can abide murder and rape, for example, what Wickeders often bring to this riverbank."

Barragor made to speak, but the tall, tawny-haired boy stepped forward and spoke his first words, in surprisingly good Straelish, "The honour is entirely ours, Elder, and, yes, we have killed, though only in our defence and only when necessary. We may once have been like the other Thorn People who came to this riverbank but that is no longer true.

"We *will* be different."

The Fjordlander Gods

Fjordland has two chief Gods, one female, one male:

Rulla, Dealer of Fates, Mistress of Owls: When Orgor first crafted the world of men (see the lesser Gods), the Gods beheld His creation and desired dominion over it. To avoid strife among the many Gods, who will pit Their will against each other, Rulla thought to order this new world. She made runes representing the Domains and obliged each of Them to select one. Because She is one of the two greater Gods, all the lesser Gods bent to Her will in this except one (see Tanat, hereafter). Rulla continues to manifest Herself in Orgor's world; upon the birth of a mortal, She selects a slate with a specific rune upon it that will guide that Fjordlander's fate. Significant events or collisions with other Gods may in fact be a manifestation of Rulla taking an interest in guiding human events, or She may actually decide to select another rune for the mortal. Events will tell which is true. The selection of a rune is seen by Fjordlanders as a path set out for the individual, but it is up to the individual to walk that path.

Hondrig the Judge. At death, He sits in judgement over whether a Fjordlander lived up to the potential of the rune Rulla selected upon birth. He weighs on His scale the rune against the accomplishments of the mortal in question. Then He allots an appropriate place in the Afterworld depending on whether the Fjordlander made the most of his or her fate, or, whether he or she made little effort to do so. Hondrig may also decide to send the soul of the Fjordlander to Skalagg, the Netherworld. Like Rulla, Hondrig also manifests Himself in Orgor's world; He will guide events to His will within any Domain if He so chooses. Again, events will show Hondrig's hand.

Lesser Gods of varying potency also populate Fjordlander theology, including:

Asgear, God of the Waves, who commands the seas.

Florri, God of Good Fortune, who controls the whims of luck.

Guliveg, Tender of the Spark of Life. It is said She wanted the Domain of the Sea but had to choose Her rune after Asgear chose His. It is also said that to spite Asgear, She may intervene to save the ship-wrecked or sailors otherwise in peril, and thus She is revered by those who ply the waves. She decides whether or not to lend succour to those whose life hangs in the balance, be it mothers and infants at childbirth, the diseased, or even the foolhardy taking some rash risk. However, She rarely manifests Herself to those locked in battle, for war is the Domain of Karn.

Heligat, Ruler of Skalagg, the Domain of the Dead, the Netherworld. Those mortals judged by Hondrig as unworthy are sent to toil for Heligat in Skalagg until the breaking of the world. It is said the invocation of a curse attracts Her attention. She is also said to send demons into the world on Her missions.

Karn, the Goddess of War. Revels in the conduct of war and is known to guide the outcome of battles based on Her whims, often manifesting Herself via Her berserkers.

Norrgi, the Master of the Winds. An active God, He controls the weather borne upon the winds. Whereas many Fjordlander sailors respect and fear Asgear, they revere Norrgi as much as they do Guliveg, though they fear Him when he is wrathful.

Orgor, the Crafter, the God who took it upon Himself to build the world. He is worshipped by all crafters and builders.

Tanat the Rogue. God of Chaos and Mischief. He oft ruins the plans of the other Gods simply for His amusement. It is said His choosing of His Domain came after many other rune slates had been chosen by the other Gods. He scorned the choosing and oft writes his own runes, depending on His mood.

Zareth, Mistress of Desire: Goddess of love, lust, and ambition.

Other spirits inhabit the Godspace and manifest themselves in Orgor's world. One that appears in this work is:

Sk'van, the Twisted, the Master of the Dark, , the greatest of all demons. He captures the souls of the living, before Hondrig's weighing, and tortures them before giving them over to Heligat.

Note: Fjordlanders will sometimes name their children after one of the Gods, though never the two chief Gods, nor Heligat.

Glossary

Bondgyld: a sum of silver given by one person to another for the safe-keeping of a third. Often paid to families to foster a neighbour.

Darknight: the celebration of the winter solstice and often used as a synonym for the solstice.

Demesne: a landed estate in Straeland owned by a particular *herg*.

Frouw: a Straelish term used as a form of address for a woman without higher honorific.

Fylgja: a familiar, usually an animal embodying the spirit of a master.

Godspace: sky.

Herg: a feudal title used in Straeland to denote a man who is the owner of a *demesne*.

Herr: in Straelish, *herr* is a weakened form of *herg*, thus used as a form of address for a man without higher honorific.

Housecarl: a Fjordlander term for man-at-arms.

Kunungr: a Fjordlander term used to denote a king, though Fjordland does not have such a ruler.

Lifgyld: a sum of silver, or life price, given by one person to another in payment for a life-saving deed. It is also the sum a Fjordlander must pay to the Sea Wolves to muster out of the Unsettled Clan.

Oberherg: a feudal title used in Straeland to denote the ruler of a province. It is the highest-ranking of the nobility after the king or queen.

Revered: what the Straels call their priests.

Tears of the Ghosts: freezing rain.

Thorn People: a term used in many parts of the northlands to describe Fjordlanders, derived from their similarity to thorns for drawing blood.

Tosk-hyr: mythical "horned men" of the high mountains and forests who bedevil unfortunate Fjordlanders.

Weregyld: a sum of silver that must be paid by one person to another - or that person's kin - upon causing a person's maiming or death, under pain of outlawry should payment not be made.

Wyrd: a person's destiny.

Also by Ian H. McKinley

The Winter Wars,
Book Three of Northern Fire

The Polgati fear for their relations with Straeland. An ambitious new Straelish *oberherg* of the north, Korgash Hasselmann, is railing against Polgatia for harbouring necromancers and Thorn People bent on spreading evil in Straeland. Even if Princess Oda is shuttling between the capital cities to calm tensions, it does not bode well for peace.

Polgatia's ruler reaches out to the Drovers of the taiga for three hundred of their famous horses to bolster his cavalry. His brother, the Dark Prince, hears troubling reports from his network of spies. On top of that, someone seems to be undertaking a campaign to murder Korgash's spies in Polgatia's capital city.

Could it be that there really is a necromancer bringing death to Korgash's agents in the alleyways and under the darkened bridges of Sar Danskaya? Could it be that the "Thorn People" against whom Korgash rails could be some Wicked Westmen that arrived in Polgatia some years previously? Could the woman among them have seduced young Prince Kilsoff, a scion of a junior branch of the royal family?

When events spiral out of control, with assassins and armies unleashed in one fell stroke, a war band arises to confront the menace. Will its determined commanders and its valorous actions turn the tide against Korgash, or will it be offered up to the Straelish noble in order to broker peace? When the time comes to settle scores, who will do the settling, and against whom?

Visit: https://lugarcomuneditorial.com/ojo-de-vidrio/